Thad offered the young woman in the sleigh his hand, but she didn't seem to see him. She's blind, he realized.

He lifted her down from the sleigh—delicate, she hardly weighed anything—and set her on her feet in the snow with care. "You're safe now."

"I know."

There was something about that voice…. He could see only her eyes between her snow-covered scarf and hood, but those eyes were a flawless emerald green.

He'd seen that perfect shade of green before— and pain speared through him at the memory. Was it *Noelle? Could* it be?

But he already knew it was true. This was the woman who had been his first love. This was the woman he'd spent years and thousands of miles trying to forget. And yet it was hard to believe this was his Noelle.

No, he reminded himself. Not *your* Noelle anymore…

Books by Jillian Hart

Love Inspired Historical

Homespun Bride #2

Love Inspired

Heaven Sent #143
*His Hometown Girl #180
A Love Worth Waiting For #203
Heaven Knows #212
*The Sweetest Gift #243
*Heart and Soul #251
*Almost Heaven #260
*Holiday Homecoming #272
*Sweet Blessings #295
For the Twins' Sake #308
*Heaven's Touch #315
*Blessed Vows #327
*A Handful of Heaven #335
*A Soldier for Christmas #367
*Precious Blessings #383
*Every Kind of Heaven #387
*Everyday Blessings #400
*A McKaslin Homecoming #403
A Holiday To Remember #424

*The McKaslin Clan

JILLIAN HART

makes her home in Washington state, where she has lived most of her life. When Jillian is not hard at work on her next story, she loves to read, go to lunch with her friends and spend quiet evenings with her family.

Homespun Bride
JILLIAN HART

Steeple
Hill®

Published by Steeple Hill Books™

STEEPLE HILL BOOKS

Steeple
Hill®

ISBN-13: 978-0-373-82782-4
ISBN-10:   0-373-82782-2

HOMESPUN BRIDE

Copyright © 2008 by Jill Strickler

www.SteepleHill.com

Printed in U.S.A.

The Lord is my shepherd; I shall not want.
—*Psalms* 23:1

Chapter One

Montana Territory, 1883

The tiny railroad town of Angel Falls was a symphony of noise. Because she was blind, Noelle Kramer had gotten the knack of separating one sound from another. There was the *chink* of horseshoes on the hard-packed snow and ice as teamsters and riders hurried on their way. The merry bell in the church steeple clanged a melody, marking the late-afternoon hour. The business-like *clip-clip* of ladies' shoes on the swept-clean board-walk was like a metronome tapping the meter. The low-throated rumble of the train, two blocks over, added a steady bass percussion as it idled on steel tracks.

It all painted a picture, of sorts, but there was so much missing. She could not see the colorful window displays of the shops. Were they bright with spring colors yet? While she could not know this, not without asking her dear aunt, who was busy fussing with their horse's tether rope, she tried to picture what she could. She hadn't been blind so long that she couldn't remember the look of things. She only had to pull it up in her mind, the main street with its cheerful window displays, awnings and continuous boardwalks.

What she couldn't picture was her friend Lanna, from their school days, who'd been in the dress shop when she and her aunt had stopped to pick up a new hat. Lanna had been bursting with happiness. The brightest notes of joy rang in her voice as she'd been fitted for her wedding dress.

Noelle closed her eyes against the pain; she closed her thoughts and her heart, too. She'd never asked what had become of the wedding gown she'd had made. The one she'd never had a chance to pick up for her wedding day.

She rubbed the fourth finger of her left hand, so bare beneath the thick woolen glove. She understood why Shelton had changed his mind. What surprised her was that her heart wasn't broken; she'd not been deeply in love with him but she'd hoped for happiness anyway.

No, what had devastated her had been his words. You're damaged goods, now. Her blindness was the reason she would never have a hope of marrying. Of being a wife and a mother. Her affliction was a burden to others. She, alone, could not tend fires and watch after servants or see to the dozens of details in the running of a household and caring for small children.

Still, she had a lot to be thankful for.

"Now, you settle down like a good horse." Aunt Henrietta's no-nonsense scolding easily drowned out the street noise. Even her gait was a sensible brisk stride and her petticoats rustled as she climbed into the sleigh.

"Is he giving you more trouble?" Noelle asked, trying to hide her worry.

"He won't if he knows what's good for him." Henrietta settled her heavy hoops and plentiful skirts around her on the seat. "I gave him a talking-to he won't soon forget. He's a Worthington now, and he has a standard of conduct to uphold. I won't be seen around town wrestling a horse for control like some common teamster."

Noelle bit her lip trying to hide the smile for she knew her aunt was dreadfully serious. To Henrietta, appearances and reputation were everything. "I'm sure he'll be fine. He's probably just not used to all the noise in town."

"I don't care what he's used to!" Henrietta huffed. The seat groaned beneath her weight as she leaned forward, perhaps in search of the lap blanket. "Where has that gone to? Wait, here it is. Cover up, dear. There's a dangerous cold to the air. Mark my words, we'll see a blizzard before we reach home, if we make it there in time."

Noelle bit her lip again. She was endlessly amused by Henrietta's drama. A blizzard? Surely that was a dire assessment of the situation. She held up her gloved hand but couldn't hear any telltale *tap, tap* against the leather. "I smell snow in the wind. It is falling yet? I can't tell."

"Nothing yet, although I can hardly hear you. I shall never get used to that newfangled contraption."

"Which newfangled contraption is bothering you now?"

"Why, the train, of course." Henrietta took delight in her complaints, for her voice was smiling as she gathered the thick leather reins with a rustle. "I can tell by the look on your face that once again my disapproval of modern progress amuses you."

"I wonder why the Northern Pacific Railroad didn't ask you before they laid track through our valley."

"That is exactly my complaint with them." Henrietta gave the reins a slap and the gelding leaped forward, jerking them to a rough, swift start. "There, now. That's more like it. I don't put up with a horse's nonsense."

Or any nonsense, Noelle knew, which was why she hadn't asked about Lanna's dress when they'd left the shop. Why she tucked away her sadness. Henrietta didn't have a mind to tolerate sadness. She always said that God knew best and that was that.

No doubt that was true. Sometimes it was simply difficult to understand.

The wind changed, bringing with it the fresh wintry scent of snowflakes. Noelle could feel them, as light as a Brahms lullaby, and she lifted her face to the brush of their crisp iciness against her skin.

Henrietta snapped the reins briskly, intent on directing their horse. "Do you smell that?"

"Yes, isn't the snow wonderful?"

"Goodness, not that, dear. It's the train. At least you're spared the ugly view of the trailing coal smoke that hovers over the town like a black, poisonous, endless snake. What are we expected to do? Expire from the discharge?"

"I doubt the men in charge of the rail company are concerned by the smoke cloud."

"Well, they can afford not to be! They are not here to breathe it in! And why do we need such progress? Gone are the days when a person labored to get to their destination. I walked beside my parents' wagon half-way to Missouri, and it put the starch in my bonnet. It's what's wrong with young people nowadays. Life is too easy for them."

The train whistle blasted, drowning out her words. And there was another more frightening sound—the high-noted terror in a horse's neigh. Noelle cringed, panic licking at her. Years ago, their mare had made that terrified, almost-human scream when a rattlesnake had startled her and she'd run with the family buggy over the edge of the road. On that day, Noelle had lost her mother, her father and her sight.

Surely, that sound wasn't coming from their horse?

She glanced around the street, as if she could see; it was habit, nothing more. She gripped the edge of the sleigh tight in reflex and in memory, but there was no time to open her heart in prayer. The sleigh jerked forward. Wind whizzed in her ears and snow slapped against her face. The sleigh's runners hit grooves in the compact snow at a rapid-fire pace, bouncing her on the seat.

"Good heavens!" Henrietta sounded deeply put out. "Calm down, you ill-behaved brute—"

The train whistle blew a second time. The sleigh jerked to a sudden stop. Noelle slid forward on the seat and something hard struck her chin. Pain exploded through her jaw, as she realized she'd hit the dash-board. Was that high, shrill bugling neigh coming from their horse? Sure enough, she could feel his huge body block the wind as he reared up. For one breathless moment, she feared he might fall on them. Henrietta's terrified gasp confirmed her suspicions.

"Quick!" She found her aunt's arm and gave her a nudge. "Out of the sleigh. Hurry! Before—"

Too late. The whistle blew, the sleigh lurched and the horse came down running. The train's loud chugging and clamoring only seemed to drive the gelding to run faster, right down the middle of Main. Shouted exclamations and the sudden rush of other horses and vehicles to get out of the way overrode all other sounds. The sleigh swayed from side to side in a sickening way. They were going too fast for the vehicle. She braced her feet and held on tight. Fear tasted coppery and bitter on her tongue. The past rose up in a colorful image in her mind's eye. Her mother's cry as the buggy broke apart. The horrible falling at great speed. The sudden blinding pain—

No. Not again. Lord, stop this from happening. Please. Panic beat crazily against her ribs. Fear felt thick on her tongue. It was too late to jump from the sleigh, and she wouldn't abandon Henrietta. She tried to make her mind clear enough to form another prayer but only one thought came. *Help us.*

Somewhere, over the sound of Henrietta's continued demands for the horse to stop and stop now, a man shouted out, "Runaway horse! Grab him!"

Maybe someone *could* stop them. Hope lifted through her panic, and Noelle clung to it. *Please, Lord, send someone to help us.*

There was no answer as the sleigh began to buck harder and rock from side to side. Had they left the road? Soft snow sprayed against her face. She held on to the edge of the seat with all her might, but her stomach gripped from the sleigh's violent rocking motion. Foliage crumpled and crunched beneath the runners.

Had they gone off the road? Fear shot through her heart. They were going too fast, they were going to overturn and the sleigh was going to break apart. Henrietta must have realized this, too, because she began sobbing. That only drove the horse to run faster. Noelle squeezed her eyes shut. A sob broke through her, and the seat bucked beneath her. They would be hurt—or worse—and she could not stop it from happening.

The Lord hadn't answered her prayer last time, either, and look at what she'd lost. Her heart squeezed with pain. She could not lose so much again, and yet she had no choice. The sleigh rose sharply upward, and tipped violently to the right, slamming her hard against the dashboard again. She felt no physical pain, only an emotional one. It was too late for answered prayers now.

Then, through the rush of her pulse in her ears, she heard something else. Something new. The drum of hoofbeats.

"Whoa, there, big fella." A man's voice, a deep vibrant baritone rumbled like winter thunder from the sky, overpowering every other sound until there was only silence. Only him. "Calm down. You're all right, buddy."

The sleigh's bumping slowed. Noelle hung on to the dashboard, drawn to the sound of the man's confident and powerful voice coming as if from the sky.

Am I dreaming this? Noelle had to wonder. None of this felt real. The sleigh tipped dangerously and listed to a stop. The dizzying sense of movement stopped.

There was only the blast of the winded gelding's ragged breaths and that soothing baritone. She could hardly believe that they were safe.

Safe. Because of him.

She heard the creak of his saddle as he dismounted. The sensations of Henrietta clutching her, the wind's low-noted howl like a lonely wolf's cry and the chill that set in all faded into the background. She was riveted to his voice; there was something about his voice, but as he spoke low to keep the horse calm over the clatter of the harnessing she couldn't place what it was. Maybe he was tethering the horse.

Relief flooded her. The remnants of fear jarred through her, making her blood thick and her pulse loud in her ears. She turned toward the faint squeaking sound his boots made on the snow. His gait was even and confident; not too fast, and long-legged. Already her mind was trying to paint a picture of him.

"Are you two ladies all right?" The man's baritone boomed.

It wasn't a cold tone, Noelle heard, but warmth in that voice, character and heart. And something more, indefinable like a memory just out of reach.

"F-fine. Considering what c-could have happened." Was that really her speaking? She probably sounded so breathless and shaky from the aftereffect of fear, that was all, and not because of the man.

Henrietta still gasped for breath, frozen in place, but still managing to talk. "We're a little worse for the wear, I d-dare say. I hate to think what would have happened if you hadn't intervened, sir. You s-saved us just in time."

"Looks like it," the rider answered easily as if it hadn't been his doing. "What's important now is that you two try to make as little movement as possible. I'm going to get you out one at a time. Don't worry, you'll be safe."

Safe? Noelle gulped. Did that mean they were still in danger? She could tell they were tipped at an odd angle, but her hearing had failed her. Her ears seemed to be ignoring everything, save for the man's voice. It was strange, as was the feeling that she ought to know him, and how could that be? If he wasn't a stranger, then Henrietta would have called him by name.

"D-dear hea-vens!" Her aunt sounded quite strained. "A-are you q-quite sure that we're not about to plunge into the river?"

The river? That took her thoughts off their rescuer. Fear shivered down her spine. Only then did she realize there was another sound above the raging howl of the wind—the rush of the fast-moving river.

How close were they to the edge? She tried to breathe but her lungs felt heavy and the air in them like mud. As her senses settled, she could better hear the hungry rush of the river alarmingly close.

"Let me help you, miss."

His voice seemed to move through her spirit and, confused, she didn't realize that he was taking her hand until suddenly his fingers closed around hers. His touch was strong and as steady as granite. Every fear within her stilled. It seemed impossible to be afraid as his other hand gripped her elbow.

Stunned, she could feel the faint wind shadow as he towered over her. She knew he was tall, wide-shouldered and built like steel. She knew, somehow, without seeing him. It was as if she was familiar with his touch. How could that possibly be?

"Careful, now." His calm baritone boomed. "Step up a little, that's right."

She could feel his strength as he lifted her out of the tipped sleigh. For an instant, she felt weightless as if there was no gravity that could hold her to the ground. As if there were only wind and sky. She breathed in the winter air, the faint scent of soap and leather and wool. Her shoes touched the snow and the impact jarred through her, although he'd set her gently to the ground.

Who was this man? The last time she'd felt like this, suspended between earth and sky, between safety and the unknown was so long ago, she dared not let her mind dig up those buried dreams.

With a whisper of movement he released her. "Stay here while I fetch your mother."

She stood wobbling on her shaky legs, feeling the kick of fear still racing through her veins. Riveted, unable to think of anything else, even her aunt's safety, she listened to the crunch of the snow beneath his boots as he moved again. The wind and snow lashed against her nose and eyes like tears. She tucked the muffler more snuggly around her face, shivering not from fear or cold but from something else.

She heard Henrietta's sob of fear, she heard the jingle of their rescuer's horse's bridle and that low reassuring baritone, although the howling wind stole his words.

Never had she so sorely missed her sight. Every fiber of her being longed to be able to see him. Then she heard the squeak of the sleigh's runner as it moved against the snow and she realized the rush she heard was the swift-running river and roar of the falls—the highest waterfall in all of Montana Territory.

A prayer flew to her lips, but before she could give it voice, she heard the crunch of her aunt's sturdy gait.

"Let me take a look at you. I have to see with my own eyes. This is like an awful nightmare." Henrietta grabbed her and turned her around, like a mother hen checking on one of her chicks.

Love for her aunt filled her—she'd learned that love made everyone perfect. What were flaws? They hardly mattered when she could have lost Henrietta as she had her parents. Emotion burned in her throat, emotion she dared not speak of, since Henrietta did not approve of outbursts of any kind.

"I'm fine," she told her aunt to reassure her. "But are you all right?"

"Worse for the ordeal but right enough. I saw you hit the dashboard. Are you bleeding?"

"I'm fine, I told you. It's blizzarding, and—"

"You ladies need to get safely home." He spoke up. "The storm is likely to get worse before it gets better."

"Young man, you saved our lives."

"I was at the right place at the right time is all." He took a step, which made it easier to keep his eye on that high-strung horse. "Are you sure you're both all right? A ride like that could shake anyone up."

"I have nerves of steel." The woman's chin firmed as she tugged at the daughter's scarf, which obscured her nearly completely. "My niece, however, is quite fragile as she's blind."

"Niece?" Not daughter. And blind at that. Wasn't that too bad? Thad thought. Sympathy filled him as he watched the aunt fuss.

"My dear, let me see. I have to make sure you've not broken anything."

"As long as you two ladies are safe enough, I'll just see to the horse then." He stepped back. His mind should be working out how to get that vehicle out of the bushes, but he couldn't concentrate on it.

There was something about the young woman—the niece—something he couldn't put his finger on. He'd hardly glanced at her when he'd hauled her from the family sleigh, but now he took a longer look through the veil of falling snow.

For a moment, her silhouette, the size of her, and the way she moved reminded him of Noelle. How about that; Noelle, his frozen heart reminded him with a painful squeeze, had been his first—and only—love.

It couldn't be her, he reasoned, since she was married and probably a mother by now. She'd be safe in town, living snug in one of the finest houses in the county instead of riding along the country roads in a storm. Still, curiosity nibbled at him as he plowed through the knee-deep snow. Snow was falling faster now, and yet somehow through the thick downfall his gaze seemed to find her.

She was fragile, a delicate bundle of wool; snow clung to her hood, scarf and cloak like a shroud, making her tough to see. She'd been just a little bit of a thing when he'd lifted her from the sleigh, and his only thought at the time had been to get both women out of danger. Now something chewed at his memory. He couldn't quite figure out what, but he could feel it in his gut.

The woman was talking on as she unwound the niece's veil. "We were tossed about dreadfully. You're likely bruised and broken from root to stem. I've never been so terrified. All I could do was pray over and over and think of you, my dear." Her words warmed with tenderness. "What a greater nightmare for you."

"We're fine. All's well that ends well," the niece insisted.

Although her voice was muffled by the thick snowfall, his step faltered. There *was* something about her voice, something familiar in the gentle resonance of her alto. Now he could see the top part of her face, due to her loosened scarf. Her eyes—they were a startling shade of flawless emerald green.

Whoa, there. He'd seen that perfect shade of green before—and long ago. Recognition speared through his midsection, but he already knew she was his Noelle even before the last layer of the scarf fell away from her face.

His Noelle, just as lovely and dear, was now blind and veiled with snow. His first love. The woman he'd spent years and thousands of miles trying to forget. Hard to believe that there she was suddenly right in front of him. He'd heard about the engagement announcement a few years back, and he'd known in returning to Angel Falls to live that he'd have to run into her eventually.

He just didn't figure it would be so soon and like this.

Seeing her again shouldn't make him feel as if he'd been hit in the chest with a cannonball. The shock was wearing off, he realized, the same as when you received a hard blow. First off, you were too stunned to feel it. Then the pain began to settle in, just a hint, and then to rush in until it was unbearable. Yep, that was the word to describe what was happening inside his rib cage. A pain worse than a broken bone beat through him.

Best get the sleigh righted, the horse hitched back up and the women home. But it was all he could do to turn his back as he took his mustang by the bridle. The palomino pinto gave him a snort and shook his head, sending the snow on his golden mane flying.

Yep, I know how you feel, Sunny, Thad thought. Judging by the look of things, it would be a long time until they had a chance to get in out of the cold.

He'd do best to ignore the women, especially Noelle, and to get to the work needin' to be done. He gave the sleigh a shove, but the vehicle was wedged against the snow-covered brush banking the river. Not that he put a lot of weight on the Lord overmuch these days, but Thad had to admit it was a close call. Almost eerie how he'd caught them just in time. It did seem providential. Had they gone only a few feet more, gravity would have done the trick and pulled the sleigh straight into the frigid, fast waters of Angel River and plummeted them directly over the tallest falls in the territory.

Thad squeezed his eyes shut. He couldn't stand to think of Noelle tossed into that river, fighting the powerful current along with the ice chunks. There would have been no way to have pulled her from the river in time. Had he been a few minutes slower in coming after them or if Sunny hadn't been so swift, there would have been no way to save her. To fate, the Lord or to simple chance, he was grateful.

Some tiny measure of tenderness in his chest, like a fire long banked, sputtered to life. His tenderness for her, still there, after so much time and distance. How about that.

Since the black gelding was a tad calmer now that the sound of the train had faded off into the distance, Thad rehitched him to the sleigh but secured the driving reins to his saddle horn. He used the two horses working together to free the sleigh and get it realigned toward the road.

The older woman looked uncertain about getting back into the vehicle. With the way that black gelding of theirs was twitchy and wild-eyed, he didn't blame her. "Don't worry, ma'am, I'll see you two ladies home."

"Th-that would be very good of you, sir. I'm rather shaken up. I'm of half a mind to walk the entire mile home, except for my dear niece."

Noelle. He wouldn't let his heart react to her. All that mattered was doing right by her—and that was one thing that hadn't changed. He came around to help the aunt into the sleigh and after she was safely seated, turned toward Noelle. Her scarf had slid down to reveal the curve of her face, the slope of her nose and the rosebud smile of her mouth.

What had happened to her? How had she lost her sight? Sadness filled him for her blindness and for what could have been between them, once. He thought about saying something to her, so she would know who he was, but what good would that do? The past was done and over. Only the emptiness of it remained.

"Thank you so much, sir." She turned toward the sound of his step and smiled in his direction. If she, too, wondered who he was, she gave no real hint of it.

He didn't expect her to. Chances were she hardly remembered him, and if she did, she wouldn't think too well of him. She would never know what good wishes he wanted for her as he took her gloved hand. The layers of wool and leather and sheepskin lining between his hand and hers didn't stop that tiny flame of tenderness for her from growing a notch.

He looked into her eyes, into Noelle's eyes, the woman he'd loved truly so long ago, knowing she did not recognize him. Could not see him or sense him, even at heart. She smiled at him as if he were the Good Samaritan she thought he was as he helped her settle onto the seat.

Love was an odd thing, he realized as he backed away. Once, their love had been an emotion felt so strong and pure and true that he would have vowed on his very soul that nothing could tarnish nor diminish their bond. But time had done that simply, easily, and they stood now as strangers.

He reached for Sunny's reins, mounted up and led the way into the worsening storm.

Chapter Two

Huddled against the minus temperatures and lashing snow, Noelle clenched her jaw tight to keep her teeth from chattering.

The whir of the frigid wind and the endless whisper of the torrential snowfall drowned out all sound. It deceived her into imagining they were being pulled along in a void, cut off from the outside world, from everyone and everything, including the stranger who had helped them. She knew he was leading the gelding; Aunt Henrietta had assured her of this fact as soon as they'd set out.

It was only concern, she told herself, because she'd been behind two runaway horses in her lifetime. She did not wish a third trip. Of course she wanted to make sure they arrived safely home and that the stranger would keep his stalwart promise to lead them there.

The stranger. She couldn't seem to rid him from her mind. Her thoughts kept turning over and over the moment she'd first heard his buttery-warm baritone and the strange, vague sense of recognition she'd felt when he'd lifted her from the sleigh.

You know who he reminds you of. She shivered against the cruel cold and swiped the snow from her lashes. No, it couldn't be her old beau. Thad McKaslin was probably in Texas by now, judging by how fast he'd left her years ago. Her heart cracked in small pieces just thinking his name.

No, there was no possibility—none—that *he* was the stranger. Their rescuer was a Good Samaritan and a dependable, mature man, not a boy who only saw to his own concerns.

"Henrietta?" Uncle Robert's bass boomed through the sounds of the storm. "Noelle! Thank God you're here safe. I was just about to ride out looking for you. Didn't you see the blizzard cloud, Henrietta? You are both half frozen."

"Oh, Rob." Henrietta stumbled off the seat with a thud and clatter.

The storm blocked any other sounds, but Noelle knew her aunt had flung herself into her husband's arms. Though stiff with cold, she waited in the sleigh to give them a private moment.

"Do you need help?"

She turned toward the sound of his voice, thinking of all the ways his baritone didn't sound like the Thad she remembered. It was deeper, more mature, made of character and depth of experience. Besides, if it was Thad, he would have said something. See, it *couldn't* be.

"Miss?"

She ignored the knot of foreboding in her stomach and answered him. "I would appreciate the help. Storms with winds like this tend to disorient me. I get a little lost on my own."

"Me, too, but I don't need a storm for that." There was a touch of warmth to those words.

She wondered if he were smiling, and what kind of smile he had. Just for curiosity's sake, of course. She began to shake the snow from the lap blanket.

"Let me get that for you."

He blocked the storm as he towered beside her. She felt the weight of the snow-caked blanket fall away. She breathed in the wintry air, the faint scent of his soap and leather and wool and remembered that boy she'd once loved.

His hand cradled her elbow to help her step out of the sleigh. Cold snow sank to the tops of her ankle-high shoes. For a moment, she felt a strange quiver of familiarity and denial seized her like a fist. Thad McKaslin here, in Angel Falls? Could it be?

She took one step, and he moved to her side to block the worst of the wind and snow. And the way he towered beside her made recognition shiver through her.

I don't want it to be him, she thought, her stomach tightening even more. But just because she didn't want it to be Thad, didn't mean it wasn't. She took another step. "Should I know you?"

"Not really," his comforting baritone rumbled.

"When a man saves a woman's life, well, two women's, she likes to know what name to call her rescuer when she thanks him."

"Maybe some things are better left a mystery." Friendly, that's what his voice was and cozy, the way a fire crackling in the hearth was cozy. "Careful, now. There's a deep drift coming up."

His grip tightened on her and he responded so

quickly and gallantly, he must have thought she was truly helpless. It was a common misconception. "Don't worry," she said, easily correcting her balance. "I've gotten used to tottering around. I'm fine."

"The snow drifts high here. Lift your steps a little higher," he said with concern.

Concern she didn't need, not from him. She tried to concentrate on feeling her way over the crest of the snowdrift with the toe of her shoe. Her feet were numb from cold, making it only a little more difficult.

"You do this very well."

She recognized the surprise in his words. "When I lost my sight, I realized I had two options. To see it as a reason to give up or as a reason to go on. Of course, I walk into a few walls and catch my toe on the top of snowdrifts, but I do all right."

"I'll say."

She could feel the flat level of the brick stone walkway that her uncle kept carefully cleared. Snow had accumulated on it, but not more than a few inches, and the walking was easier. She released her rescuer's arm. "Thank you, but I can get in from here."

"No, I should see you to the door."

"You've done enough all ready."

"But you're blind."

"Yes, but I'm not incapable."

"No, I see that." What did he say to that? Thad didn't have the slightest notion. It was breaking his heart in every way. He cleared his throat to ask the question most troubling him. "How long have you been like this?"

"Tripping in the snow? Or blind, do you mean?"

"I'm sorry for your loss of sight." Her smile was still

the same, he realized, modest and sweet as the finest
sugar, and how it transformed her lovely face the way
dawn changed the night sky. But something *had*
changed. She no longer held the power to render him
a love-struck fool. No, he thought stoically, her smile
had no effect on him whatsoever.

"It's been over four years, now."

"Four years?" That surprised him. He'd been gone
just about five.

"I hit my head when our buggy rolled and I lost
my sight. It wasn't the worst thing I lost. My parents
were killed."

"I—I'm sorry to hear that." It surprised him that the
venom he'd felt for Noelle's parents vanished. Whatever they had done to him aside, they had loved their
daughter dearly. She was their greatest treasure. Hard
to blame them for it; harder now that they were gone.

The venom had died but not the bitterness. It was
hard to keep it buried where it belonged. "I guess that
had to be hard for you."

A single nod, nothing more.

His feelings aside, he knew it had to have been an
unbearable loss for her. She had loved her parents
deeply, which was one reason why he'd made the
decision he did five years ago and why they stood
together now as strangers. The only decision he could
have made.

Despite her condition, she looked well. Very well.
Soft lamplight glowed from the wide windows, gilding
her in light. Snow had gathered like tiny pieces of grace
on her hood. She looked beautiful, more lovely than ever.
Vibrant and womanly in a way he'd never seen her before.

She's happy, he realized with a punch that knocked

the air from his lungs and every last speck of regret from his heart. He'd done the right thing in leaving. Her father, rest his soul, had been right.

He didn't like what that decision had done to him, but he'd learned a hard lesson from it. Be wary of the woman you give your heart to.

He took a moment to capture one last look of her, happy and lovely and matured into a sweetheart of a woman. Knowing this only made him feel colder. Glad for her, but cold in the way of the blizzard baring its teeth.

"Won't you come in? You must be half frozen." Concern was there on her face for the stranger she thought he was. "Come in and warm up. We have beef soup and hot tea."

"Can't. My horse is standing in this cold."

"You could put him in our stable."

"No." Would she still ask him in if she knew who he was? What did she think about the man who'd broken his promise to elope with her? Did she even remember him?

Probably not. The bitterness in him won out, but it wasn't *only* bitterness he felt. That old tenderness, a hint of it, remained. No longer a romantic tenderness; that had been surely destroyed, but his feeling of goodwill surprised him once more.

He lifted her free hand, small and disguised by her woolen glove. He knew by memory, still, the shape of her hand from all the times he'd held it in his own. It was with well wishes for her future that he pressed a gentleman's kiss to the back of her hand.

"Now that I've got you and your aunt home safe and sound, I've done my good deed for the day."

"Only one good deed per day?" She withdrew onto

the brick walk. "You remind me of an old beau of mine."

"Pardon me, but he couldn't have been the brightest fellow. I can't imagine any man passing you by."

"I must be mistaken, then." She shook her head. Why had she been so sure? But as she swiped the snow out of her eyes, she realized he hadn't answered her question. "How long have you lived in Angel County?"

"I, uh, just moved back to the area. Haven't been here long."

So, it was as she thought. The voice she remembered had been an eighteen year-old's voice, manly, yes, but still partly boyish, too, not in full maturity. This man's voice was deeper and confident and wholly masculine, but still, it was Thad's.

"Miss, you take care of yourself. No more riding behind runaway horses."

"I think my uncle will see to that."

"Where is your husband? Shouldn't he be the one seeing to your safety?"

"My husband? No. I've never married." Was he moving away? The wind was gathering speed so she couldn't hear him move. "The blizzard is growing worse. You can't go out in that."

"Don't worry your pretty head about me, Noelle."

Noelle. The way his baritone warmed like wild honey around her name made her absolutely certain. "Thad?"

But there was no answer, just the moan of the wind and the hammering of snow falling with a vengeance. It pounded everywhere, on the top of her hood, on the front of her cloak, on the steps at her feet, and the sound deceived her.

Had he already disappeared into the storm? She
couldn't tell. She stood alone, battered by howling
wind and needle-sharp snow, feeling seventeen again.
Those feelings of love and heartbreak and regret were
a lifetime ago. She'd had enough of all three these past
years to last her a lifetime. She knew it was foolish of
her to wonder about Thad McKaslin now. He had
rejected her, too.

She turned on her heels and waded through the snow
to the covered porch steps. They were icy, so she took
them with care. It was best to keep her mind focused
firmly on the blessings in her life. On what was good
about this moment and this day. No good came from
dwelling on what was past and forever lost.

"Young man, where do you think you are going?"
Henrietta demanded from, what sounded, near the
bottom of the porch steps. "You'll come back here and
warm up with a cup of tea in front of a hot fire."

"I've got stock to see to before the storm gets much
worse. Good day, ma'am." Thad's voice came muted
by distance and the thick veil of snow.

"Mark my words, you'll freeze to death before you
make it to the end of the driveway!" Henrietta humphed
when no answer came. "What a disagreeable man. He
may have saved us, but God help him. We'll likely as
not find him frozen solid on the path to town come
morning. Terrible thing," she said, leading the way into
the house.

Apparentlys back to her usual self. Noelle gave
thanks for that.

After following her aunt into the warmth of the house,
she found herself wondering about Thad. He'd disappeared back into the blizzard, just as he'd come to them.

* * *

A narrow escape.

He wasn't bitter, Thad told himself as he nosed Sunny north. No, he was as cold to the past as the wind. But he was unprepared. Unprepared to have seen her. Unprepared to accept the fact that she'd said the words that kept playing over and over in his mind. I've never married.

Wasn't that why he'd left Angel Falls? To do as her father wanted and get out of her life? So she could marry the right kind of man? Because there was no way an immigrant's son like him could give Noelle the comfort she was used to. There had been many times over the last lonely years that he'd seen the older man's point.

The love he thought they had was a fool's paradise. A dream that had nothing to do with the hard reality of life.

They'd been two kids living on first love and dreams, but the real world ran on hard work and wages. He'd driven cattle from all over the West to the stockyards, from California to Chicago. He'd eaten dust and branded calves and tucked away every spare dollar he could and, except for a few months every winter, he'd lived out of his saddlebags. He'd learned what life was about.

The icy wind gusted hard, pulling him out of his thoughts. He'd gone a fair ways down the driveway. There was nothing around him but the lashing wind and the pummel of the iced snow, which had fallen around him like a veil. He gave thanks for it because he couldn't see anything—especially the house he'd left. Noelle's house. The twilight-dark storm made it easier to forget he'd seen her. To forget everything. Especially those early years away from her and how his heart had bled in misery until one day there'd been no blood left. Until he'd felt drained of substance but finally purged of the dream of her and what could have been.

Sure, there had been times—moments—since then when he'd thought of her. When he saw a woman's chestnut hair twisted up in that braided fancy knot Noelle liked to wear. Or when he saw an intricate lace curtain hanging in a window, he would recall how she'd liked to sit quietly in the shade on the porch and crochet lace by the hour. Any time he heard a piece of that fancy piano music she liked to play with the complicated chords and the long-winded compositions, he would remember.

It was the memories that could do him in, that were burrowing like a tick into his chest. He tried to freeze his heart like the winter's frost reaching deep into the ground. Usually that was the best way to handle those haunting thoughts of her and of the past.

He would never have come back to Angel Falls except for his kid brother. The boy didn't know what kind of a sacrifice Thad was making in coming back here and in his decisions to stick around, help the family and start to put down roots for a change.

Roots. He'd been avoiding doing that all this time, aside from the money it took to buy the kind of land he wanted—because settling down would only remind him he wasn't building a life and dreams with her.

Don't think about Noelle. He willed the words deep into his heart. Now, if only he were strong enough to stick by them. Whether she was married or not, their past was dead and gone. He was no longer that foolish boy thinking love was what mattered. He was a man strong enough to resist making a mistake like that—like her—again.

The white-out strength winds blasted harder; Sunny shied and veered off the faint path of the road. Not a great sign. Thad pulled his mustang up, so he wouldn't lose his sense of direction. It wouldn't take much for a man to get himself lost in a blizzard like this. He shaded his eyes from the wind-driven downfall to try to get a good look, but he couldn't see a thing. Still, he dismounted, to make sure. Something could be in the road—like another rider driven off track by the storm in need of help.

The curtain of snow shifted on a stronger gust of wind, and something red flashed at the roadside only to disappear again. Keeping hold of Sunny's reins and his sense of direction, Thad knelt to find a lady's hatbox tied up with a fancy red ribbon and, next to it, a small flat ice-covered package.

Must be Noelle's things, he figured, scanning what little he could see for landmarks. This sloping slant of ground was probably at the junction of the main road. The sleigh had made a sharp turn onto the driveway here. Combined with the wind, the goods had probably slid right over the edge of the sleigh.

It looked as though he wasn't completely done with Noelle yet. The small package fit into his saddlebag, but not the bulky hatbox. That he had to hang over his saddle horn by the ribbon.

Just his luck. Now, as he nosed Sunny north into the storm and toward home, there was a reminder of Noelle he could not ignore. The blizzard grew with a ruthless howl, baring its icy teeth. He was cut off from the world. He could see only gray wind, white snow, brutal cold and the cheerful slash of a Christmas-red bow, making it impossible not to think about her. To wonder, but never to wish.

No, not ever again.

Shivering between the cold sheets, Noelle burrowed more deeply into the covers. Her toes found the metal bed warmer heating the foot of her bed. Ah, warmth. Above the background drone of the blizzard, she heard the hiss of the lamp's flame as it wavered, pausing to draw more kerosene up its wick.

On the other side of the bedside table, her cousin's mattress ropes groaned slightly as she shifted, probably to keep the lamplight on her Bible page. "'The Lord does not look at the things man looks at. Man looks at the outward appearance, but the Lord looks at the heart.'"

There was a gentle whisper of the volume closing and the rasp as Matilda slid her Bible onto the edge of the table. "I didn't want to say anything when Mama was around, but did you two almost drown in the river? You know how she exaggerates."

"We didn't fall into the river. The sleigh stopped before that could happen. Fortunately." Noelle knew she would never understand why this runaway horse had been stopped short of disaster, when another one hadn't. Why the stranger had been in the right place at the right time to help them—this time. There was a greater mystery troubling her, though. Their rescuer. She wouldn't stop wondering about that man—against all reason and all wisdom.

"Divine intervention, beyond all doubt." Matilda

sounded so sure. "Mama said that man was an angel. She said she wasn't sure how he'd been able to come through the storm like that and to stop that new horse of Papa's just in time. Then he disappeared like he was called up to heaven."

"He took my hand to help me out of the sleigh and, trust me, he was a man and nothing more. He was no angel."

"Then how did he disappear?"

"It was a blizzard. All he had to do was walk three feet and he would be invisible. You know how your mother is."

"Yes, but it's a better story that way." Matilda sighed, a girl of nineteen still dreaming of romance. "Do you think they exist?"

"Angels?"

"No, of course *they* do. I mean, dashing, honorable men who ride to a lady's rescue."

"Only in books, I'm afraid."

"But the stranger, he—"

"No." Noelle cut her cousin off as kindly as she could and pulled her covers up to her chin. "He was probably mounted up and at the edge of town when the gelding broke away. I heard other men shout out to try to stop the horse. He himself said he only did what anyone would do."

"You don't sound grateful."

"Oh, I am. Deeply." She'd done her best to try to keep her calm; as she'd told her aunt, all's well that ends well. But the truth was, about midway through supper the calm had worn off and she'd trembled in delayed fear and shook through most of the evening. Now, she felt worn-out and heartsick.

Why hadn't Thad introduced himself? Why had he used her blindness against her? He knew she couldn't look at his face and recognize him, so he'd chosen to stay safely in the dark. Certainly no hero, not in her book, she thought, knowing that was the broken pieces of her heart talking, apparently still a bit jagged and raw after all this time. He'd been the one to leave her waiting at her window, with no note, no one to break the news to her, nothing.

She squeezed her eyes shut, as if that could stop the hurt from flooding her spirit. It was a long time ago, and it didn't matter now.

Put it out of your mind, she ordered, but her heart didn't seem to be listening. She would never forget the way it had felt to wait through the heat of the September afternoon and into the crisp twilight and refuse to give up on him. Vowing to wait however long it took, that's how much she believed in him. How strong her love. But as the first stars popped out in the ebony sky and the cool night set in, she'd had to accept the truth.

Thaddeus McKaslin, the man she'd loved with her entire soul, had changed his mind. Not the strong stalwart man she'd dreamed him to be, but a coward who couldn't tell the truth. Who couldn't commit. Who'd changed his mind, broken his promise and left town without her.

Why was he back after all this time?

Sharp footsteps knelled in the hallway. "Girls! I know you're in there talking. Lights out! It's past your bedtime."

"Yes, Mama," Matilda answered meekly.

Noelle knew her cousin was rolling her eyes, greatly burdened by her mother's strict role in her life. She herself had been that way once, but it had taken tragedy and maturing into an adult for her to understand the love that had been behind her mother's seemingly controlling behavior. Love, the real kind, was what mattered.

"Good night, girls." Henrietta's steps continued down the hallway to check on her other children.

"Good night, Matilda." Noelle curled onto her side, listening to the rustle of bedclothes and the squeak of the mattress ropes as her cousin leaned to put out the light.

She tried to let her mind drift, but her thoughts kept going back to Thad. To his questions as he'd walked her to the door. He'd asked about her blindness and her parents and her unmarried state. She added one more silent prayer to the others she'd said, as she did every night before she fell asleep, kneeling beside her bed moments earlier. *Please watch over him, Father. Please see to his happiness.*

If a tear hit the pillow, then she was certain it was not hers. The storm droned and, finally warm enough, Noelle let sleep take her.

Thad put away the last of the dishes and hung the dish towel up to dry. "You all set for the night, Ma? Is there anything else I can do for you?"

"Not one thing. You've been a great help. You've had a long day, too. You go put your feet up and read some of the newspaper with your brother."

His older brother, Aiden, gave him a forbidding look over the top of the local paper.

"I'll go on over to the shanty, then, where my books are. Good night."

"I'll make pancakes tomorrow morning just the way you like them." Ida glowed at the prospect and untied her apron. "Good night, son."

Aiden didn't look up from his reading. "'Night."

The clock was striking nine as he closed the back door behind him. He had to fight the blizzard across the yard and through the garden to his dark, frozen shanty. Typical Montana weather, snowing just when you thought there couldn't be any more snow left in the skies.

He found his home dark and empty and cold. As he knelt to stir the banked embers, air fed and sparked the coals. They glowed dull red and bright orange and he carefully added coal until flames were licking higher and bright enough to cast eerie shadows around the tiny simple dwelling.

He left the door open and the draft out, keeping his eye on the fire as he pulled the match tin down from the high corner shelf. Ice shone on the nail heads in the walls and on the wooden surface of the table. The lantern was slick with ice when he went to light it.

This was not the Worthington manor. Then again, he wouldn't want it to be. He hooked his boot beneath the rung of his chair and gave it a tug. Noelle was as unwelcome in his thoughts as the bright red hatbox on his corner shelf.

Just showed that what he'd come to believe in the last five years was true. The good Lord had better things to do than to watch over an average working man like him.

The shanty was warmer, so he closed the stove door and drew his Shakespeare volume down from the bookshelf. While he read of lives and love torn apart for the better part of two hours, Noelle was never far from his thoughts. He knew she never would be again.

When the shelf clock struck ten, he closed the book and got ready for bed. He shivered beneath the covers trying to get warm, and he prayed for her as he did every night. As he had for the last five years.

Chapter Three

"Three whole days trapped in this house by that blizzard." Aunt Henrietta bored through the parlor like a locomotive on a downhill slope. Crystal lamp shades trembled on their bases with a faint clink and clatter. "Three whole days I could have been sewing on Matilda's new dress, and instead I had to spend them in idleness."

"Well, not in complete idleness," Noelle couldn't resist pointing out as she paused in her crocheting to count the stitches with her fingertips. "You spent a lot of time composing letters to the local newspaper and to our territorial lawmakers."

"I hardly expect them to listen to a woman." There was a *thwack, thwack* as Henrietta plumped one of the decorative pillows on her best sofa. "But I will have them know what a danger that contraption is. What newfangled invention will they think up next? I shudder to think of it."

"Well, you should," Noelle said as kindly as she could. "With that dangerous contraption on the loose, do you think we ought to risk another trip to town?"

"It gives me pause." Henrietta moved on to pummel another pillow on Uncle Robert's favorite chair. "I must post these letters of complaint immediately. Noelle, I am sure, poor dear, you are frightened beyond imagining. Perhaps you ought to stay home with Matilda. No sense the two of you endangering your lives. I shall be fine."

Across the hearth from her, Noelle could hear Matilda struggling to hold back a giggle.

"I'll come with you. I'd like the fresh air." Noelle gathered her courage. Driving was a fact of life. She couldn't stay afraid of one thing, because she'd learned the hard way that fear easily became a habit. It had nearly consumed her after she'd first gone blind.

"No, I won't risk it." There was that smile in Henrietta's voice again. "Although my trusty mare is now reshod, so we shall not have to take that wild gelding, there is no telling what peril we could meet with."

"If that's true, then I must come, or I'll sit here worrying over you the entire time you're gone."

"You are a sweetheart." Henrietta blew a loud kiss across the room. "Now then, I've got my reticule. It's a shame about your new winter hat. Perhaps we can find another."

"The one I have is serviceable enough." Noelle carefully anchored her needle in her lacework, so she wouldn't lose any stitches or her place in the pattern, and folded it into the basket beside her chair. The floorboards squeaked beneath her weight as she stood.

"Maybe you'll catch word of the dressmaker's nephew," Matilda whispered, sounding a little breathless and dreamy. Perhaps she wasn't aware that her affections for the handsome teamster weren't well hidden. "Or, maybe you'll happen into the stranger's path again. If he's new to town—Mama didn't recognize him and you know she makes it her business to know everyone—then perhaps he's looking to settle down. Homestead. Marry. He did rescue *you*."

"He stopped a runaway horse, it was nothing personal. Besides, he's probably already settled down with a wife and kids at home." But Thad married? She couldn't imagine it. She told herself it wasn't bittersweetness that stung her like an angry hornet as she crossed the room. Because she was steeled to the truth in life. It was best to be practical. She almost said so to Matilda but held back the words.

Once, like her cousin, she'd been young and filling her hope chest with embroidered pillow slips and a girl's dreams. Maybe that was a part of the way life went. Maybe she would be a different woman if she'd been able to hold on to some of those dreams, or at least the belief in them. She reached for her cloak on the third peg of the coat tree.

"Goodness! I've never seen such poor manners!" Henrietta burst out and threw open the door so hard, it banged against the stopper. "You! Young man! Where do you think you're going? You get back here and do this properly."

Thad. Noelle knew it was him. Somehow, she knew.

"Uh, I didn't want to disturb, ma'am." His baritone sounded friendly and uncertain and manly all at once. "It's too early to call, but I was on my way to town and didn't want to make a second trip to drop this by."

"Still, you ran off before we could properly thank you the other evening."

"There was a blizzard raging, ma'am. I had livestock

I had to get back to. The storm was growing worse by the second."

He sounded flustered. She really shouldn't take any pleasure in that. If only she could draw up enough bitterness toward him—but now that he was here she realized that she couldn't.

"I'll have to forgive you, young man, seeing as I am standing here alive and well to scold you, because of you." Henrietta's voice smiled again. "Are you coming in?"

"I, uh, was planning to get on with my errands."

Noelle could feel his gaze on her like the crisp cold sunshine slanting through the open door. She wanted to say his name, to let him know she had figured out who he was and that he couldn't hide behind her blindness any longer. She also wanted to hide behind it, too. It made no sense, either, but it was how she felt.

Maybe it was easier to let him go back to his life, and let it be as if their paths had never crossed. What good could come of acknowledging him? What good could come from not?

Henrietta persisted. "We are on our way to town, too, but I'm willing to put aside my pressing concerns to thank you properly. You should come in. I'll have the maid serve hot tea and you may meet my oldest daughter."

"Uh, no thank you, ma'am." Thad scooped up the box and package he'd left on the swept-clean porch. "I found these in the road on my way out the other night."

"Oh, the new fabric. And, Noelle, your hat. How good of you to bring them. And to think we thought we'd lost these forever. It wasn't a tragedy, mind you, but a bother to have to go back to town and risk whatever peril would befall us this time around. Bless you for sparing us that."

"No trouble at all, ma'am." Thad wasn't sure what to make of this woman who stood as straight as a fence post and had the air of an army general, but there was one thing he did recognize. The way she was sizing him up and down as a husband candidate. He could spot a matchmaking mama a mile away. This one was so eager, she was giving off steam.

Or, he thought, maybe that was from his near state of hyperventilation. He was no good at social calls. "I'm more at home in a roundup, ma'am, or riding a trail. I don't get invited into parlors much."

"Then you're not married." She sounded real happy about that.

"No." He reckoned she would be glad to help him remedy that, so he backed up a few steps doing his best to escape while he could. Dragging his gaze from Noelle, who looked even lovelier in the soft lamplight. He didn't want to bring her more pain. Best just to leave. "Well, I've got to be on my way. Nice seein' you again, ma'am."

"Soooo," she dragged the word out thoughtfully. "You're *not married*. We have not been properly introduced. I'm Henrietta Worthington, that is my lovely daughter, Matilda, in the parlor and you already know my niece, Noelle."

"Yes. Good to meet you, miss." Tongue-tied, he tipped his hat, backing away, avoiding looking at Noelle again. The frozen tundra of his heart remained solid. In place. It was probably best if he didn't notice how her apple-green dress brought out the emerald flawlessness of her eyes and emphasized the creamy complexion of her heart-shaped face. Or how the dark hints of red in her chestnut hair gleamed in the firelight from the hearth.

No, it was best not to notice all that. Which was why he'd planned on leaving the goods on the front step and riding away without announcing himself. Too bad it hadn't turned out that way. He didn't know how, but he had to disappear from Noelle's life the way he'd come into it. He hadn't forgotten that he'd been the one to leave her waiting to elope with him.

"Let him go, Aunt." Noelle looked at him with a quiet, confident air as if she saw him perfectly. Her gently chiseled chin hitched up a notch. "I'm sure you have Mr. McKaslin trembling in his boots at the thought of being alone with so many eligible young ladies."

So, he hadn't been as nameless as he'd hoped. She *had* recognized him. Don't let that affect you, man, he told himself, but it was impossible. He'd hoped to spare her this, nothing could come of digging up the past, rehashing things that could not be fixed. They were both changed people now. Strangers.

Why, then, was the small flame of tenderness in his chest struggling to life again? It was tenderness in a distant sort of way, in a wish-her-well sort of way. It could never be anything more. He wouldn't let it be.

All he had to do was to look around. When he'd been here before, a blizzard's heavy downpour had cut off his view of this grand home, the elaborate spread, the plentiful fields that would yield quality wheat. Such a place could not compete with the claim shanty he lived in now, behind his brother's modest home. Such a place could not compete with the land he planned to buy—when he found the right place that he could afford, that is.

No, there was no storm now to hide the differences between him and Noelle. The differences, which had always separated them, always would.

Henrietta Worthington gasped. "Noelle! Shame on you. You've known who this man is this entire time? Why haven't you said anything? And why don't we know this friend of yours? Come in—"

"He is no friend of mine. Not anymore." She cut off her aunt with her gentle alto, giving no real hint of the emotion beneath.

Anger? Bitterness? Or was it nothing at all? Probably the latter, Thad realized. Lost love first left hurt and anger in its wake, then bitterness, and finally it was forever gone, leaving not so much as ashes to show for it or an empty place for all the space and power it had taken over one's heart.

Proof that love was simply a dream, not real or lasting at all.

"I'd best be going." He gave Noelle one last look. Figured this would be the last time they would come face-to-face. He didn't intend to spend much time on this side of the county. He didn't intend to play with fire; he'd only get burned if he tried. He knew that for certain. All he had to do was gauge it by the narrowing of the aunt's gaze, as if she were taking his true measure.

And Noelle, what would she see in him now if she had her sight? Probably the man who sweet-talked her out of one side of his mouth and lied to her out of the other.

He took a step back, already gone at heart. "Not that

it's my business, Mrs. Worthington, but don't go driving that black gelding again. He's no lady's horse. It's not worth your lives if he bolts a second time."

It was Noelle who answered, who'd stepped into the threshold with her wool cloak folded over one arm, staring directly at him. "That sounds as if you care, and how can that be?"

"My caring was never in question." He took another step back and another. "I'll always want the best for you. Take good care of yourself, darlin'."

"I'm not your darling." She tilted her head a bit to listen as he eased down the steps. "Goodbye."

His steady gait was answer enough, ringing against the board steps and then the bricks and the hard-packed snow. She felt the bite of the cold wind and something worse. What could have been. Thad was a lost path that would be forever unknown, thank the Lord. She thought of all the reasons why that was a good thing, but his words haunted her. Was he simply saying the easiest thing, or part of the truth, or was there more truth to tell?

She told herself she wasn't curious. Truly. She didn't want to know the man he'd become. So why did she wait until she heard the creak of a saddle and the faint jangle of a bridle, a horse sidestepping on the icy crust of deep snow before she stepped back into the warmth and closed the door?

"Noelle Elizabeth Kramer!" Henrietta burst out. "Why didn't you tell me you knew that man?"

"I don't. Not any longer. That's simply the truth." Why did she feel emptier as she hung her coat back on the tree? "I knew Thad long ago before, from my school days. As it turned out, I did not know him very well at all."

Henrietta fell uncharacteristically silent, and Noelle wondered if her aunt was compiling a list of questions on the man's character and wealth. Which would be completely expected, but Thad was bound to be a disappointment to her aunt's high standards for an acceptable beau for one of her daughters.

From the corner of the parlor, Matilda gasped. "Do you mean he once courted you?"

"No, there was no courtship." No official one. Why it shamed her now, she couldn't begin to explain. It had all seemed terribly romantic to a sixteen-year-old girl with stars in her eyes and fairy tales in her head, to secretly meet her beloved.

Oh, it had been terribly innocent; Thad had been respectful and a complete gentleman, had never dared to kiss her even after he'd proposed to her. But now, looking back with disillusionment that had forever shattered those fairy tales and dimmed the stars, she could see a different motive. Not a romantic one, but a less than noble one. He'd courted her behind her parents' backs, purposefully fooling them, and for what?

In the end, he'd chosen to run instead of marry. In the end, if there had been any truth to his courtship, then his affection for her had paled next to the strength of his fear. At least, that was the way she'd rationalized it. That's why his words were haunting her. *My caring was never in question.*

Perhaps his caring had been only that. Caring and not the strong, true love she'd felt for him. Either way, it hardly mattered now. She knew his true measure beneath the handsome charm and solid-appearing values. Thad McKaslin was not a man of his word. He was a coward. A man who ran instead of stayed.

"What about his family? Does he own property?" Henrietta persisted. "That's a fine young man. And handsome. Don't you think, Matilda? Noelle, you must tell me what you know about him. Here's your cloak. We're still attending to our errands in town. I'll not be put off my cause, you know."

Noelle fumbled with the garment Henrietta pressed into her hands. Certainly she knew that; why had she rehung her cloak in the first place? It simply went to show how tangled up her emotions were. A mess of them, threads of old hurt and confusion and the sharp tang of lost love were as hopelessly knotted. "I'm afraid I know very little about Mr. McKaslin. He left town long ago. I never knew what became of him. I never cared to."

After she'd finally accepted that he'd broken his vow to her. That he'd left her waiting for a promise he'd never meant to keep.

"Perhaps he left to make his fortune." There was the rustle of wool as Henrietta slipped into her coat. "Perhaps he has very respectable family back East."

"I'm afraid I don't know." Noelle lost count of her steps and had to reorient herself. Three more steps and she was at the door. The handle felt warm from the radiant heat of the fireplace, which was blazing on this frigid, late-winter morning—like her emotional tie to Thad. "But if I were you, I wouldn't depend on Thad McKaslin as a reliable kind of man."

When she stepped outside, the still morning air seemed to wait expectantly, as if some wonderful thing were about to happen. But what? She lived a quiet life teaching piano and crocheting and sewing for her five cousins' hope chests. The days, while happy, were predictable and routine. Why did it feel as if something was about to change?

Simply her wishful thinking, no doubt. Before she'd lost her sight, she had a love for romantic novels. Or, she reasoned, maybe spring really *was* right around the corner. It was, after all, late January. A month and a few weeks more and March would be storming in. It had been her father's favorite time of the year.

Her father. She missed him so strongly, it was like taking an ax to her midsection. She gripped the rail and froze a moment, drawing in the fresh, icy air. He'd been at her side when she finally accepted that Thad had abandoned her. He'd run away from marrying her. After she confessed, her father had comforted her and reassured her as she cried for the pieces of her shattered heart and broken dreams. Only the death of her parents had hurt with that same keen-edged grief.

I miss you, Papa. She felt the lonesomeness for him as solidly as the boards at her feet. Her knees felt weak as she tripped down the steps. Thad had brought all this up. Simply waltzing into her home, pretending he was such a good dependable man. Why the pretense? She already knew the kind of man he was.

An opportunist, her father had said to her, kindly, while she'd sobbed. She remembered how her mother had come into her room with a steaming pot of tea for all of them. She sure ached for her parents' comfort, their company, everything. They had held her up after her innocent illusions had been so thoroughly destroyed.

If they were still alive, they would be the first to reassure her and to send Thaddeus McKaslin back on his way to wherever it was he'd run off to. Good riddance.

But as she reached the brick walk, she heard the low, deep-throated nicker of a horse's greeting and the chink of steeled shoes shifting in the ice-crusted snow. Was it Thad's horse? Was he still here? And why was she allowing herself to be so upset by him that she hadn't paid enough attention to remember if she'd distinctly heard him riding away or not?

The horse's bridle jingled and she could hear him take a step her way. She held out her hand and the steel-shod hooves padded closer. This time the low nicker was accompanied by the radiant warmth of a horse's big body, and the tickle of whiskers against her fingertips warned her a second before the horse scented her palm and rubbed against her.

Oh, she loved horses. She cherished the warm-silk feel of his muzzle and stroked the animal's nose.

"You are a handsome one," she said, running her fingers over the length of his nose to his forelock. He snorted as if in answer and pressed into her touch. Joy, warm and quiet, flowed through her. "I miss riding the most but you'll just keep that secret, right? My aunt does not approve of women horseback riding, even sidesaddle."

The horse seemed likewise offended as he snorted and leaned in, lowering his head to give her better access; at least that's how she chose to think of it. "It's a pleasure to be with a well-behaved horse. That's not usual around here now that my uncle has—"

An angry, buglelike whinny shattered the morning's peace. Noelle spun toward the sound—the stable. That new stallion of Uncle Robert's was so spirited, he was dangerous. "—has decided he's a horseman," she finished.

Please, don't let my uncle get hurt, Lord. She took a step off the brick walk and stopped, unsure of the uneven drifts of snow that would be no challenge if she could see them. Not that she could help if there was a problem, but she wanted to help. Robert knew next to nothing about horses, although he was certain he knew everything, the poor, dear, misguided man. Perhaps that's where Thad was, giving her uncle a hand and a word of advice. Robert needed it.

The front door slammed shut and Henrietta barreled down the steps with the speed of a tornado. "Where is my horse? Why hasn't Robert brought out Miss Bradshaw?"

"I don't know why your mare is not hitched up yet. It sounds as if he's having problems with the stallion again."

"The stallion? What about my mare? He'd best not even contemplate the possibility of my driving to town behind that—that creature! As if that new gelding hadn't been bad enough of an experience. We shall meet peril for certain. Wait here, dear." Henrietta tromped by on the walk, her shoes striking against the brick and then muffled by the snow.

Noelle imagined her aunt lifting her skirts and wading through the snowdrifts like a Viking conquering the fjords. Since she had to stand alone in the cold, she may as well get better acquainted with Thad's horse. As if the horse agreed, his bridle bit jingled— perhaps he was shaking his head—and then he nosed her hand for more affection.

How could she resist? She savored the little joys of it. The alive feeling of the warm, velvet coat. The rhythmic breathing hot against her hand. The ticklish muzzle whiskers. The heart of the horse as he politely lipped at the pocket of her cloak. She liked him; it was hard not to. Once, in simpler times, she had dreams of horses and living all her life with them—and Thad.

Thad. At least she didn't have to worry about him lingering around, or coming back into her life to stay. His leaving was a certainty. She ran her fingers through the horse's coarse forelock. What was keeping Henrietta's sleigh?

Chapter Four

Seeing her haloed by the frozen mist and chatting with his horse was like being kicked by a bull. He'd been kicked several times, so he knew exactly how it felt. The sight of her knocked the wind from his chest. She looked like his dreams. She looked like his idea of heaven. Always had. Always would.

"So, McKaslin," Robert Worthington said from the finely built stable's main aisle where he fastened the last buckle on a docile mare's harness. "What do you think of my fine purchase in that stall over there?"

Thad looked up and down the aisle; only a few stalls were occupied and one by a white horse showing his teeth. He wasn't sure exactly what to say to compliment the ill-tempered colt. The scent of newly cut wood and fresh shavings at his feet told him this enterprise of Worthington's was brand-new.

Noelle's aunt marched into sight. "Is that fine purchase the reason my sleigh is not ready? Poor Noelle is out there half-frozen in this cold. She's fragile, you know that."

"I know, dear. Just had a bit of a problem is all. McKaslin gave me a hand."

"A problem? It looks like a wild bull got loose in this stable—"

Noelle. Thad's attention swung back to her and stayed there. She was petting Sunny. The mustang was no fool. He was nosing her hand affectionately, looking as though he wanted nothing more in the world than to win a smile from her. Poor fella. Thad knew how he felt. He'd once felt the same way.

Seeing her again— Whew. He froze in place. He'd wanted to avoid her this morning so he wouldn't cause her any pain, but now he realized he wasn't as tough as he liked to think.

He could resist making a mistake like her again, but what he couldn't seem to do was to stop the pain. Why, it was impossible to forget how his love for her had once filled his spirit the way a rising sun filled the hollows of a mountain's peak.

Time to leave, man. He nodded in Worthington's direction. "Good luck with that wild boy of yours."

Robert looked up from rechecking the bridle buckles and grinned. "You say that like you think I need good luck."

I think you're gonna need more than that. Thad glanced at the big white stallion, teeth bared and ears plastered flat against his head, and was glad he didn't have to deal with that animal. "I hope you got a good price for him."

"Cost me a pretty penny."

That's what Thad was afraid of. "I meant a low price, sir."

"Well now, he's got excellent confirmation. And his pedigree. Why, it's about as impressive as it can be."

"I'm not about to argue with you, but personally I like a horse who isn't keen on biting me when I get anywhere near him." Thad tipped his hat. "Good day to you, ma'am."

"Uh, well, thank you, young man." With the ferocity of an army general the fine lady squinted her eyes and looked him up and down. "Do you have relatives up north?"

"I believe so. My father's side of the family."

"Very well. It showed a fair amount of character to deliver our lost packages. You went out of your way when you didn't need to."

"I just did what anyone would do." He took a step away before she could invite him back into the parlor for supper or some such nonsense. He didn't figure that she'd want much to do with him if she knew the truth about the way he'd treated Noelle. "Again, good luck, Mr. Worthington. You be careful when you're handling that stallion."

"I intend to." Robert straightened and took the mare by the bit to lead her, but seemed frozen in midstep. He glanced through the wide, open double doors to the picture Noelle made, befriending the gold-and-white mustang. "You wouldn't know a good horseman you could recommend to me, would you? I could use some help around here."

"I, uh—" *Me.* He clamped his mouth shut before the words could escape. He needed a job, but not that bad. Besides, Noelle wouldn't like that idea. And the notion of facing who he was every day—the man she made him remember. The man she saw as a coward. That's what he felt like, even though he knew it wasn't true.

Maybe Noelle's opinion of him meant more than

he'd ever thought. He steeled his chest and took a step back, staring hard at the ground, at his scuffed boots, anywhere but where she stood, framed in silver light. "I'll let you know if I hear of anyone."

He left the husband and wife to their chatter, keeping his eyes low, feeling the ache of regret tug at him. There she was. He could sense her somehow like warmth on a spring breeze. What did he do? Walk up to her and make pleasant conversation? He didn't reckon she wanted that. He didn't, either.

The trick was to keep control of that spark of caring in his heart. Keep it small and eventually it would snuff right out. That was his hope anyway.

She must have heard him coming because she turned toward him. There was no smile on her face and she stood in shadow. He'd always remembered Noelle as she'd been when he'd left her—she'd never aged or changed for him in memory, but time changed everyone.

He saw that now. The way hard loss and sorrow had changed the shape of her mouth and eyes, no longer wide with an easy, assumed happiness. Her face was as soft as a rose blossom still, but leaner. Time and maturity had sharpened her high cheekbones. Her emerald-green eyes, still so lovely, did not twinkle and smile at him with good humor, the way they once had. The way they never would again.

She was lovelier than ever, but changed. It was the change now he saw, not the similarities to the young woman he remembered.

"You have a very polite buddy," she said gently, politely. "Unlike my poor uncle's horse."

"Sunny's the best. I'm lucky to have him." He didn't

bother to hide the affection he felt. "Pardon me, your uncle seems like a fine man but not that good with horses. I'm worried about that stallion in there."

"As am I. My uncle is inexperienced with horse handling. He's city raised." She turned her attention back to Sunny, who didn't seem to mind more petting a bit. "My aunt is not pleased with this notion of his to quit the bank and realize his dream of raising horses."

"Pleased? Nah. It's worse than that. When I left, she was lighting into him real good." Thad came close to reach for the reins. "Doesn't a family like this have hired stable help?"

"We're between hands right now. Henrietta disapproved of the last one's interest in one of her daughters—my cousins. Two are in town at school, and two more were sent away to finishing school. That's where Angelina will be next year, especially if another stable boy becomes interested in her again."

"Of course. I suppose a family has to be careful of its reputation."

"My aunt seems to think so. Listening to her, it would be impossible to find anyone good enough for her daughters to marry." Noelle kept a careful lid on her heart. Hearing the creak of the saddle and the jingle of the bridle as he obviously gathered the reins so he could mount up, she stepped back so he could leave. Good. She didn't have anything to say to him that hadn't already been said.

He was the one who seemed to be lingering. "Well, now, I'd better get along."

"Yes."

Perhaps she'd answered too quickly. Perhaps that single word had been too sharp. She hadn't meant it to be, but it was too late to change the awkward silence that settled between them like the frigid air. She was sorry about that. "I shouldn't have—"

"No, don't." He stopped her with a hand to her arm. "You have every right to hate me."

She didn't hate him, but she couldn't seem to correct him, either. His touch made a sweet, heartfelt power sweep through her, and it was unsettling. In memory came the summer's heat beating on her sunbonnet, casting a blue shade from the bonnet's brim, the scent of fresh cinnamon rolls and ripening wild grasses, and the pleasantly rough texture of Thad's large hand engulfing hers. Grass crushed beneath her summer shoes as they left their picnic basket and strolled near the river's edge.

The memory of color and shape and sight came, too. She remembered the way Thad's thick, collar-length hair shone blue-black with the sunlight on it. His eyes were the honest blue of the Montana sky before sunset. She could see again the shape of his sun-browned, handsome face, rugged with high slashing cheekbones and a strong blade of a nose. His jaw had been cut square and stubbornly; she supposed it still was.

The horse—Sunny—gave a low nicker of complaint. Thad's hand fell away from her arm, the bridle jingled and Thad spoke. "Looks like your horse and sleigh are ready to go."

The past spiraled away, bringing her solidly into the present with not even the memories of images and color before her eyes.

In darkness, she stood shivering in the cold, listening to the *clip-clop* of the mare, Miss Bradshaw's gait and the faint hush of the sleigh's runners on the icy crust of snow. Hurt rose up like a cold cutting fog until it was all she could feel.

As if from a great distance she heard her aunt and uncle saying goodbye to Thad, she heard the beat of his steeled horseshoes on the icy ground and felt the tears of the girl she'd used to be, the girl who believed in love and in the goodness of the man who was riding away from her. Even now.

Please let him move on, Lord, she prayed as Henrietta's no-nonsense gait pounded in her direction. *Please take this pain from my heart.*

She didn't want to feel, especially after all this time, the ragged pieces of her spirit broken. She'd waited at the window for Thad watching the moon rise and the stars wheel across the sky. She stood waiting, shivering as the September night turned bitterly cold. Still she'd waited, believing in the goodness of the man she loved—a goodness that didn't, apparently, exist. She'd believed in a love that wasn't true.

Now, five years later, she felt the burn of that old heartache and gulped hard to keep it buried. The pieces of that shattered love still cut like tiny shards of sharp glass.

At least I know he will move on, she thought. *Please, Lord, let that be soon.*

Her world was dark and pragmatic. She set her chin, gathered herself and turned toward her aunt's approaching steps. "You have your letter? I wouldn't want you to face such a perilous trip to town and realize you'd left the letter behind."

"Exactly." Henrietta sounded cheerful and it was no trouble at all to imagine her delighting in the prospect of more drama. There was a rustle and shuffle as she gathered her skirts. "I certainly pray we shall not run into any further trouble. Now that Robert has agreed to take that beast of a runaway to the sale this very day, I am most relieved."

"Yes, but think of whoever buys the gelding," Noelle pointed out, struggling to put a smile on her face, as Robert took her elbow and helped her into the sleigh. "There is more peril awaiting that unsuspecting buyer."

Robert chuckled, warm and deep, a sure sign he was amused. "I will make it clear the gelding has certain training problems, so that we won't have that on our consciences."

"Good." Noelle patted his hand before she let him go. "Thank you for that. I don't want anyone to get hurt the way—" she swallowed hard, forcing the past back where it couldn't hurt her "—we almost did."

"And I'll drive you two lovely ladies to town myself, just to make sure there are no more mishaps."

Henrietta's humph of disapproval was loud enough to disturb the placid Miss Bradshaw. The mare side-stepped in her traces with a quick *clip-clip* on the ice. "Robert, you'll not hitch that beast to this vehicle!"

"Now, my dear, I'll just tie him behind the sleigh. There will be not a single thing to worry about."

"We shall see when we get safely to town. *If* we get safely to town." Henrietta gave the lap blanket a sound snap, shaking it out.

Noelle felt the rasp of the blanket fall across her knees. Whatever her losses and lessons in her life, she was so grateful for her wonderful aunt and uncle. Their love, their acceptance and their funny ways reminded her of her own parents. She hooked her arm through Henrietta's and held on tight.

By noontime, the freezing fog had been blown apart by a cruel north wind bringing with it the look of snow. Thad reckoned the growing storm cloud in the northeast might bring another whiteout. With the responsibilities at the home place partly his now, too, Thad worried about the livestock. He blew out a breath, knuckled his hat back and glanced around the busy town street.

Angel Falls was still a small town by most standards, but it had grown in the time he'd been away. There were more shops, and the look of the street was fancier, as if the whole place, despite the current recession, was managing to thrive. Fancy ribbons brightened up one window, colorful ladies' slippers another, even here at the far end of Second Street, making him feel out of place as he looked for the land office. But he did spot a bookstore. He'd have to go in there another time.

Was he on the right side of the street? He tugged the piece of paper from his trouser pocket and squinted at the address Aiden had scribbled down for him. A woman's gruff voice lifted slightly above the drone of noise on the street. A familiar voice.

"I shall never become accustomed to this weather!" Mrs. Worthington was climbing out of their sleigh a good half-dozen shops up ahead. "You're likely to freeze sitting still in this wind. You must come in, dear."

"I have a difficult time in a crowded place. No, I'd best stay here and try not to freeze in the wind." There was a note of humor to Noelle's voice.

A note that was like an arrow to his heart. Just a hint

of humor, but without the brightness and the gentle trill of laughter he remembered so well. They truly were strangers, he reminded himself, surprised how much losing the last little piece of Noelle—the way he'd kept her in memory—hurt. So much for the notion of love. Not only was it ashes, but even long after the ashes had scattered, blown into nothing by the wind, the scar from the burn remained.

Yes. He rubbed at the center of his chest with the heel of his hand. The burn remained.

Mrs. Worthington hadn't see him; her back was to him as she marched along the boardwalk and disappeared into a doorway. He stared at the numbers written on the paper. Sure enough, he'd have to head in Noelle's direction. The last thing he wanted to do was to hurt her more. Chances were he could walk right by her without her knowing, since she could not see him. The boardwalks were fairly busy, and the noise from the street would disguise him well enough.

He headed on in her direction. It was best not to say howdy to her, or the burn on his heart would start hurting fresh. He kept his gaze focused on the icy boardwalk ahead of him and did not look her way, but there she was in his side vision, alone and lovely and sitting in the cold, blind and alone. He had to fight the powerful urge to stop and stay with her, to watch over her until her aunt's return.

She's not your lookout, remember? Not when her father forced him out of town the way he did. Not when her father had threatened his family's land. The trouble was, his heart didn't seem to care about all those sensible arguments. His spark of caring remained. There was a brightness within him that remembered, that would always remember, the schoolgirl who'd laughed so easily, saw wonder and joy everywhere, hummed with every step she took and was full of love and dreams.

Maybe his notion of love being nothing at all was a poor one, when put to the test. Seeing Noelle made his heart cinch up tight. Did she still matter to him?

The embittered part of him wanted to say no. No a thousand times. But as a gust of wind hit him square in the chest, he had to admit the truth.

He'd gone through a lot of misery for her sake. He'd left home, his family and everything he'd ever known. He'd slept on hard ground in freezing weather and in mostly unheated bunkhouses come winter. He'd ridden hard from sunup until sundown in blazing summer heat long day after long day. He'd lived a life he did not like or want because somewhere beyond his unhappiness was her joy, bright and shining and everything she deserved.

Yep, a wise man would just keep on walking and not give her another thought. He forced his boots forward on the icy boardwalk and kept on going.

"Thad?" Her gentle voice said his name the way it always had.

He could tell himself he didn't remember, that she was a stranger to him, that the past was past. It didn't matter so much for deep down in his heart, he would always know her.

She turned toward him as if she saw him. Her sightless eyes looked at him but did not see him. He stopped in the middle of the boardwalk. "How did you know it was me?"

"I'd know your gait anywhere. Do you see my uncle? He's at the horse sale." She sounded hopeful.

She looked that way, too. She might not notice how easily her emotions played on her lovely face. He might not want to think about how easy it was for him to read her feelings. It always had been for him.

Aching at all the things that had changed between them, he leaned over the hitching post to peer down the alley. Robert Worthington in his fancy tailored suit stood out in the crowd of cowboys and ranchers. "He's right ahead, but he's looking at a half-crazed mare. Doesn't he have any horse know-how at all?"

"My poor uncle means well, but he's city born and bred. He's spent his life reading books on wranglers and cowboys, so he has a lot of fictitious notions in his head." Fondness shaped her soft face. "It's been a lifelong dream of his to be a great horse trainer. The poor man has no notion of ranching or real experience handling horses."

"Where does he hail from?"

"St. Louis."

"Your parents came from here," he remembered.

"Yes. When they passed away and I was so injured, Henrietta came straightaway. She took charge of everything until Robert could settle things enough at his work to come help. He took over Papa's interest in the bank, started managing my investments, which I had inherited, and finally sold my family home."

Her family home? It had been a mansion and not a home, but he didn't comment on that. To her, it must have been jammed full of memories. "Was it too painful to live there, afterward?"

"Yes. You *would* know that about me." There was no mistaking the sorrow shadowing her face. "Robert moved his whole family to Montana Territory. He didn't want to take me away from this country where I grew up."

"You had to have been gravely injured."

"Yes, at first, but then I began to recover. God spared me my life, and I am thankful. I have to believe He has some purpose for my life yet."

"I'm sure of that, Noelle." He sounded so sincere, it was impossible not to believe him, impossible not to be touched by that. He shook his head once and cleared his throat. "Well, now, this mare looks much more suitable for a lady's driving horse."

"Yes, that's Miss Bradshaw. She's very sensible."

"So I see." His step drummed closer. "Miss Bradshaw?"

"Henrietta doesn't believe in calling a horse by his or her first name. She prefers a more formal relationship."

"Best not tell her all the nights I slept beside my horse."

"Best not." Noelle couldn't think of more to say; at least more that she wanted to. She wanted to be unaffected, beyond the pain of her schoolgirl's broken heart and above holding on to old anger. She'd healed from his betrayal and moved on, truly. But there, beneath the lid she kept on her heart was something more devastating than anger. She didn't know how to fill the silence between them.

And what a silence it was. Five long years of silence. She didn't know how to break it. She was fairly sure she didn't want to. It wasn't easy holding back the memories of how wrong she'd been about him, about love.

"McKaslin!" Robert's bass boomed cheerfully above the noise and motion on the street. His boots drummed quickly as if he were in grand spirits. "Glad to see you're still here. I was just telling my wife how well you handled that stallion. I've never seen anything like it."

"It was nothing. I've been around horses all my life, is all." A note of humility deepened his baritone.

Noelle knew he was being modest; Thad had a way with horses and an understanding of them she'd always thought was a divine blessing.

Not that it was her business anymore. She carefully drew the lap blanket more tightly around her, leaning to listen. Even when she told herself she shouldn't want to hear. His voice was deeper, manlier and rang with integrity, enticing a long-forgotten part of her to want to believe in him again. But she could not let down the guards on her heart.

"Say, Thad," Robert boomed out jovially, "you're good with horses. You wouldn't happen to be looking for work?"

Noelle's heart forgot to beat. No, her uncle couldn't be about to hire Thad. No, that was simply not possible—

"Rob!" Henrietta scolded above the sudden staccato of her steps. "How can you offer Mr. McKaslin a job? It's as if he isn't successful in his own right."

Noelle could hardly hear anything above the panicked rush in her ears. Surely, Thad would not accept Robert's offer. He had no interest in anything permanent, she was certain.

Thad's friendly chuckle rumbled with amusement. "Pardon me, ma'am, but do I look successful to you? I'm a simple cowboy, nothing more."

Noelle fisted her hands around the hem of the lap blanket. A simple cowboy? He had never been that.

"You can't fool me, son," Robert answered. "You are a born horseman. I've never seen anyone calm down a horse as fast as you calmed the stallion this morning in my stable. You must make your living training horses."

Noelle felt as cold as the rising wind as she waited for Thad's answer, although her heartbeat filled her ears so loudly, she didn't know if she would be able to hear him when he answered. She turned toward where he'd been standing on the boardwalk and wished she wasn't wondering. Wished she didn't want to know the pieces of his life and if he'd found his dream without her.

"No, sir," Thad said at last, his baritone heavy with regret. "I've been making my way as a drover. Riding cattle is hard work but it pays well enough."

"Cattle!" There was no mistaking the excitement in Robert's voice.

Noelle gulped in a bite of air, feeling oddly lost. She wasn't sure if it was worse to know Thad hadn't lived out his dreams than hoping he'd found them without her.

"I imagine that's a hard life, living on the trail," Robert went on to say. "Imagine you've gained a lot of experience."

"Yes, sir. I'm a good all-around man. I know my way around a cattle ranch. I mostly rode cattle. Spent March through October in the saddle on the trail."

She hadn't known she was holding her breath until the air rushed out of her lungs. Riding cattle? Was that what he left her for? To live a cowboy's life wandering from job to job far away from his responsibilities to his family and his promises to her?

Maybe she hadn't forgiven him as much as she'd

thought. Shame filled her. There was this hardness in her heart she hadn't realized was there. She shivered beneath the layers of wool and flannel she wore. Determined, she tucked the sheepskin-lined robe covering her lap neatly around her and anchored it so the wind wouldn't creep beneath it. It didn't help. She still felt as cold as a mountain glacier.

Thad's words, calmly spoken, continued to ring in her ear. "Yes, I did like it very much. It's a tough life. Not as romantic as the dime novels make it seem."

"I should think not!" Henrietta humphed as she marched up to the sleigh, her steps quick and confident. "Not at all a preferable livelihood."

Judging by her uncle's chuckle, he was completely amused. "I keep telling my wife that it's the mark of a man how he handles hardship, not what he does for a living."

"Robert! You know that I don't completely disagree with you." By the sound of her voice, half shocked and half smiling, Henrietta was probably shaking her head fondly at her husband.

She could also imagine Thad standing quietly, hands on his hips, in that patient way of his.

"Riding cattle." Robert sounded impressed. "Now, that's excitement. Is it like they say? Singing the cattle to sleep and using your saddle for a pillow?"

"I mostly use my saddlebag, as it's a might softer." Thad's baritone rang with an equal amusement.

That was the sound she recognized—the ring of Thad's easy, warm, good humor. If she'd met him anywhere else, and not in a blizzard with fear thrumming in her ears, she would have recognized him no matter what.

"A saddlebag, eh? That doesn't sound much better. I suppose it's true what they say about the dust in the air and those long hot days."

She waited for Thad's answer, realizing that the lid on her heart was a little ajar. Had Thad found whatever he'd been looking for? Down deep, beyond her disillusion and her hurt, she truly hoped he had.

"Sir, that doesn't begin to capture it. Hundred degrees in the shade, a herd of cattle, say anywhere from a hundred to a thousand kicking up dust, why, it makes a Montana blizzard look like a clear day."

"That does not sound quite as thrilling. I imagine there's a lot of gain to that lifestyle despite its hardships. Sleeping under the stars must be nice."

"It surely does make for a good night's sleep. Nothing like having the heavens and the wonder there for your roof."

Yes, there was the Thad she remembered from long ago. A pang of longing and remorse knelled through her, and she was surprised by the intensity of it. It was a longing for that sweet, innocent time in her life when the world had been so sunny and colorful. When her future was nothing but a long stretch of happy possibilities.

Not anymore. Noelle heard the catch in her throat, like a sob, although it wasn't. She hadn't realized how much she had changed from the girl who knew how to dream, that was all. How much she had lost.

"Goodness, are you all right, dear?" Henrietta dropped onto the sleigh's seat, all motherly concern. "Are you catching a chill? I predicted the wind was too cold for you to sit here and wait for me, and now I fear the worst."

Ashamed, Noelle nodded. What was wrong with her? She did not know, and she had the feeling that if she did, she could not find the right words to describe it. She cleared the regret from her throat before she could speak. "I'm not too cold. Truly."

She feared Thad had noticed, that he was watching her even now. What did he think about her blindness? Did he pity her? Did he think that she was damaged, less than whole? How could he not? "D-did you post your letter?"

"Certainly I did. Robert, untie Miss Bradshaw for me. I intend to get Noelle out of this bitter wind. In her delicate state, this cold cannot be good for her. If she does not succumb to pneumonia, I shall be amazed!"

Robert's chuckle was loving. "Yes, dear, go on. If you two lovely ladies wish to frequent the dress shop, I'll come by for the horse and sleigh and fetch the girls from the schoolhouse."

"Mind you don't be late! The school bells ring promptly at four o'clock." Henrietta took up the reins with plenty of shuffling. "Good day to you, Mr. McKaslin."

"Good day to you both." Kindness enriched his voice.

She imagined he was tipping his hat's brim once, the way he always used to do. She tried to picture more of him, tried to imagine the young man she'd known, in his prime now. It was hard to do, for he had surely changed as much as she had. Maybe more.

"Goodbye, Noelle."

His words sounded so final. "Goodbye, Thad."

As the cold wind scorched her face, she listened to his boots strike crisp and steady on the boardwalk as he walked away. She could not allow herself to imagine how his wide shoulders would have broadened, how his lean frame would have filled out with muscle and a cowboy's strength. Something cold struck her cheek as she tried not to see—and yet could not help drawing up the image—of how he would look seasoned by experience and a rugged, active life.

"It's snowing yet again." Henrietta's voice carved into Noelle's thoughts. "When will winter end? I shall never become accustomed to these Montana storms."

"Yes, sadly we are all likely to be snowed over until Armageddon if this continues." Noelle knew that dire prediction would make her aunt happy, who huffed decidedly, pleased to have such problems to discuss.

Determined to leave Thad McKaslin out of her thoughts, Noelle set her chin and swiped at the cold wetness on her cheek—tears, and not snow after all. "Then your letter shall never reach the territorial governor."

"Exactly my brand of luck. Listen to that! That contraption! How blessed we are to have a sensible mare who will not bolt at the clamor and dank coal smoke."

Only then did Noelle hear the clatter of the incoming train and smell its choking coal smoke. She did not notice much else, not the harmony of the traffic noise or the melody of the town's people going about their busy ways.

Her heart was too heavy to hear any music. Snow began falling in earnest with sharp, needlelike hits that had no rhythm or song as they fell, driven on a bleak wind.

Chapter Five

As Thad circled a dappled gray mare at the sale—he'd let Robert Worthington talk him into giving his opinion on a few animals he was considering—not even the steadily falling snow could clean away the grit of emotion that clung to him.

This wasn't how he'd reckoned things would be. Seeing Noelle again was going to happen—he knew that when he'd made the decision to come back to Angel Falls. But he figured she'd be a wife and a mother, busy with the fanciful tasks that kept privileged women occupied, like book clubs and church fund-raisers and whatnot. What he didn't figure on was having to realize how complete her father's plan had been. Mr. Kramer, rest his soul, must have known that Noelle would never understand or forgive, even with her generous heart. He'd hurt her then, and he was hurting her now. He hated it. He wished—well, he didn't know what he wanted, but he would do anything, or be anything, to keep her from hurting.

Impossible, he realized. His nearness made her sad. It was as plain as day.

"McKaslin, what's your opinion?"

"Wh-what?" He blinked, realizing he must have been staring at the horse's withers for a rather long time. The sights and sounds of the busy horse sale chased away most of his trail of thoughts, but not all of them.

"She's too old but, McKaslin, you seem to like her better than the gelding."

Thad knocked back his hat and the snow accumulating on the brim slid off, giving him time to think of the best way to answer. "You'd do well to go with an older horse. This mare is a little long in the tooth, but she's steady and gentle."

"I suppose I like the brash younger ones. More of a challenge."

Yep, Worthington had even less horse sense than he'd figured on. "Well, sir, you might not want to gamble your womenfolk's well-being like that. This old mare has a lot of good years in her, she'll be suited to pulling a light sleigh or buggy. Besides, look at the kindness you'd be doing. If no one buys her, she might be sent to the stockyards. That is one sad end for a nice horse."

Robert gulped at that. "I hadn't considered that before. I'm glad I asked your opinion. You have sound reasoning and a lot of knowledge. You know I'm looking to hire a good horseman to teach me what I haven't learned in books. If it's stable work you mind, I'll find someone to muck out the stalls—"

"You've got that wrong, Mr. Worthington. I don't mind stable work." Thad shoved his fists into his coat pocket, Noelle filling his thoughts. She was the biggest reason he had to say no, but there were others, too. "Truth is, I've got family trouble to help straighten out and then I've got my own plans."

"I understand." Robert pulled his billfold from his pocket. "I need permanent help, but more than that, I need someone like you. It's hard for a man like me to admit, but this horse business is not like banking."

"No, sir, it's very different. Stacks of money don't kick you in the chest."

"You're right there. I don't want to tell my wife how many times I've come close to getting seriously hurt. Maybe you'd consider working temporary, if that suits you. I'd be grateful for as long as you could stay."

It sounded mighty fine, except for Noelle. Remembering the look on her face whenever he was near cinched it. Nothing could make him hurt her like that.

"I see you're considering it." Robert sure looked pleased.

Thad cast his gaze around the sale. Rows and rows of horses standing in a spare lot between a boardinghouse and the smithy. Men and boys milled through the aisles, the sounds and colors muffled by the softly falling snow.

He thought of what to say to Robert and then of the land office he had yet to get to. He didn't know if he had a blue moon's chance of finding and affording his own place.

"Then come work for me. You can start right now by helping me figure out a good price for this mare."

"It's sure tempting, but I can't take the offer." There was no other answer he could give. "I wish I could."

"Could I ask what the reason is?"

"It's personal, sir." Out of the corner of his eye he caught sight of his older brother ambling along the boardwalk, probably heading to the land office, where they'd agreed to meet.

Best to hurry this along. He'd spent over an hour with Worthington, and the man had yet to take his advice. "Robert, buy this mare. I'd offer low first, say twenty, but she's worth more. If you pay seventy-five for her, it's not too much."

"Well, I appreciate that." Robert tipped his hat as Thad did the same.

He left the man bargaining with the horse trader and waded through the fresh snow to the boardwalk. Aiden was leaning over the rail, one eyebrow arched in question.

"I heard that." He didn't blink, and his dark eyes kept careful watch as Thad hit the icy steps.

The ice gave him something to put his mind on instead of Noelle. "What did you hear?"

"Worthington trying to offer you a job." Aiden pivoted and crossed his arms over his chest. "Why would you turn down a good wage? Even if you find land to buy around here—"

"Land that I can afford," Thad pointed out. That was the catch. He'd worked long and hard to put aside every dime he could of his wages, and it didn't add up to nearly what he needed it to be. "I'm not going to work anywhere near Noelle Kramer."

"Ah, so you've seen her. I wondered what would happen when you did."

"You could have told me."

"About her blindness? You could have asked. You left town before because of her." Aiden nodded in the direction of a shop two doors down from the postmaster's. "Are you going to be leaving for the same reasons now?"

"No. I gave you my word I would stay and I will." Thad let his brother fall in step with him. There was a lot he hadn't told his brother five years ago and now. Time to change the track of the conversation. "How's Ma?"

"She's at the mercantile buying fabric to start sewing for Finn." Aiden didn't sound too happy about that.

Thad had learned that Aiden wasn't too happy about anything. "We'll make sure he doesn't let her down this time."

"We'll do our best. I got his train ticket taken care of. He ought to be arriving two weeks from tomorrow." Aiden's wide shoulders sagged a notch.

It was quite a burden. Thad could feel it, too. "I'll do my best, too. We'll get him straightened out."

"It all depends on how the territorial prison has changed him."

Thad didn't know what to say about that. Life had a way of changing a person in the best of circumstances. "I wish I would have come back sooner."

"The wages you sent home made the difference between losing our place and keeping it, so put that worry out of your mind. Between us, we've got enough of them as it is." Aiden checked his watch. "Let's hurry up. I've got to pick up Ma and take her to her church meeting in thirty minutes."

"Hey, I thought you were going to look at property with me."

"I'm not going to leave you to do this on your own, little brother. You need a wiser man's opinion."

"And where would I be gettin' this wise opinion? Surely not from you?"

Aiden smirked—the closest to a smile he ever got. "I've been keeping an eye on the land prices around here. Figured we would take a peek at the sale sometime, too." He gestured toward the sale. "When Finn gets home, he's got to have something to ride. He's not using my horses."

Or Sunny. Thad nodded in agreement.

Aiden cleared his throat as they started walking. "You wouldn't be thinking about beauing that woman again."

"Noelle?" Beauing her? There was an outlandish thought. "No. I learned my lesson and I learned it well."

"Now it's time for me to worry about you, brother. If it's not Miss Kramer, then what else has put that look on your face? There are the Worthington daughters. A few of them are of a marriageable age."

He'd hardly noticed the one in the parlor—then again, he would never notice anyone else when Noelle was in the same room. The pang that ached in his heart was best left unexamined. He spotted the land office. "The real question is, brother, why are you mentioning those daughters? Say, you wouldn't be sweet on one of the Worthington girls, would you?"

"Me?" Aiden spit out the word. "You've been gone a long time, brother, or you'd remember my opinion on most women."

"I remember just fine. But I reckon that you've been alone a long time. That might have changed your opinion some." Thad tried to say the words kindly, knowing his brother hurt for the wife and the newborn son he'd buried. Years hadn't chased the haunted look from Aiden's face. "Even I think about marrying now and again."

"You?" Aiden's jaw dropped in disbelief. "Didn't figure that would be likely."

"Now, I didn't say I was serious about it right this moment, but I've considered marriage from time to time." He stepped to the side to allow two women to pass by on the boardwalk. "The real trouble is finding a *sensible* female."

"Brother, there isn't a one of them on this green earth. God didn't make a woman that way, and if you think otherwise then you are just fooling yourself."

"Spoken like a man destined to live alone for the rest of his life."

"And you aren't?"

"No, not me." Thad blinked against the sudden sharp glare of wintry sun as the road curved northeast. "I'm holding out for the kind of woman a man can count on. Maybe someday I'll find a woman who understands that life is a battle you've got to fight every day."

"Good luck with that one, little brother." Aiden shook his head. "You've been riding the trail too long. You've forgotten what females are like. They're not like us."

"And you've been working in the fields alone too long."

"Then there's no doubt about it, little brother. We are a pair."

That was something he couldn't argue with. He did his best to steel his heart, to let go of what was past and hope that there would be a new start in life awaiting him. The truth was, he could never forget the pain he'd put on Noelle's lovely face. He had to do his best to stay away from her, for both their sakes. Knowing his luck, there wouldn't be land he could afford—at least the kind of land he wanted—and he'd be moving on after things on the home place were better.

The land office was nearly empty, he noticed as he yanked open the door, but the potbellied stove in the center of the room glowed red-hot. Thankful to be out of the bitter cold, Thad shook the snow from his hat and stepped inside.

"I can't tell you how this cheers me up!" There was no disguising the joy in Uncle Robert's voice from atop the mare he'd just bought for himself at the sale. "I feel alive again, I tell you."

Henrietta tsked as she pulled closed the dress-maker's door. "Robert, of course you are alive. You are driving me to distraction with this nonsense. You are no longer a young man, no matter how many ill-mannered horses you purchase."

Noelle felt a strange chill shiver down her spine, although perhaps it was the turn of the wind. Another storm was on the way, she could smell it brewing in the air. While her aunt and uncle battled good-naturedly, which was not unusual for them, her cousins spilled ahead of her down the steps and into the family sleigh. Their footsteps and chatter, lively and pleasant, coun-terbalanced the worry she had for her uncle. She wanted to ask Robert to dismount and join them in the sleigh, but it was hard to get a word in edgewise.

"*Two* more horses?" Henrietta sounded stunned. "How many horses will we need to pull our sleigh?"

"Now, Henrietta, you know I'm trying to start my own ranch."

"Yes, but you're a banker," Henrietta pointed out. "This is lunacy, Robert."

"Our Matilda is old enough to drive. The gray mare is for the girls' use."

"What? For us?" The chatter halted and footsteps herded away from the sleigh, Noelle presumed, where the old mare was tied.

"What's her name?" Angelina cried out.

"She's sweet!" fourteen-year-old Minnie cooed.

"She's really ours?" Matilda's hand slipped from hers.

Noelle froze in place on the sidewalk. So, Robert really had taken Thad's advice. That was a relief, but now she felt, well, grateful toward the man. She didn't want to feel the hint of gratitude toward the man. A hard knot coiled up in her stomach, and she wished, how she wished, it would stop. Her normally placid emotions were all snarled up ever since Thad had ridden back into her life.

Without Matilda to guide her, she dared not take a step for fear of falling on a patch of ice. She stood alone, waiting while the family inspected Matilda's new mare. Why was one ear searching the sounds on the street for Thad? Searching for his confident, steady gait, and for the low rumble of his voice?

Longing overtook her. Longing for those sweet, carefree days of her youth, for the dizzy happiness she'd felt when Thad had been beauing her, and for the shining future she'd wanted with him. The shining future she could not have now.

It was all Thad's doing, she realized. Making her remember her lost dreams. Making her look at memories filled with color and love. He made her realize how dark her life and how alone her future. Because of him, she saw her future so clearly—a future she tried not to look at.

"Noelle?" Matilda's touch at her elbow drew her from her thoughts. "Are you all right?"

"Y-yes." It took all her strength of will to bury her feelings. She turned in the direction of her cousin's voice. "No need to worry about me. Do you like your mare?"

"She's a darling. Papa promised he'd teach me to drive once the weather turns warmer. I'm so excited. I've been waiting to learn to drive for ever so long. Mama still thinks I'm twelve."

"She loves you," Noelle said simply.

"I know. I'm glad I finally get to learn." Matilda sounded as if she was glowing. "Oh, I wonder if I'll be able to drive to Lanna's wedding. Probably. It will be the first wedding of the year!"

"Probably, although learning to drive might also mean that you have to fetch your sisters to and from school now and again."

"True, but I don't mind." Matilda fell silent, and the chatter from the rest of the family remained a background symphony of conversation. "Perhaps there's a good chance I'll run into the dressmaker's nephew while I'm out driving."

"That would hardly be proper," Noelle cautioned, remembering. With all the pieces of her heart, she was remembering her own mistakes. Mistakes she wanted to wipe out of her life like chalk from a blackboard, to rub away every flaw, every wrong choice and every foolish romantic notion. "It's one thing to admire an available man's good qualities—but you don't want to get yourself into trouble, Tilly."

"What trouble could I get into?" Matilda said, all innocence, for she'd been gently raised.

As Noelle had. So innocent, she could not imagine all the consequences of one innocent crush on a nice man. Somehow, Noelle could not separate the feeling that if she'd never fallen in love with Thad, if she'd never strayed from her parents' expectations for her, if she'd never been so headstrong and determined and stubborn, then her parents would still be alive. And she would still have her sight.

Right now, she could be sensibly married to a fine, dependable man, and have several children of her own. More lost dreams that were hard to swallow. Her arms empty, her heart empty, she swallowed hard to keep it from sounding in her voice. "We're commanded to honor our parents, Tilly. You oughtn't to be placing so much importance on something as frail as love. It's like a snowflake in the air, lovely while it's swirling on the wind, but it melts and vanishes into nothing."

"Oh." Matilda sounded stricken. "I didn't mean to disrespect Mama and Papa. I only meant—" She sighed. "I'm not sure what I meant. I just want to be married and happy."

She fell silent. Noelle didn't know what to say. More remorse filled her up. She hadn't meant to hurt her cousin. "I know you do, Tilly. I pray every day that the right man will come calling for you."

"And I appreciate it." There was a smile in Matilda's voice, as if trying to cover her hurt.

"I shouldn't have been so harsh. I didn't mean—" She felt the brush of snow against her cheek, as gentle as grace. This is what came from being anywhere near to Thaddeus James McKaslin. Everything was upside down. Her sensible life, her sensible thoughts. She was choking on the pain and memories she'd buried for good reason.

She squared her shoulders and said as kindly as she could to her cousin. "Am I hearing this right? Uncle Robert *doesn't* want to drive us home?"

"He wants to ride that beautiful new mare of his home. Oh, she is a beauty." Matilda sighed. "Jet-black. She's so well formed, even I can see it. She's like perfection. Except she keeps trying to bite everyone."

"Is she tame?" Was it a mare Thad had approved of?

"Aside from trying to bite, she *seems* well trained. Come, I'll help you to the sleigh."

The late-afternoon chill seemed to blow right through her layers of warm clothing and penetrate her very bones. "I'm sorry I was so harsh, Tilly."

"No, I appreciate your guidance, Noelle. I just—" Sad. That's how Matilda sounded. "I want to believe there's a real hero meant for me. A great man who will love me for who I am and will never let me down."

"It's a nice dream, Tilly." But it was only a dream. Noelle knew that for a fact, but she held back her words. She didn't know what to say to protect her cousin; and the last thing she wanted to do was to take away her hopes for happiness. "There is a good man out there for you. I'm sure of it."

It was best to accept love for what it was, and marriage, she realized, her aunt and uncle's dissatisfaction with one another adding a sour note as the girls climbed silently into the sleigh.

Thad knocked the snow from his hat brim and felt his hopes fall to the ground, too. The land he was looking at—even buried in snow—was in sorry shape. The fencing—what was left of it—was tumbling over from neglect. The stable was sod. The house nothing more than a tumble-down shanty with no roof. If his guess was right, then where he was standing would be marshland when spring came. Most of the hundred and sixty acres were in a gully, which made him worry about floods from winter snowmelt and spring and autumn rains.

Yep, it was far from ideal property and for an unreasonable price, too.

Aiden ambled over from inspecting the buildings, leading his horse by the reins. "I hope you aren't thinking about laying down good money for this place."

"No. It would be hard to raise a profitable crop here. Livestock can't graze if the pasture's knee-deep in water."

Aiden nodded in acknowledgment, casting his gaze around, frowning severely. "The barn is ready to fall in. This place isn't worth what the bank wants for it."

And this was the last property on his very short list. Thad blew out a lungful of air and stared down at the toes of his scuffed boots. "I want to pay cash. I'm not going into debt for land. Not after what we've been through with the home place."

"Wise decision." Aiden cleared his throat, choosing not to speak of what they had struggled with.

The family mortgage had been the leverage Noelle's father had used to fully convince Thad to leave town without her. His ma was fragile; she had always been. The family had been desperate—Aiden's wife was expecting and sick with the pregnancy, and they needed their home and their land to make a living on. Thad had vowed he'd never let anyone have that kind of hold on him again, especially a banker.

He swallowed hard, glad he'd done the right thing— the only thing he could do. And yet, remembering the pain on Noelle's beautiful face, it had been the wrong thing, too. He'd been caught between a rock and a hard place, and he still was.

"I guess I'll look farther out in the county. Maybe the prices will be better there. Something close enough to ride in and help you with the wheat—and our brother, but far enough away from bad memories." That and the fact that he could see the county road from here, the road the Worthingtons also used to go to and from their spread. A lone horse and rider cantered along the lane.

"Sounds sensible." Aiden mounted up and swung his horse toward the driveway.

Some days reality was a tough thing. Thad gave one last look at the property. His hopes had been higher than he'd thought. He eased his boot into the stirrup and grabbed hold of the saddle horn.

"Would you look at that fool?" Aiden sounded concerned. "He's gonna get himself killed."

Thad slid into the saddle and looked up. Sure enough, it did look as though that horse and rider were in serious disagreement. They'd come to a stop in the road. The black was head down, tail up, bucking like a wild bronco. The man clung to the saddle. There was something familiar about that man. Thad reined Sunny toward the driveway, fighting a bad feeling in his gut. Robert Worthington had a brown wool coat like that, and he was not in control of his horse.

Aiden had already pressed his mount into a fast trot. "That man needs help. Is it—that looks like Mr. Worthington. He's a banker, not a horseman. What's he thinking?"

Thad couldn't answer, as he pressed Sunny into a

fast gallop. Could he get there in time to help? The long stretch to the road seemed a hundred miles. Sunny's mane and stinging snow lashed his face as he pushed the mustang faster.

Hold on, Robert. Thad watched the black horse's nose nearly touch the snowy ground as the hind end rocked up high and then higher. Thad was close enough to see Robert scrambling to stay on, but he was slipping. Looked as if he was clinging to that horse with all his might. Chances were that Worthington was going to be unseated. Since he didn't know how to sit a green-broke horse, then he likely didn't know how to take a fall from one, either. Didn't he understand how dangerous that was?

"Faster, Sunny." Thad willed the mustang on, and Sunny went full out, his gallop so fast, they could have been flying.

It was not enough.

With the cold wind in his ears and tearing his eyes, it was hard to tell the exact moment Worthington went flying. But the bad feeling was back in his gut when he saw the man lift off the horse's back end and take a hit from those powerful, carefully aimed rear hooves.

Worthington hit the ground like a rag doll and didn't move. The black, freed from its rider, didn't run, but stayed, stomping and bucking and rearing up to paw the air, dangerously close to the fallen man. Thad winced, hurting for the man, knowing what this could mean. Robert looked unconscious. Maybe worse. Maybe dead.

Please, Lord, not that. A rare prayer filled his heart.

Adrenaline chugged through his veins as Sunny's hooves ate up the distance. The instant Sunny hit the main road, he swung out of the saddle, keeping one eye on that black horse. His boots hit the hard-packed snow and he dodged just in time to miss a well-aimed, angry kick to his head.

Thad stood between Robert and the enraged horse and caught the mare by one rein. The instant his fingers tightened on the leather strap, he yanked straight down, pulling the bit with him. The mare fought him with an angry scream, sidestepping and half kicking and baring her teeth, fighting to get in a good bite.

"Whoa there, filly. Whoa, now." Beads of sweat broke out on the back of Thad's neck, strong-arming the powerful horse farther away from Robert. The man was still unconscious. Sunny stood by the fallen man, nosing him gently. Where was Aiden? As the mare fought, trying to knock him off balance, he heard hooves striking nearer.

"I said whoa, girl." The beads of sweat began to roll down his back. His arm muscles burned as if they'd been set on fire. He stood his ground, gritting his teeth, trying to use what leverage he had to force the mare even farther away from Robert.

"Hold on," Aiden called out from behind him.

Not sure how much longer I can do that. Teeth gritted, the mare surged upward into a full rear. His feet left the ground. Pain shot through his arms. C'mon, Aiden. He couldn't hold on much longer.

A lasso whizzed through the air and hissed around the mare's neck. The rope yanked tight. Thad's feet hit the ground, and he shortened the rein.

Thank the Lord. Out of the corner of his eye he saw his brother riding close, keeping the rope taut. Free to let go, Thad left the mare to his brother and ran.

Sunny, standing over the unconscious man, gave a snort of alarm. Thad dropped on his knees at Robert's side. His guts clenched. Blood stained Worthington's hair, chest and the snow around him.

Was it too late? Hard to tell. It didn't look as if he was breathing. Thad, dreading the worst, thought of Noelle as he tackled the buttons on the man's thick wool coat. What would she do if she lost her uncle, too? Who would take care of her? Protect her? Look out for her?

Thad tore back the coat, icy fear making his fingers clumsy. Robert's chest was still—too still. And then there was the faintest movement. Shallow. Slow. Unsteady. But it was a breath.

Relief nearly drowned him. Worthington was alive. There was some hope to cling to.

"Robert!" He unwound his scarf. "Mr. Worthington, can you hear me?"

No answer. No movement. Nothing. He was hurt bad, Thad knew it. Sweat broke out on his brow. The icy air made him shiver. The snowflakes landed on his nape as he leaned forward to try to bandage the wound.

"I'll go for the doc!" Aiden drew up his horse. Behind him, the temperamental mare, squealing in angry protest, was tethered to a fence post. "Or, is it too late?"

"He's alive. Barely." Thad nodded toward his mustang, who stood patiently waiting at Robert's feet. "Best that you take Sunny. He can run faster than your draft horse."

"I'll be fast." Aiden slid off and gave the old draft horse a fond pat on his neck before he took Sunny by the reins. He mounted up, leaving without another word, for there was no time to waste.

"Robert?" Still no response. Thad shrugged out of his coat, debating what to do. At least those years of experience on the trail would come in handy. Thad figured the cut to Robert's head looked bad enough, but it was the blow to his chest that troubled him. He'd been around enough of this kind of injury to know it was often lethal. His heart could have been damaged.

The wind gusted, blowing colder. It was likely to be worse before it got better—and not good for Robert. Thad whistled for Clyde.

The big gentle Clydesdale ambled close, his nostrils flaring at the scent of blood, but he wasn't startled. He was a wise horse as he stood and blew out his breath in a whoosh, as if accepting his new burden.

The wind was kicking up, and the snow began to fall like rain. In the haze of the downpour, Thad took a moment to gaze down the road, where the Worthington ranch lay.

Noelle. He hurt for her. He knew that she loved her uncle very much.

Clyde nickered, scenting the wind. Someone was coming. Thad was no longer a religious man so to speak, but that didn't mean he wasn't given over to prayer now and again. He sent one more plea heavenward, *Lord, let that not be his family. Let them not see this.*

A dark horse broke through the veil of snow. There was no mistaking Miss Bradshaw's fine lines and sensible demeanor. He leaped to his feet and grabbed the horse's bridle bit. "Whoa there. Is that you, Mrs. Worthington?"

The snow shrouded her, and her voice was sharp. "Who dares stop us? We have no money, for we spent it all in town. Unhand my horse, you—"

"Thad?" Noelle's gentle voice seemed louder than the storm. She was already moving out from beneath the lap blanket, looking at him as if she clearly saw him. "Something's wrong. What is it?"

"It's Robert." So much for his prayers, Thad thought, steeling himself to face her again. "The horse threw him. He's in the road, and we—"

"Robert?" Mrs. Worthington cried out. "What's happened to my Robert?"

"No, stay where you are, ma'am." He released the bit to stay the woman's arm. "He's injured. I need you to stay collected."

"Injured?" The woman began to hyperventilate, breathing deeply and rapidly.

"Noelle, my brother's riding for the doctor, but we cannot leave him in the road. I was about to put him on the back of this horse, but the sleigh would be best for him."

"Of course." She looked stricken. Instant grief had carved its way around her emerald-green eyes. "Minnie, crowd the lunch pails and books into the backseat. Tilly, come help me. Angelina, see to your mother."

Thad turned on his heel, rushing the few paces back to the fallen man's side. There was so little he could do for Robert, but do it he would. He crouched down beside the fallen man and knocked aside the snow. A fine layer had begun to accumulate on Robert's body as if he were already gone.

Taking gentle care with the injured man, Thad lifted him carefully, determined to get Robert home. With the big man's heavy weight in his arms, he gave one final prayer. *Help him, for his family's sake. Noelle has had enough losses.*

A low note rose in the strengthening wind, and he feared his faith was not strong enough to lift his request to heaven's ear.

"Thad, lay him here." Noelle had deftly collected the lap blankets and had lined the center seat.

As the wife and daughters caught sight of their loved one, battered and bleeding and unconscious, their renewed cries rose up and echoed around him. Thad hardened his heart, fearing a sad outcome, and carefully laid down his burden, holding the man's head in one hand so there would be no further injury.

He was concentrating so hard, he didn't notice Noelle's touch until her hands bumped his. Her fingertips feathered over the blood-soaked makeshift bandage.

"We've got to wrap him up well." Thad spied the last lap blanket lying over the back of the front seat and pulled it onto the unconscious man. "Make sure to keep him as still as you can. I'll be riding right behind the sleigh."

Noelle nodded. Snow clung to her everywhere, gracing her with a pure white luminescence. Her sadness eked into his stone-hard heart and he gruffly moved away, leaving so much—leaving everything—unsaid.

"Getup, Miss Bradshaw." He reached out to give the mare a light pat on the flank and the mare took off, drawing away the sleigh and Noelle.

His Noelle. He could tell himself a thousand times that she was no longer his. That he didn't love her, wouldn't care about her, that the past was done and gone.

The truth was not so simple. The truth left him

feeling as hopeless as the bitter winds howling in from the north. He mounted up and pressed Clyde into the teeth of the growing storm.

Chapter Six

Noelle had never felt so useless. While they waited for the doctor to come, the maid and cook hustled back and forth from the bedroom to the kitchen and back again bringing all sorts of necessary items. The best thing she could do was to sit in a chair by her uncle's bedside.

"Robert? Oh, my Robert, please wake up." Henrietta clutched her husband's hand, tears streaming down her face. "You wake up. You hear me? It's the least you can do for not listening to me. If you had, you wouldn't be d-dying."

Lord, please don't let that happen. Noelle swiped at a falling tear. She sat straighter on the ladder-back chair the maid had brought up for her and steepled her hands together.

Please let him be all right.

She could not see to bind his wounds, cook and prepare a poultice or tend to cleaning his abrasions. The most she could do was to keep out of the way of those who could. The only thing she could do with her hands was to pray. As important as that was, it didn't feel like enough.

"If you l-leave me, Rob—" Henrietta choked on a sob "—I shall never forgive you. Mark my words! I will hold it against you for all eternity, that's wh-what I'll d-do."

Her aunt broke down again, all tears and incoherent fear. Noelle unfolded her hands from prayer and rose to find a fresh handkerchief from the top bureau drawer. The eerie, waiting silence of the room and of the house made her padding footsteps seem louder than a herd of horses at feed time.

"Here, Henrietta." She felt her way to the other side of the bed, where her aunt sat sobbing. "What more can I do for you?"

"There's nothing you can do, child. All I want is to see my Robert awake and alive and as good as new. That's what I want." She took the handkerchief and blew her nose with a trumpeting sound. "That man! Why did he go and do that? Mr. McKaslin told him not to buy that mare. Not a lick of sense. He's at *that* age."

Knowing her aunt needed to talk, that it would comfort her, Noelle knelt on the wood floor. "What age?"

"Selling the house in town, moving out here to this wilderness is trouble enough. But he quit his job at the bank. Quit. We still have our girls to raise and marry off, every single one of them. This is not the time to begin a horse ranch. Weddings are expensive and we'll have five of them, *and* Lydia's and Meredith's finishing school costs. Next year Angelina will be attending the academy in Boston, and the year after that Minnie. How will we find good matches for the girls and their lasting happiness if we cannot afford it?"

Noelle found Henrietta's elbow and from there, took

her aunt's hand in both of hers. She knew her aunt well enough to know it wasn't the finances she was so distraught over. Henrietta's love was so deep for her husband she could not speak of it.

Noelle wished she knew how to comfort that kind of pain. She felt inadequate as she gave Henrietta's hand a loving squeeze. "One worry at a time. You're not alone, my dear aunt."

"You are a blessing to me." Henrietta sniffled. "What is keeping that doctor? Doesn't he know my Robert needs him? What kind of a physician takes his own sweet time? I should write a letter of complaint."

She heard the echo of an approaching step at the far end of the hallway.

"The doctor's riding up now." Cook charged into the bedroom, breathing hard with her exertion. Water sloshed in a basin and she plunked it down on the top of the bureau. "Out of the room, missy. The doc will need room to work."

Yes, she was in the way. Noelle released her aunt's hand and pressed a loving touch to her uncle's forehead. He was such a good man. He had taken her in when she'd had nobody else. He was a good husband and father.

As she slipped from the room the doctor was hurrying up the stairs, perhaps let in by the maid, Sadie, and once again, Noelle was in the way when she wanted so badly to do something to help. She took several paces back and waited in the hallway's cool corner until the medical man strode through the doorway in a great hurry and clatter.

Only then did she make her way downstairs. With a trembling step and a heavy heart, she retreated to her chair in the parlor. The low crying and quiet sniffles told her she wasn't alone in the room. The fire was low, judging by the dull hum of the flames and the lazy occasional pop, but she could not see to add wood to the grate.

"Matilda? Would you like me to pray with you?"

Another quiet sniffle. "N-no. I just left Minnie and Angelina praying in the library. I j-just hurt s-so mu-uch."

"What can I do for you?"

"There's nothing that you can do. Only the d-oc-tor. And G-god."

"Should I make you some hot tea?"

"That would be l-lovely." Matilda stifled a sob. "Cook's lemon mint?"

"Of course." Relieved to have something constructive to do, she headed to the kitchen, counting her steps as she went, ticking off the number of paces from her chair to the dining room and from the table to the swinging kitchen door.

Thad. She knew he was there by the change in the air, by the scent of horse and leather and hay. Against her will, her heart tugged as if he'd cinched a rope around it.

Split wood tumbled into the fuel box with a roll and thunk. She waited, holding herself very still as Thad's movements seemed loud in the still and empty room. The fire's voice grew to a crackling roar.

"That'll do." Cook's grudging approval was a rare sound. "That was mighty Christian of you, Mr. McKaslin."

"Just helping out while I'm here." His baritone tensed, as if he knew she was in the room. "I guess I'd best see to the other fires in the house."

His footsteps knelled closer with the unhurried, strong beat that she knew so well.

She stepped aside, knowing she was in the way and

expected him to walk on by. After all they'd been through, what could there be left to say? She wouldn't trust him, wouldn't allow a friendship, would do nothing but to wish him well. She was certain he felt the same way.

But his gait halted, and she could feel his calming presence towering over her.

"I'm sorry for your uncle," he said gruffly. "I don't suppose there's any word from the doc yet?"

Her eyes watered at the tender caring in his voice—a tender caring she well remembered through all the years and disillusionment. It had been the great gentleness in the powerful man that had once won her heart completely.

If only her heart did not remember that now. She nodded, not trusting her voice, wishing him to go on his way before the burning in her eyes turned to tears.

"I'm no longer much of a praying man, but I've been keeping him in prayer."

"That means a lot." One hot tear rolled down her cheek. "More than you know."

"I care more than you know."

The rough, callused pad of his thumb brushed featherlight against her cheek to stop her single tear. He'd moved closer, and he leaned in closer still. She could hear the rhythm of his breathing and smell the faint scent of soap on his shirt.

"I know Robert is like a second father to you. I don't want you to lose him, too."

Noelle shook her head, too overcome to speak. She recognized the soft note in Thad's tone, and she knew how his face would look, his eyes caring, his jaw squared, a combination of strength and heart that had always dazzled her.

Another tear rolled down her face, and he caught that one, as well, brushing it away with a kindness that made her ache with all that she had lost. All that had never been.

"Are you going to be all right?" Thad was all the stronger, in her view, for his kindness. "I can sit with you."

"No." How did she tell him the truth? She ought to be crying for her uncle, but the tears were for herself. For him. For the fragments of the past she'd never truly let go. She held on to those bright pieces of joy like a miser did his last pieces of gold. They were slivers of happiness she could not stand to remember. They were bits of sorrow she could not forget.

"N-no." The word scraped against her raw throat. "You go on home. I shall be fine."

"All right, then, but I'm not about to leave. You sure you're okay?"

"S-sure."

"You don't look all right."

Those pieces of sorrow felt brighter, bigger. It was not him she needed.

The door swished open and shut, Thad was gone, and she was achingly alone. She could hear the striking of Cook's shoes on the stairs echoing rapid-fire. Dully, she heard Thad pass through the house before the kitchen door swung shut and cut off the sound of him.

She felt adrift. She longed for the comforting words of her Bible. She ached for the days when she could have run her fingertips along the edges of the fragile, gold-edged pages, treasuring all those wonderful words and passages.

It was no trouble to locate the everyday teapot in its

place on one of the many kitchen shelves or the tins of tea. A few quick sniffs helped her to find Tilly's favorite blend.

While she worked, she heard the younger girls clattering down the hall from the library and questioning Cook.

What had the doctor said? She plucked an oven mitt from the top drawer next to the stove and strained to listen.

"The doc has said nothing yet, only that the fall should have killed him. Perhaps there is still hope."

"What if Papa n-never w-wakes up?" Minnie's thin, fragile voice held a note of pure anguish.

Footsteps pounded up the stairs, drowned out by sobs.

"Angelina, Mama said we all had to stay downstairs," Minnie called out. "Angelina, I'm telling on you."

"I don't care." The strike of shoes on the staircase had to be Angelina's, while Minnie cried.

I know exactly how much it hurts to lose a father. Lord, I hope You can spare her, spare them all, that pain. She hurt for them in too many ways to count, this loving family who had taken her in as their own. She had done her best to accept a similar hand the Lord had dealt her, but she truly prayed that the Worthington family would have better favor.

She carefully located the teakettle's handle and lifted it with the mitt, intent on keeping the kettle level so as not to spill boiling water all over the stove, the floor and her dress. She was concentrating so hard that she didn't notice a strange burning smell until after she'd returned the kettle to the back burner. Her skirts had gotten too

close to the hot stove, and she'd scorched the fabric—
again. She touched the hot fabric with her fingertips,
unhappy with herself for not remembering to check her
dress.

The door chose that moment to whisper open.
"Don't worry, it's not bad. Just a small spot."

"Thad." She felt foolish fussing over her skirt, and
she straightened, knowing her face was flushed.

"What are you doing at the stove?"

"Trying to be useful."

"Seems to me you don't need to be in the kitchen
to do that."

There it was, his kindness again. It was harder to
confront than all the ways he'd wronged her. A lump
formed in her throat. Before she could search for something—anything—to say to break the silence between
them, a flurry of steps rang in the stairwell. The girls'
voices rose in a clamor. The doctor had come down.

"Guess you'd best get in there." The hinges whispered and silenced.

He had to be holding the door for her. She smoothed
down her skirt, set her chin and salvaged what she
could of her composure. She would not allow herself
to imagine how tall and dark and handsome he looked
and the way his steadfast kindness only made him more
so.

She breezed through the doorway without a word
and did not look back.

The doctor had left, saying he'd done all he could.
It was up to Robert now, and up to God, whether he
would awaken or if he would not. All anyone could do
for him was to wait and to pray. Their reverend had

come, and after supper and a sustaining prayer session, he left, too.

The evening had ticked by and midnight was near. Noelle was still dressed—she'd changed into a garment that wasn't scorched—and, alone in the parlor, she worried who would ride for the doctor if Robert needed him. Matilda did not know how to drive, the other girls were too young, and Sadie, the maid, was afraid of horses. With Cook gone home, that only left Henrietta, and heaven knew the woman was too distraught, and rightly so, to do anything.

At loose ends, she settled into her chair by the hearth. The heat was fading and the fire was nearly silent. She tried to open her heart in prayer, but the words didn't come. Only fear did.

Life was a fragile gift, and all it took was one moment in time, one rattlesnake or one poor decision to buy a horse for it to change in a moment and forever. If only Robert had bought a saddle horse as tame as the little old mare he'd gotten Matilda.

That brought her thoughts right around to Thad again. His words had been haunting her all evening long. *I care more than you know,* he'd said with a ring of honesty that confused her.

"Noelle?" A familiar baritone rumbled low and quiet in the midnight stillness, and it was as if she'd dreamed him up. But it was his step coming her way and no dream, echoing in the room and not in her hopes.

"Thad? What are you still doing here? I thought you went home."

"No, I thought I'd stay around and help out. Try to be useful." There was a smile in his words, small, but sure, a warmth she could not deny still lingered somehow, impossibly, between them. "After Aiden fetched the doc and saw to my ma in town, he brought in the mare. I got her settled and then gave the stable a good cleaning. The animals are snug for the night. Thought I'd come in and bank the fires so the house will be safe for the night."

"You've been here the whole time?"

"Yes. Sadie brought a dinner plate out to me while I was working. I'll be staying the night in the stable."

"But it's freezing outside."

"I've got my bedroll, thanks to my brother. I'll be fine."

"You won't be fine." She couldn't say why she was so upset over the image of him bedding down with the horses. "You should stay in the house."

"Nope, I don't feel comfortable with that. I saddled the doc's horse when he left. He said Robert murmured Henrietta's name a few times, so that's hopeful."

"Yes, but it's a bad sign that he still hasn't roused." She thought of the other warnings the doctor had left them with. Robert's condition remained a grave concern. "Henrietta is sitting at his bedside in case he—" Died. She couldn't say the word.

"That's why I'm staying. If you need to send word to the doctor, I'll be here to ride for him."

"Oh, Thad." That was all she could get out, simply his name, when his thoughtfulness meant so much more. Why was she having a hard time telling him that much? She folded her hands tightly together, not moving from her chair. She listened to the fire crackle lazily in the hearth and tried to find safe words—ones that would not leave her vulnerable. "That's a comfort knowing you'll be here. That you're here to help if he needs it."

"Good. I want to make your load lighter. If you're gonna be up, I can feed the fire for you."

"No, I'm about ready to go upstairs. I was just catching my breath." She didn't mention she'd been trying not to think about all that could go wrong for this family she loved.

"It's been a tough day."

"Exactly."

"You won't mind if I bank the embers?"

"Not at all."

The leather of his boots squeaked slightly as he eased down beside her. Over the clank of the fireplace utensils, he spoke. "I've been trying to keep out of your way. That's why I've kept to the stable, for the most part. I know it's gotta be hard having me near."

She couldn't deny it, but she didn't want to say the words, either. She steepled her hands in her lap, feeling raw and worn. "I'm grateful for you. You made a difference for Robert. Matilda said she saw your shadow through the snow this afternoon. She said it was hard to be sure, but it looked as if you were protecting Robert. That you could have been as badly hurt, too."

"An injury like Robert's is serious business. I've seen quite a few in my line of work."

"I imagine you have."

"Not many pull through with a head injury and a bad kick to the chest, but I *have* seen it." There was another click of the shovel against the grate. "How's your aunt holding up?"

"She refuses to leave his side. For all her confidence and bluster, I think she would be lost without him. I'm scared for him. For my family. You know what that's like."

"I do." He'd lost his father more than ten years ago, and Bo McKaslin hadn't been the good, strong father Noelle was used to. The real loss in his life would always be her.

He stood, doing his best to hold in his feelings. "I have a good suspicion that Robert will be all right."

"It's g-good of you to stay."

"It's my pleasure. Good night, Noelle."

"At least let me send some blankets out with you."

"No. Sleeping indoors is treat enough for me. I'm used to bedding down in unheated bunkhouses and on the trail. I can't tell you the number of summer nights a storm rolled in when we were in the high country and I got snowed on."

"Didn't you sleep in a wagon when the weather was bad?"

"What wagon? There was usually the chuck wagon, and that was it. Besides, it wouldn't have been good for a cowboy's reputation to act as if a little bit of snow could trouble him."

"Cowboys are overly concerned about their reputations, are they?"

"The tougher you act, the better cowboy you can fool yourself into thinking you are."

"I suppose you fooled yourself into thinking you were a very fine cowboy?"

"I surely tried." There it was, the hint of a grin in his voice and it warmed her a little in the hopeless places where she felt so cold. "I'll be right enough out there. Don't you worry. If your family needs anything, send word to me."

"Fine." She rose. Her skirts swirled around her ankles as she took a stumbling step. When she was sure she'd put a safe distance between them, she stopped and turned toward the front door, where she supposed he must be. "Tell Sunny good-night from me and to keep warm tonight."

"I surely will. I know he'll be glad to know you wish him well."

Something in Thad's voice made her believe he knew she was speaking not only of the horse. She could feel her heart unraveling string by string. She took another step, careful to skirt the edge of the end table next to Henrietta's favorite sofa. "He's rather a good man for helping out tonight."

"I'll tell him. I know that means a lot to him, that you think he's a great man."

"Good, not great," she was quick to correct.

"Right, I'll let him know that he's got some proving up to do." His voice had a hint of a smile again, warm and wonderful and so substantial it was hard to believe he'd ever let her down.

"Definite proving up." She took one step and realized she was lost.

She'd forgotten to count her steps.

"Good night, Thad." She set her chin, hoping she looked rather as if she meant to stand somewhere in the parlor like a statue.

His steps moved away and the hinges of the front door whispered open. "Good night."

The way he said it sounded more like goodbye. She waited until she heard the knob click shut before she groped her way in the dark. Once she'd found the end post to the staircase she lowered herself onto the bottom stair, feeling alone in the dark. So very lost and alone.

Her heart ached, her spirit ached, her very soul felt

cracked apart. She sat a long time in the dark, until the clock struck one, before she went upstairs to check on her aunt.

Chapter Seven

From her uncle's bedside, Noelle heard the faint chime of the downstairs parlor clock marking the early hour— five chimes. She'd been up all night. She thought Henrietta had fallen asleep in the chair on the other side of the bed, but she wasn't sure.

It was hard not to let all the worries in. She had personal ones for her dear uncle, for it had been a blow to her head that had stolen her sight. She prayed harder than she ever had before for him to awaken and be fine.

Exhaustion pulsed through her, and she fought another yawn. She would stay with Henrietta as long as she was needed. The embers popped in the bedroom's hearth, and she thought of Thad. How had he fared in the stable? She wasn't exactly sure why he'd stayed, but she was deeply grateful to him.

Grateful. The hard nugget of emotion—of the thing she hadn't forgiven—hurt like a blister. And it made it easier for her to remember past the hurt of Thad's abandonment to the time before, when she'd been so happy. Happy, because his love had made her that way.

She was no longer the kind of woman who believed that love was strong enough to build anything on, for it was only a dream. But the girl she'd been, who had believed, remembered and mourned.

"Why, I must have drifted off for a moment there." Henrietta broke the long-standing silence. "Oh, my heart stopped. He's still breathing. I vowed I'd not take my eyes from him, and here I am, drowsing in this chair."

Noelle could feel her aunt's anguish. "It's been a long night for you."

"You would know, as you sat up every moment with me. Unnecessary, dear one, but terribly appreciated." Henrietta's voice broke and she cleared it, but perhaps failing to clear away all the emotion, went on to say nothing at all.

How hard it had to be for a loving wife to fear every ticktock of the clock that passed. The doctor had warned that Robert's head wound was not the most serious of all his injuries. The kick he'd sustained to his ribs had damaged him deep inside. There was no telling if he could heal from that.

"I've been reciting what I can remember from Ecclesiastes." Noelle searched with her fingertips along the bedside table, where she'd put the family Bible for safekeeping, and handed it in her aunt's direction. "Perhaps you ought to resume where I left off."

"Your voice likely needs a rest." The chair creaked as Henrietta took the treasured book. "Relax, dear. I'll read until our reverend arrives. He promised to stop by first thing."

Noelle squirmed in the uncomfortable wooden chair. Her spine burned as if someone had set it afire. She couldn't find a more comfortable position, gave it up as hopeless and set her mind on ignoring her discomfort.

The pages flipped softly. "His color looks to be improving. I'm most certain of it. The doctor said his making it through the night would be telling, and I am sure beyond all doubt that my Rob is going to be fine."

If will alone was strong enough, Noelle knew that her aunt's would be. "His breathing sounds steadier."

"His pulse strengthens, too." The pages stopped ruffling. "For once I am thankful for newfangled ways. The doctor is newly out of medical school back East. Do you suppose he is married?"

Noelle bit her lip, taking comfort in Henrietta's irrepressible concerns. "Don't you think it would be more appropriate to wait until Robert can give his permission before you go marrying off one of your daughters?"

"It's a woman's duty to marry. Would you like me to start quoting passages and verses?"

"You can't fool me, my dear aunt. I know down deep you are a true romantic. That's what's behind all your hopes for your daughters. You want them to know happiness the way you have."

"I'll not admit to such weakness as soft feelings. True love." Henrietta tsked. "Well, perhaps you've caught me at a rare moment of weakness. The greatest gift *is* to be loved as I have been loved. As I love." Her voice trembled and she fell silent.

Noelle fell silent, too. Love was the last thing she wanted to think about. She was glad when Henrietta began reading, in a quiet steady voice. "'To everything there is a season, and a time to every purpose under heaven.'"

She felt Thad's approach like a touch to her spirit, just as she'd used to. Her heart was aware of him long before his familiar gait tapped quietly through the house. He hesitated outside the open doorway, waiting for a break in Henrietta's reading to speak, and her soul leaned toward him, the way a blooming rose faced the sun.

It took Henrietta a moment to notice him, for she was absorbed in her reading. When she did, it was with a gasp. "Oh! Mr. McKaslin. I did not see you standing there."

"Good morning, Noelle. Ma'am. Want me to build up your fire?"

"That will be fine, young man. I take it you've started the fires downstairs?"

"That I have."

The confident, lighthearted jauntiness to his baritone had changed, Noelle realized. This Thad sounded like a seasoned man sure of his worth and capabilities, and through it all he still had his positive humor.

Not that she ought to be noticing so much about him. She sat straighter in the chair and smoothed her skirts with her hands, straightening imaginary wrinkles, since she couldn't see them. It did give her something to do other than to listen to the easy pad of his step and the rustle and whisper of his movements as he knelt down to stir the ashes.

Thad. Why did it feel as if her heart could see him? She wondered if he'd been warm enough or too uncomfortable to sleep; if he had shaved or if a day's growth whiskered his jaw. She could not allow herself to ask.

"Mr. McKaslin?" Henrietta broke the silence. "Might I prevail on you for another favor?"

"Sure, ma'am. What do you need?" His voice lifted higher, and Noelle could feel him towering behind her, his breadth and height and strength undeniable.

"After the house is awake, you come back," Henrietta instructed. "I'm going to need a more comfortable chair if I'm to continue to stay by my husband's side. My back is paining me something terrible, and I must keep up my strength for him."

"That'll be no trouble at all. I'll be back."

When he walked away, he left behind the sweet scent of hay and an impossible longing within Noelle's heart. If only he had been the kind of man she could have counted on.

Henrietta returned to her reading. Noelle struggled to sit straight in her chair and let the Bible's beautiful words comfort her.

As Thad went around the Worthington place doing chores in the stable and later in the house, he couldn't get Noelle out of his thoughts. Seeing her sitting quietly in the hard-backed wooden chair with her hands clasped in her lap, listening patiently while her aunt read from the Bible gave him a new view of her.

It was an image that subdued him as he considered which chair would fit into the space between the Worthington's bulky bed and the bedroom wall. While he considered his options in the parlor, solemn and subdued voices drifted in from the nearby dining room. The Worthington girls were up and taking breakfast, but it was Noelle's quiet alto that he picked out like a melody from the other voices. Her dulcet voice was his most favorite sound in the world.

Once he'd chosen a chair and hefted it up the stairs, his ears strained to keep hearing her. She grew fainter with every step he took and by the time he'd managed to reach the Worthington's bedroom door, he could no longer hear her. Every bit of him seemed to strain, searching for her.

Henrietta looked up from her Bible and squinted at him appraisingly. She looked exhausted and sick from worry.

His heart softened toward her. "Where would you like this?"

"Where my chair is now. You'll have to take the wooden one back down to the dining room."

"Be glad to." He eyed the doorway and angled the chair to wedge it through in one try. The missus seemed to watch him carefully, perhaps she was concerned about him scuffing her fancy woodwork, but she needn't have worried. He set the heavy chair down with as much care as he could and took away the wooden one. "Will that do, ma'am?"

"I'm grateful, Mr. McKaslin."

"No trouble at all, ma'am." He stopped to take a glance at Robert, who lay ashen and motionless against the stark white sheets. "He's been stirring?"

"No." The strong woman who looked as if she could have commanded the army now looked frail.

"I'm sure he'll be rousing soon, ma'am." It was the only kindness he could offer her. "I've seen it before." He backtracked to the door. "You need anything at all, you send word."

"Of that you can be sure."

As he hooked the ladder-back chair over his shoulder and headed down the narrow hallway, he had to admit the Worthington's marriage was clearly based on a deep love. The kind he'd forgotten could exist in this world. The kind he didn't want to admit did exist, because it would make him see how empty his life was.

. What did a man do when he'd lost his only chance at a deep, true bond? He knew that whenever he eventually married, it would not be to Noelle. He'd lost his dream. The best he could hope for now was someone sensible and compatible.

The expensive rug at his feet led him to the staircase, where once again he heard Noelle's voice as soft and sweet as lark song. He tried to harden his heart so he didn't have to feel a thing. It was better that way.

He did his best not to look her way the moment he stepped into the fancy dining room. Knickknacks and breakables were just about everywhere, so he moved the ladder-back chair with purpose. He didn't want to lower Henrietta's opinion of him by breaking some of the expensive whatnots. The Worthington girls fell silent. The silence felt painful as he kept his eyes down and slid the chair into place at the foot of the table.

He didn't dawdle, but headed straight for the kitchen door. He had intended to check with the maid to see if any errands needed to be done in town, but he went straight toward the back door. The pressure building so strong in his chest was likely to choke him. He had his hand on the door handle when he heard Noelle padding quietly behind him.

"Thad?"

She looked shadowed and forlorn, and the pressure in his chest detonated like a keg of dynamite in a mountain tunnel. His willpower crumbled along with every bit of his steely self-discipline.

"What can I do for you, darlin'?" He feared she could hear it in his voice.

She took a small step back. "I need someone to tell my piano students I won't be teaching t-today. Most likely for the whole next week."

"You mean you teach piano? But how can you…?"

"Easily." She shrugged simply, unconsciously, gentle as always. "I don't have to see to hear a bad chord or a wrong note. The keys are always the same whether I can see them or not."

"You've got some lucky students, learning from you."

Her chin dipped. "I'm immune to your compliments, Mr. McKaslin. I'm the lucky one, as I need to make what difference I can in some way and I can't think of a better purpose for me."

"Whoa, there. You need to make a living?"

"Why do you sound so confused about that?" She tensed up some again, as if he'd hit a sore spot with his words. "It doesn't seem to be in God's plan for me to marry, and it's not right I rely too much on my aunt and uncle's generosity. I support myself and I contribute to the household."

"But—" He shook his head and gripped the edge of the counter. "I heard news of your engagement. I'm sorry you lost him, too. In the buggy accident?"

"No, he's alive and well living in town with his wife and newborn son." She let the notes fade to silence, holding her hands still as her heart. "He followed in your footsteps. After my accident, he broke our engagement. He didn't want to marry a blind woman. Or, damaged goods, to use his words."

"*What?* You're not damaged. I—I can't imagine it. I am sorry."

"It wasn't in God's plan for me." She fought the punch of sorrow that would always seize her—not at Shelton's loss but because she'd so wished for a family of her own—something else that could never be. "What about for you?"

"Me? Marriage?" His note of panic was revealing. "Now I'm not sure there is any plan—divine or otherwise—but I'm hoping for a wife one day. Someone who sees life the way I do. You work hard, try to do what's right and at the end of the day rest up for another hard day on the ranch."

"I see." Maybe more than she ever had. "Excuse me, I must get back to my aunt—"

Footsteps thundered down the stairway like cannon fire. Noelle fell silent, icy fear spilling into her veins as she heard the girls at the dining room table cry out in alarm. Henrietta's racking sobs rose above the other noises in the house. The door swung open; Noelle could hear the hinges and feel the breeze the door made against the side of her face.

"Mr. McKaslin! There you are." Sadie was out of breath and panicked sounding. "Quick! Ride for the doctor. Mr. Worthington is awake."

"Awake?" Noelle stumbled over the word, it surprised her so. "He's all right?"

"Has his wits about him, if that's what you mean—"

The door thudding open against the wall broke off her words. Thad's boots rang on the wood floor. "Noelle, make a list, and I'll take care of your students when I'm back with the doc."

The door slammed shut before she could answer. He was gone, leaving her wrestling for control of her heart as she hurried upstairs.

* * *

After he'd alerted the doc, Thad had pressed Sunny into a brisk pace and nosed him toward home. The long ride and the quiet time in the barn as he rubbed down his horse gave him plenty of time to mull things over. By the time Aiden found him, he pretty nearly had things puzzled out.

"You're home." Aiden stopped in the aisle to give him a grim look. "Didn't see you ride in or I would have come to help you."

"No need. Almost done here." Thad released Sunny's rear hoof and stood. "Just need to fetch him a little water."

"I'll get it." Gruff, Aiden strode away and said nothing more.

Thad scratched the back of his neck. His brother wasn't in the best of moods and probably for good reason. He patted Sunny on the flank before stepping over the gate bar. When he caught sight of Aiden at the back pump, he headed his brother's way.

"Don't blame you for being mad at me," he said by way of an apology.

Aiden turned from the pump and shrugged one big shoulder. "Not mad. I'm concerned."

"Concerned?" That threw him like a wild horse. Thad took the bucket. "Robert woke up this morning. He'll recover from his other injuries."

"Good to know, but that wasn't what I meant." Aiden cleared his throat and pushed the barn door closed once they were through. "You're going to get sweet on that Kramer girl again, and that'll be a mistake."

"No one knows that more than I do." Thad made his way back to Sunny's stall. "I'm helping out is all."

"Fine. Christian duty and all that." Aiden fisted his hands. "How about I take over at the Worthingtons. You hold down the fort here."

"You? At the Worthingtons?" That was almost laughable. "You know there's nothing but women over there? A cook, a maid, those daughters and Mrs. Worthington?"

"And that Kramer girl." Aiden quirked one eyebrow as if to give those words special emphasis. "I'm unaffected by her. By any woman. I'd best take over in your stead for a couple of days, at most. I suppose more family are coming to help?"

"Don't know." Thad smiled at Sunny's nicker and poured a quarter of the bucket into the trough. Sunny took a look at that and shook his head in argument. Thad rubbed his nose. "More later, buddy. I'll come back with some warmed mash for you. Is that acceptable?"

Sunny seemed to consider it and dipped his muzzle into the cool, fresh water.

Satisfied his horse was cared for, Thad left the bucket on the aisle floor and turned to face his brother's displeasure. "I'm not going to make old mistakes."

"I'm not so sure."

"Doesn't matter." Thad grabbed his saddle pack from the rail he'd slung it on and hefted it onto his shoulder. "I've got a duty, is all, Aiden. Surely you understand duty."

"What I understand is that look in your eye."

"What look?" Thad shouldered open the side door and barreled out into the harsh weather. He didn't have any look in his eyes. What he had was conviction. He would always do right by Noelle. It was as simple as that.

"Why, Thad!" The lean-to door swung open and there was Ma clutching her shawl closed at her throat and standing in the cold. "You came back. Just when I was starting to worry why we hadn't heard from you."

"Couldn't keep away from the prettiest ma in all of Montana Territory."

She sparkled, despite her worrying paleness. "It's good to have you home, son."

"It's good to be home." He kissed his mother's cheek and followed her into the lean-to.

"I've got a hot pot of coffee on," Ma said as she slipped through the kitchen door, where it was warm and snug. "I've got some cinnamon rolls from yesterday's baking. I'll warm those for you boys, too."

"Thanks, Ma," Thad said.

Aiden, who stepped in behind him, said the same.

Not wanting to pick up the conversation they'd been having in the barn, Thad kept his back to his brother and stepped around the morning's supply of stacked wood to fit his boots on the bootjack. "What's the news on Finn?"

Aiden didn't say a single word, but Thad could *hear* his scowl, it was such a strong one.

"That bad, huh?" Thunk, went his boot on the floor. Thad fit his other boot in the jack, his foot slipped out and that boot, too, fell loudly in the awkward silence. He bent to retrieve both and set them against the outside wall. "What? He's still coming home, isn't he?"

"Looks that way." Aiden turned away and thunk, went his boot to the floor. "Ma picked up a letter at the post office yesterday. Finn got himself into some trouble at the prison. A fight of some kind."

Of course. That boy was more trouble. Thad

shrugged off his coat and hung it over a peg before he hiked into the kitchen.

Warmth surrounded him. The golden lamplight and the polished shine of the wood floor and table was a welcome sight, but not more than the view of his ma at the stove. She hummed while she worked in a calico work dress and apron. It felt right being back here after all this time. He'd missed her and his home so much.

Heart brimming, he joined his mother at the stove and took the coffeepot out of her hand. "You're not well enough to be waiting on me. You're supposed to wait for Aiden or me to do the cooking. You know that."

"Nonsense! I'm your mother. It's my job." She might argue, but this close, he could see she'd gone from pale to ashen.

"Why don't you sit and let me bring you coffee and rolls?"

"I'm not helpless, young man." Gently said, and lovingly. "But I won't say no to your offer."

"Good." Fixing breakfast had taxed her, he knew. He held out her chair at the table. "You've overdone things, since no one was here to stop you."

"Oh, you know me. I'm not happy unless my hands are busy." Ma settled into her chair. "This illness has been a hardship in many ways, but the hardest seems to be all this idleness."

The door swung open, and Thad went back to the stove. He grabbed three cups by the handles and set them onto the table. By the time he'd returned with the coffeepot, Ma had set the cups in place and Aiden had taken his chair, still scowling.

"How is that nice Kramer girl?" Ma asked, while he poured her cup first.

"Fine enough," he answered, and shot Aiden a warning look. The subject was one that had to stay closed.

He moved on to Aiden's cup, prepared to set his brother straight if he brought up Noelle again. He'd taken all the hurt he could.

He hardened up his heart, fetched the cinnamon rolls from the oven and let his ma take first pick.

This was his life, this was the way it would always be. Fine enough, he supposed, but never as good, never as vibrant, never as meaningful without her.

Chapter Eight

The parlor clock was striking the noon hour as Noelle counted out four of the everyday plates from the kitchen shelves to be carried in to the table. Henrietta and the girls were upstairs by their father's side, and it was as if the house itself had breathed a sigh of relief. Robert was holding his own. She thought of everything Thad had done for her uncle, protecting him from the bucking mare, bandaging him, staying the night. And now, back in the stables at work after delivering notes to her students, according to Sadie.

Thad. His words kept rolling through her mind. *I'm hoping for a wife one day. Someone who sees life the way I do. You work hard, try to do what's right and at the end of the day rest up for another hard day on the ranch.*

"I'm taking a tray up to the missus." Sadie tapped her way closer. "You're a dear to help me, but you needn't do it."

"I'm happy to be useful." She shook all thoughts of Thad from her mind and set the small stack of dishes on the worktable centering the room. She added another plate for him.

"I think he's been out there working with one of those crazy horses." Sadie's voice made clear her opinion on horses that could not be trusted. "Someone needs to take them in hand, I suppose."

Thad. The knot in her chest yanked tighter. She did her best to keep her feelings still and slipped another plate from the shelf. The plates clacked together, Sadie's step retreated to the kitchen door and she was alone again. Her mind was a muddle of stray, troubling thoughts. Exhaustion vibrated through her like a plucked cello string. Sadie's steps faded away, leaving her to think about the one man she should not be thinking about.

When she heard Thad's familiar gait coming from the lean-to, she had only a moment to brace herself before the door opened. She wished that her senses did not focus on him even before he stepped into the room. She knew the brush of his movements, the rhythm of his breathing and the beat he took to pause before he spoke. Again, her spirit turned toward him and her traitorous heart followed.

"Messages delivered," he said with a smile in his voice. "I didn't realize you taught so many students."

"It surprises even me." She couldn't say why she was almost smiling back. She shook her head, gathered up her common sense and blamed her reaction to Thad on the fact that she had yet to sleep after being up all night with Henrietta. "Thanks for delivering my messages."

"I didn't mind, and I got to see more of the country-side." There was a rustle, as if he were taking off his coat and then hanging it on the hooks by the door. "A lot has changed since I've been away."

"A lot has stayed the same, too." She ran her fingertips along the edge of the worktable and followed it to the corner. "Would you like me to get you some coffee? I'd offer you tea, but Cook has commandeered all the kettles for my uncle's medical needs."

"Is that what that awful smell is?" Thad's wry humor made his baritone more intimate and cozy. "I thought a skunk somehow got loose in the house. I was just about to offer to go hunt it down for you."

"How gentlemanly of you, but as you can see, we won't be needing your hunting services." She felt her way along the upper shelf for a cup and found nothing with her fingertips. She went up on tiptoe to search some more. "Is that a yes to coffee? I just helped Cook wash and dry a dishpan of cups. They ought to be here."

His steps beat near, and she froze as he came close and then closer. Until she could smell the bite of winter wind and fresh snow on his clothes. Until she could remember what it had been like all the times he'd been this close to her.

Memories stirred up like a kick of wind in dust, limiting her clarity, taking her back in time. How safe she'd felt when her hand was tucked snugly within his larger, work-roughened one. How full her heart and soul had been every time he said her name. How her love for him was as endless as a summer's blue Montana sky.

"Here's one, pushed all the way to the back." His voice rumbled like spring on a late-winter's storm.

Warmly, her heart responded against her will. She took an abrupt step away from him, putting a careful distance between them. Now, if only she could do the same with her feelings. Her throat was tight.

"The rest of the cups are on the drain board, just so you know."

"Y-yes." She knew that somewhere in the dust cloud of her mind, but all she could think of was how she wished more than ever that she could see. Just for one glorious moment, that was all, so she could look at the man who made her spirit stir.

"Am I making you uncomfortable?" His question was blunt, but his words were kind.

Her hands trembled as she turned to the stove. "It's not easy having you so n-near."

"I understand. It's a bad wound between us. It's as simple as that. Nothing in the world is going to change that."

She nodded, unable to agree. Unable to disagree.

"Believe me, the last thing I ever want to do—the last thing I would ever do is hurt you, Noelle. I'll eat in the kitchen and keep my distance from you."

She had to fight to keep her feelings still. She had to fight not to let her own honesty show.

There he went again, closing the distance between them, leaning near and then nearer as he took the coffeepot from the stove. Ironware clanged against the trivet and his muscled arm brushed against her shoulder. "I don't want you to burn your pretty dress again."

She blushed. She couldn't help it. Why did she feel so awkward about being near to him? "I don't scorch my skirts every time. Just now and then."

"I imagine being near a stove is tricky for you."

"Yes, tricky."

"Is that your cup on the table? Then I'll fill it, too." He moved away, already speaking over the sound of coffee pouring. "I stopped home and packed my saddlebags for another night's stay."

"Not another night out in that cold barn."

"Only until Robert's out of risk. I wouldn't feel right about leaving you ladies here by yourselves tonight. If all goes well tomorrow, then I'll head home."

"Th-that's decent of you, Thad." And more than she expected of him.

The coffeepot landed on the trivet with a clang. "Your uncle is going to be bedridden for awhile. Is there any family you can send off to and ask to come help?"

"I'll m-mention it to Henrietta."

"I'll pitch in until then."

No matter how hard she fought against it, she could not keep her emotions still. They rose up like a lump in her throat. She swallowed hard, trying to ignore them, praying they would go back down into the dormant place within her heart. "But aren't you needed at home?"

"It's true, I have obligations." His baritone dipped, low like an invitation to lean and listen.

"What kind of obligations?" The question rolled off her tongue before she could order herself not to ask it.

"I would have thought that you'd heard."

"Heard what?"

"My younger brother's had some trouble with the law."

"Finn? Oh, I didn't know." Noelle choked the words out past the expanding lump in her throat. She swallowed but it refused to budge. "Is it very serious?"

"Serious enough or I would have never come back to help my ma and Aiden out."

Of course. His exciting cowboy life. Impossibly, the emotions tangled up in her throat expanded more, and she could not speak.

"Where do you want your coffee?"

"Oh, I can carry it." She'd never felt so awkward.

"I don't mind. Besides, I filled it awful full."

"The parlor, then."

"Follow me." His steps struck like thunder in the whir of her mind. Somehow she made her feet carry her around the table and through the door, which he held for her.

"I came in to check the wood boxes," he told her, talking uneasily. So, he did feel the awkwardness between them. "Is there anything else that needs doing? I might as well make myself useful as long as I'm here."

Throat aching, heart aching, she could only shake her head once in response. His boots were a slow and sure rhythm in contrast to her own.

She almost forgot to count her steps as she left the corner of the dining room table to make the long path to her armchair by the hearth. The familiar cadence of his gait, his scent of hay and winter and horses, the rustle of his movements and the coziness of his presence all sweetly affected her, and against her will.

"On the table by the chair?" he asked.

"Please." She slipped into her chair.

"There's a Bible on the table, too." His tone dipped with tender understanding. "You must miss being able to read that."

"Very much. The Bible was my mother's, and it's a comfort just to have it near." One of her questions about him rose to the surface like a soap bubble. "I remember you said you're no longer much of a praying man. Why?"

"It's complicated, like most things."

"Yes, faith is complicated. I wrestled with it for a while after the buggy accident."

"I imagine so. It's hard to understand why God would let someone as gentle and kind as you be blind."

Always kind and gentle, that was Thad, too. She hadn't realized how much she'd missed him. "I've learned to accept it."

"Seems to me that would be awful tough."

"It was for a while, but I'm blessed in so many other ways." That was a dark time she tried not to think about. She had learned to accept. "Whatever you're struggling with, you should never let anything come between you and God."

"Don't you go trying to bring me back to my faith. I'll find my way, don't you worry." His footsteps retreated. "Tell the maid I'll be out in the stables if Robert should need the doc again."

"Thad?"

"What is it, darlin'?"

"There is one thing you could do for me. There's a sorrel mare in the corner box stall."

"I know the one. She's a sweet thing. If I don't miss my guess, she'll be foaling in a week or two."

"Would you keep a careful watch on her? Solitude is special to me."

There was a moment of silence. "Then you can count on me."

Was it her imagination or were his words heavy with regret? Or was it sadness? She listened to his steps fade and the kitchen door whisper shut. Even if she sat perfectly still, she could not stop all the ways her heart felt for the man.

And all the ways she didn't.

She reached for her Bible, careful not to disturb the full cup of steaming coffee, and hugged the treasured volume to her. *You can count on me.* Why did Thad's words trouble her? This wasn't the first time he'd said something that seemed to have a deeper layer to it.

The last thing I ever want to do— The last thing I would ever do is hurt you. His words puzzled her. She could not reconcile Thad's sincerity with the man who'd shattered her heart.

How would a man who had knowingly broken her heart also be the man who stayed to clean the stable, see to the horses, chop wood, run errands and ride for the doctor at a moment's notice? The real truth was that he had always been hardworking and sincere and caring. Except for that one terrible point in time.

The fire popped and crackled, and, exhausted, she laid down her Bible and reached for the bracing cup of coffee. A wave of chatter floated down from upstairs, bringing with it notes of measured happiness and hope.

That happiness could not penetrate her deeper sorrow.

Thad put off going into the house as long as he could. He'd scrubbed the water troughs, washed out the feed trays, took note of what feed was running low and even spent some time working with the new mare. She had a long way to go before she was a reliable horse, but he had faith in her.

He especially made sure to keep a careful watch on

the expecting mare, as Noelle had requested. He imagined she didn't ride anymore. That was too bad since she loved horses so much.

As he trudged through the snow to the house, he couldn't think of anything else. Only her. She still amazed him. She was more beautiful and as good as ever.

How could love be there all long and he hadn't known it? Against all common sense, he wanted to take care of her and cherish her. Every fiber of his being longed to protect her with all of his devoted heart.

You are a sorry case, Thaddeus McKaslin, he thought as he beat the snow off the steps. Hadn't Aiden said it? *You're going to get sweet on that Kramer girl again, and that'll be a mistake.*

And what had he told his brother? *No one knows that more than I do.*

It didn't seem as if he knew that now. No, the past and its mistakes and pain seemed to be forgotten whenever he was with Noelle. It was a mistake to let himself care about her again. Plain and simple.

But did that stop the spark of tenderness in his heart when he remembered her in the kitchen with her scorched skirt and determination to be helpful to her family? That flame of tenderness grew until it had warmed his cold winter's heart. He wanted to make her smile again. He wanted to put happiness back into her life. He wanted to love her the right way for every minute of every day to come.

Whoa there, his thoughts were like a wild horse running away with him. He leaned the shovel against the siding. For a moment there in the kitchen, it had been almost like old times. Words had come easily, there had been a zing of emotional connection between them and a moment of understanding that made him hope, just a little, that *maybe*—maybe—she could forgive him.

He knocked the snow from his hat brim and stomped his boots on the back step. His pulse was rattling in his chest, and he felt as if he were about to step in front of a speeding train as he opened the door. The lean-to was chilly but the kitchen was warmer. As he shrugged out of his winter wraps in the empty room, he had to admit that he'd been half expecting to see her here, doing what she could to help out.

That skunk smell had faded some, but not enough that he wanted to linger in the kitchen. He marched past the huge worktable, the rows of counters and the wall of glass shelves, and found himself in the dining room. It, too, was full of polished wood furniture and shelves of fancy doodads. But no Noelle.

He didn't spot her until he stepped foot into the parlor. She was asleep on the couch, stretched out the length of those stout-looking cushions, her head resting on a throw pillow. Her hands were pressed together beneath her chin as if in prayer.

An overwhelming lightning bolt of affection hit him. Left him thunderstruck.

He loved her. Beyond all rhyme and reason, beyond all good sense and possibility, he loved her.

Quietly, he took the afghan off the back of the couch and covered her. She didn't stir. He gently tucked the warm knitted wool around her and stood over her, watching her sleep. Hopes came to life in his soul— hopes he could not let himself look at—but they were there all the same.

No good could come from his feelings and he knew it. But that did not keep the love in his heart from growing until it was as solid as the Montana Rockies and just as lasting. Until nothing in this world could alter it.

He resisted the urge to brush away wisps of pure chestnut from her face. The thick coil of her braid fell over her shoulder, and she could have been a painting, framed in the soft spill of the lamplight and the glow from the fire. His chest cinched with a physical pain as he backed away.

He might be low on faith, but he was starting to believe there was a reason God had led him back to Angel County. Maybe he was meant to be here to help her through this time. Perhaps he was meant to watch over her until her uncle was able to do so again.

And then what? Did he have a chance with her?

As he climbed the stairs in search of the missus, he couldn't rightly see how Noelle was ever going to forgive him for jilting her. He had to be sensible. As much as he wanted her to forgive him, it wasn't likely she would ever trust him again.

His steps were heavy as he headed down the long hallway. He had a lot of work to do before nightfall. Maybe it would be best if he concentrated on that.

The school bell's final tones lingered on the crisp February afternoon as she tried to avoid the deep drifts of snow between the school yard and the road. She didn't want to ruin her new shoes, so she'd hiked her woolen skirts and flannel petticoats up to her ankles. She was in the middle of taking a shockingly unladylike step over the drifts when she heard a familiar chuckle.

"Careful there, you might slip."

Noelle's shoe hit the ice on the street side of the snowdrift, and for one perilous instant she felt the heel of her new shoe slide. If she fell on her backside in front of the handsome Thad McKaslin, she'd have to let Mother send her off to finishing school in Boston, as she'd been threatening to do for the last year, because she could have never faced him again.

Heaven was kind to her because her shoe held, she heaved herself over the drift and realized Thad had stopped his horse and was standing beside his sleigh. He tipped his hat to her, and a quivering hope sprinkled through her like the snow through the sky.

He held out his gloved hand. "This is my lucky day. I was just in need of some help."

"You need my help?"

"Yep. I just finished building my sleigh, and I need to see how she drives with two passengers."

"I see. You couldn't find anyone else?"

"Who else? I don't see anyone. Only you."

One look at that grin of his, wide and dimpled had her smiling, too. A gaggle of smaller schoolkids went screaming past them, and Noelle didn't tell him the school yard and the street were both crowded with lots of other students.

"I know exactly what you mean," she told him shyly as she placed her hand on his palm. "I don't see anyone else, either."

His fingers closed over hers, and the tenderness she felt in his touch showed in his blue eyes, too. His eyes were blue as her dreams. As blue as forever.

Thad. Noelle woke with a start and a heart full of longing. The fringe edging of an afghan tickled her chin. When she sat up, it slipped to the floor with a swish. The vibrant images of her dream clung to her. The blue sky and brilliant snow and handsome man faded in clarity and color until there was only darkness. Disoriented, she realized where she was by the steady tick of the clock, the lick of the fire in the big fireplace, and the sofa beneath her.

She wasn't sure what had awakened her, but her heart wouldn't stop aching like an open wound that could not heal. She bowed her head, folded her hands and prayed with all of her might. *Please, Father, take the memories of him I can no longer bear.*

There was no answer but a pop of wood in the hearth and the eerie howl of the wind kicking up against the north side of the house. She shivered, although she could not feel the cold wind, and she wished, how she wished that Thad McKaslin had never come back into her steady, placid, safe life.

She had to stop thinking of him. She had to bank that tiny light of caring within her. He was not the right kind of man. He'd *never* been the right kind of man. She— a woman grown and wise to love and life—did not want Thad McKaslin. No, these feelings were coming out of what was past, out of memory of the schoolgirl she used to be, nothing more.

She felt for the heap of the afghan and lifted it off the floor. She stood, holding her heart still, banishing all thoughts of Thad as she briskly folded the length of wool and tossed it somewhere on the couch—she heard it land with a whisper. She couldn't sense much beyond the roiling longing in her heart and the wishes she could not let herself give voice to. How did you stop remembering what had hurt so much? And what had, once, brought her so much joy?

This is not good, Noelle, you must stop this. She felt as if she were suffocating and could not get air, so she headed straight for the door. Careful not to make any noise to wake the house, she grabbed her cloak on her way out the door. Cold air hit her with a bitter force, sapping all her warmth and chilling her feelings like a sudden freeze.

Ice crunched beneath her shoes. The cold moan of the wind swirled around her and filled in the lonely, empty places where her future and her dreams used to be. She pulled a pair of mittens from her pocket and tugged them on.

The wind was picking up, bringing with it the promise of more snow. Winters were long by tradition in Montana Territory, and she knew it, so why then was she longing for spring? She breathed in the heavy scents of wood smoke and dormant trees and ice. The temperature was falling, and she breathed in the air cold enough to burn the inside of her nose and tingle in her chest. Today the world was especially dark to her, and she sorely missed the colors and look of things and the comfort in them.

The rail was thick with ice and she curled her hands around the thick board. The wind was against her left side, so she knew she faced westerly. The great rim of the Rocky Mountains should be straight ahead of her. She remembered how they speared upward from the prairie's horizon. Night was falling, and the air smelled like falling snow. She knew how the sky would look— thick clouds, white with snow and dark with storm, spiraling together.

What she could not know was the look of this sky at this moment and the exact shade of the mountains as they changed to match it. She hadn't realized how her memory of color was fading with time. Was the sun still out? She strained to feel its cool brush against her cheek and felt none. Had it already sunk behind those oncoming clouds, and what colors had the sun painted them? She tried to imagine it, could not.

Thad. Why was it that when she was with him, she could? She couldn't explain it, so she breathed in the feel of the late afternoon and listened to the near silence of the plains.

Memory took her over in a sudden wash of color and light. A late-winter's afternoon much like this one with the promise of a storm. The sky was a hue of fluffy dove-gray. Every shade of white spread out in the landscape around her. Sunshine glossed the polished miles of snow like a hundred thousand diamonds. Thad had taken her hand to help her into his little red sleigh. At a gentle slap of the leather reins, his gelding carried them forward across the jeweled snow with a twinkle of merry sleigh bells.

She realized that the musical clink of steel shoes on ice wasn't in her thoughts. Someone was riding up to the house from the stables. Thad. If she looked into her heart she could see him, the way his head was down and his eyes low. He always sat his saddle straight and strong.

"Howdy, there." His baritone could warm every sliver of ice away. "Isn't it a little cold for you to be just standing there?"

"It's not any colder out here for me than it is for you."

"Yes, but I have a sheep-skin lined coat."

"My shawl is warm enough for now. You needn't worry about me, Thad."

"Sorry. Can't help myself."

He didn't sound sorry at all, and she ought to be upset about that. She didn't know why she wasn't. "Are you going to town on errands for my aunt?"

"Yep. Got some business at the feed store, and then a stop for a few supplies the doc recommended. Your uncle's looking better."

"Is he? I haven't seen him recently. I must have fallen asleep on the sofa instead of going upstairs to sit with everyone."

"The way I hear it, you were up all night with Henrietta. Robert's still as gray as ashes, but he's looking better. He ought to be riding green-broke horses in a few weeks' time." The saddle creaked as if he'd shifted in it.

Had he been in the house while she was napping? Had he seen her sleeping? Remembering the afghan and how she'd woken up with thoughts of him in her heart, she knew. He had been the one to cover her up.

A horse nickered, and it sounded like a scolding. She couldn't believe she had forgotten the mustang.

"Sunny, please forgive my manners," she said, feeling her way along the rail. She kept one firm grip on the banister in case she hit an ice patch and moved to a much safer subject. "How are you doing this fine day?"

The horse gave a snort, and his bridle jingled as if he'd nodded his head to say "fine."

"He's looking forward to the long ride to town," Thad answered for his horse. "I promised to give him his head so he can pick the pace."

"You do that often?"

"I'm not lord and master of this horse." He said the words as if there was more, a story behind it, and a question she was supposed to ask.

A question she could not, would not ask. She had to keep Thad at a distance—there was no other choice. She tugged off her glove and was rewarded with Sunny's warm, velvety muzzle. She rubbed his nose gently. He exhaled into the palm of her hand, tickling her.

Laughter vibrated through her. Making her feel like her old self again. But only for a moment. She fell silent when she felt Thad's gaze like a touch to the side of her face.

Why did a tiny spark of caring quiver to life within her? It was impossible to go back and repair the past like a rip in a seam. It was impossible to forget how he'd shattered her down to the soul. There was nothing to be done but to turn around and head toward the house, which is what she had to do.

"Goodbye, Thad. Have a safe trip," she said over her shoulder.

"I will. You get some more rest, darlin'."

His caring was like a knife cutting deep. With every step she took away from him, the longing for him grew. And for what could have been.

That's all this is, she told herself as she closed the door shut behind her. All that could never be for her. Even if the past did not separate them, even if Thad had not jilted her, she was blind. Having a good husband to love her, her own home and children to look after was not possible for her. She'd accepted that years ago. Why was she upset now? God had chosen this path for her. She had to walk it.

She shrugged out of her cloak and hung it with care on the tree. The warmth of the fire lured her closer and when she was safely in her chair, she held her hands in the direction of the hearth to warm them. Thoughts of Thad came with her, too. It was not easy knowing the best part of her life was behind her—and would always be.

Once her hands were warm, she tucked away her feelings and headed upstairs to check on the family she did have, the people she was deeply thankful for.

Chapter Nine

The days began to blur together as her uncle slowly improved. Life had stood still for the two weeks Robert had been bedridden and in so much pain he could scarcely breathe. Gradually life returned to some normalcy. The girls started back up at school, the minister's visits were more social than serious, the doc was openly optimistic when he'd last driven away, and Noelle's piano lessons resumed.

One thing remained constant. Thad arrived twice a day to care for the horses and tend to other chores. When she was in her music room, she could hear him the best. Sometimes the wind would snatch his voice and carry a snippet to her. Or the rhythmic beat of a horse on a lunge line would interrupt her concentration during a lesson. The scrape of a shovel on the brick walk, the spill of wood into a metal bin, the low rumble of his voice in the kitchen when he returned a tray Sadie had made for him.

It wasn't easy keeping her feelings tucked away. She made sure Sadie packed a few treats for his mother to take with him at the end of the day. A loaf of freshly baked bread. A pan of cinnamon rolls. A plate of oatmeal cookies.

The day Robert took his first few wobbly steps with a cane marked an occasion for celebration. Henrietta ordered a celebratory meal, sending Cook into a flurry. The morning was suddenly in chaos, and no fire had been lit in Noelle's music room.

She pushed through the kitchen door in search of the maid and heard the faint ring of an ax outside the back door. Thud, thud, thud, chink. The sound repeated itself like a refrain, over and over in nearly perfect rhythm. Thad was here again.

"Noelle." Sadie's voice came from somewhere near the kitchen hand pump. "I meant to light the fire in the music room, but there was not enough wood. I'll have it done soon enough."

"Thank you, Sadie." Noelle hesitated, drawn by the sounds of the ax. "Hasn't Henrietta hired someone to take care of things yet?"

"I believe she's certain the mister will be fit as a fiddle in a few more days and can do it all himself."

Henrietta, bless her heart, was not thinking clearly. "Robert has several broken ribs and a broken calf bone. He's not going to be able to clean the stable for some time to come."

"Between you and me, you're right. I wonder what the missus is thinking. She refuses to hire anyone. I must tell you all about last night. I caught her and Thad in deep conversation."

Uh-oh. "That cannot be a good thing. She wasn't trying to marry any of us off to him, was she?"

Sadie chuckled. "I wouldn't have been surprised,

but she was offering Thad money for his work here, but he wouldn't take a cent." There was a clink of ironware and a rustle as Sadie moved closer. "He said he wasn't the kind of man who stayed on to take advantage of a family in need."

That did not surprise her in the least. That was the man she used to know. "Did he say why?"

"He said as much as he needed a wage, he wasn't helping out for money." There was a clatter and clink of ironware. "Considering the way Thad looks at you, I thought you ought to know."

Emotions swelled in her throat until she could scarcely speak. "How does he look at me?"

"Like you are Sunday morning dawning, all bright and new. Well, now, I've got to get this up to the mister." Sadie breezed on by and left the door swinging in her wake.

The *thud, thud, thud, clink* seemed to echo in the stillness, and the emotions tangled in her throat hurt until her eyes teared. Why was he doing all this? And for no gain for himself? This was the Thad she'd fallen in love with all those years ago.

She forced her feet to carry her forward and down the cool hallway. The north wing felt especially cold this morning. She shivered, but it wasn't the kind of cold a fire could warm. With every step she took, the sound of Thad's ax faded into silence. She was thankful for that.

Leave the past where it belongs, Noelle. She ran her finger along the hallway wall, counting the doorways so she could find her way. Silence seemed to close in around her, bringing with it all the sore, raw edges of the questions she was too afraid to ask. She could no longer deny the hard sheath of anger around her heart, like the tough outer shell of a seed. Anger at him for hurting her. Anger at him for breaking every belief she'd had in him. Anger now at the way he behaved like the man she'd once known him to be.

Although the music room was cold with the chill of the morning, she went straight to her piano. Her fingers yearned for the comfort of the familiar keys. Her heart ached to let music move through her and push away all this bound-up confusion. She settled on the bench, uncovered the keys and let her fingers go.

She amazed him, all right. Thad halted outside the open doorway. That sweet complicated music drifted across the hall, the notes too tangled up for a cowboy like him to figure out, but it was nice. Noelle had always had a hundred pieces of music stored in her memory. At least her blindness did not keep her from playing.

He had a perfect view of her at the piano, the morning sun haloing her like a dream. Lost in her music, she didn't hear his approach. He watched her unguardedly, savoring the sight of her. Her hair was a sleek fall of gleaming cinnamon, held back with a ribbon tied at the crown of her head. The soft locks framed her heart-shaped face. She still had that goodness within her shining up and it was the most beautiful sight.

The lilting sweetness of the music stopped in midnote. She lifted her gaze to meet his, as if she saw him clearly. "Thad?"

"How did you know?"

"The scent of hay and freshly split wood."

"That was mighty good piano playing. Don't stop because I'm here."

Sunshine streamed through the long bank of windows, polishing her with a golden light. She was radiance and everything dear to him as she returned to her playing, caressing beauty from those mysterious white and black keys. He felt gruff and too big and too awkward for her and for this fancy room full of expensive things. Some things, it appeared, hadn't changed a whit.

Her music followed him across the room. Maybe it didn't much matter how many years passed, he would always be able to easily see into her heart. Right now hers was closed up tight to him—and it always would be. He had to face that, too. There was no way to repair the hurt he'd caused her. There would never be a chance she would trust him again. No way he could ever be sorry enough.

That took a piece out of him. His heart, as cracked as it was, broke a little more.

He emptied the wood into the bin, noticing that her playing faltered for a moment. She went on playing, so he knelt at the stone hearth. He drew back the screen and looked around, trying to figure out where the matches were.

The piano playing stopped. As the last notes of the chord faded in the room, she pushed back the bench and breezed toward him. Her skirts and petticoats rustled like the softest music.

"Are you looking for the match tin?" She lifted a box from the shadowed corner of the mantel behind some fancy doodads. Her movements were pure grace as she leaned close, holding the tin in her small hand. "It sounds like it's full. Sometimes the maid gets busy and forgets to fill it."

"I imagine keeping up with Mrs. Worthington's standards is a very demanding task."

"She has overwhelmed more than one maid. It became such a situation that Henrietta couldn't find a single girl to work for her in the whole county."

He whisked the tin from Noelle's hand. "Did she have to advertise outside the territory?"

"She wasn't taking any chances of being without hired help again, so she brought Sadie from back East. She can't go anywhere until she's paid off the cost of her trip out here."

"That's one way to solve the problem." He lit the match and set it to the crumpled paper and dry cedar kindling already in the grate. At Noelle's smile, the tundra of his emotions thawed some. "A fancy house like this should have one of those heaters, what are they called? Furnaces."

"Henrietta doesn't approve of them. She won't allow a single coal heater anywhere in the house." She smiled, looking not as guarded as she spoke of her aunt.

Probably not because she was starting to like him again.

"It's an ongoing discussion of ours." She shrugged as if it was more amusing than anything else. "She believes it's not natural for a house to be so warm. She thinks newfangled inventions make life too easy for us. She is a firm believer that hardship builds character."

"It doesn't hurt it, that's for sure." He watched the paper melt before the flames and the fire lick up through the kindling to snap and pop greedily. He opened the damper. "Is there anything else you need me to do?"

"You've done more than enough." She tilted her head slightly, as if using the sound from the fireplace to orient herself in the room. Her rich chestnut locks shimmered with the movement and drew his gaze.

The woman she was now captivated him. It took all his inner strength to hold back his heart and the many ways he wanted to care for her. She moved away from him with a swirl of wool skirts, and his self-discipline melted like sun on ice.

He stood and put the match tin back on the mantel piece. "My ma said she appreciated the baked goods Sadie's been sending home with me, according to your instructions."

"That Sadie was sworn to secrecy." Noelle didn't look too troubled as she felt for her piano bench and settled onto it. She sat so straight and tall and poised the way she always did, it took his breath away.

"You can't get too het up at Sadie." It was tough being smitten, but he did his best to hide it. "She means well. Those cookies and cakes and breads have been a real treat for my mother. For all of us."

She slid her forefinger along the edges of the ivory keys to find the tiny carving to designate middle C.

"I am glad your mother is recovering. She was always kind to me. I remember she was the sweetest lady and had a smile for everyone, whether she knew them well or not. It must have been hard being away when she was so ill."

"It was." He fought the pressure rising in his chest, the pressure of all he wanted to say and everything he could not let himself feel. "I was making a much better wage than I could hope to find in these parts. Better wages helped out more at home, but it left Aiden to shoulder the burdens of the ranch on his own."

"I remember him as a very friendly, outgoing young man. I heard of his loss. They belonged to the other church in town, but I went to the service. It had to be so hard for him to lose his wife in childbirth."

"It changed him forever."

"Understandably." Soft curls fell across her face, hiding her expression as she traced one fingertip along the edges of the piano keys. "How is he doing now?"

"Unable to let go of the past. Like a lot of us."

She nodded and said nothing at all. Her fingertips brushed at the piano keys, drawing out a harmony of music that rose sweetly before fading to silence. "You've sent money home? It must have been hard. Wages never go as far as you need them to."

"Never. I've been sending over half of my pay home since I first went away."

"Truly? All five years?"

He nodded and steeled his chest. He could tell her the truth right now, but at what cost? Her happiness? The high cost of protecting it was taking a big gnawing bite of him.

Best to change the subject. "I've been keeping a careful eye on the mare, like you asked me to. Solitude doesn't have much longer to go."

"Really?" Her reserve fell away. "I've been worried about her after Robert fired the last horseman. Is there a chance that she'll foal before you have to leave us?"

He could not say no to her, hands down. "I'll make sure the mare is all right. I'll be right here, even if your aunt finds someone else to hire or she calls in family from St. Louis to help out. How's that?"

"I'm grateful, Thad." She brightened like dawn. Nothing could be lovelier. "Solitude is such a sweetheart of a mare, and she means so much to me. I can't be around horses the way I used to, but I..." She shrugged, falling silent, as if unable to finish.

"You love them." He understood her. Always had. Always would. He couldn't stop his feet from carrying him forward. Just as he couldn't stop caring for her. "It's got to be hard, to have given up so much of what you used to love."

"It's just the way life is. I've grown to be terribly practical, I'm afraid."

"Me, too. Hardworking, sensible, no time for fancy. That's me."

"We've grown up, you and me. Time has been kind to you." As if suddenly shy, she bowed her head and her hair fell down to hide her face.

He saw her meaning clearly. The heartache and bitterness battling within him vanished like sun to mist. There was something new in his heart. Not the old tenderness for her he'd always carried within his spirit, but more. A new love for the woman she was now.

He was not practical after all. The hard lessons in life and the rough trails he'd ridden were forgotten when he gazed into her beloved face.

He hated that she'd known hardship. His leaving hadn't spared her from that. The loss of her parents, her broken engagement, an accident that had almost taken her life. It made a man wonder about fate—about God's design for a single life. Was it His intention for Thad to have left the way he did? Or had God meant for them to be together?

If Mr. Kramer hadn't interfered, would they have found happiness? Would he be married to Noelle right now? Would she have been saved from her losses and blindness?

It was a funny thing—a single decision in a man's life could irrevocably change everything else that followed it. He'd lost more than his heart on that September night long ago when he'd been forced out of town. He'd lost his belief in the goodness in people. He'd lost his belief in love and that a simple man could be honest, work hard, do the right thing and it would turn out all right for him.

He was no longer that naive young man but a man full grown who knew how the world worked and the people in it. But being near Noelle, seeing how she was still so good and bright at heart, made him wish he could be the young man he'd once been.

"I'd best get back to the stable." It wasn't the easiest decision to walk away, but it was the right one. "I'd best keep an eye on the mare."

"Yes. You'll keep me informed?"

"Count on it." He left while he could still hold on to his heart. Noelle started playing and her music followed him out into the hall.

It sounded suspiciously, impossibly, like hope.

Noelle hesitated outside her uncle's bedroom and listened. If Robert were napping, she didn't want to wake him. But she heard the creak of the leather chair, so she counted her steps into the room. "Henrietta said you were sitting up."

"And glad to be, too." His voice was stronger. "I didn't know a horse's hooves could pack such a wallop. It's one thing to read about being injured like that. Another entirely to experience it."

"I'm just thankful you are here to tell the tale." Noelle smiled, knowing that comment would please her uncle. "You must be careful not to overtax yourself right now. Do you need me to call for the maid? We can get you lying down again."

"I've done enough of that. Sitting up like this is doing me good."

"All right, then. Henrietta would only take a nap if I promised on my very soul to sit with you every moment and not let you take up your cane and wobble down to the stables."

Robert's chuckle was warm with love. "That wife of mine knows me too well."

"That wife of yours refused to leave your side night and day until she knew you were going to be all right." *That* was love. The right kind of love. The rare kind of love. The kind she'd once dreamed of. She'd seen a glimpse of that dream today.

Don't think of Thad. She cut off her thoughts like a piece of thread.

"I'm a very blessed man, and I know it." Robert paused and the breath he took sounded strained. "I've always known how much, but never more than in the instant when I saw that mare's rear hooves kicking out and I knew I couldn't get away in time. I was in big trouble. That one minute stretched longer than my lifetime, or so it felt, and my last thought was what a fool I'd been, chasing dreams when all I truly wanted was to be with my wife and daughters."

Noelle's heart cinched up tight. He sounded ashamed and regretful. She knew something about those experiences. "Do you mean as the practical bank president who had unerring good sense?"

"That's the man." Robert's voice sounded glad and sad at the same time. He fell silent as the fire in the grate roared and crackled.

Tiny pings against the window glass announced that it was snowing again. Henrietta's words drifted through Noelle's mind. *The greatest gift is to be loved as I have been loved. As I love.*

It was a while before he broke the silence between them. "There's nothing wrong with dreams and trying to make them come true, Noelle. I might not know what I'm doing when it comes to horses, and I always might make a better banker than a horseman, but at least I got to try. I would be wise to go back to the bank, I suppose."

"Didn't you just say that you decided that it was foolish to chase dreams?"

"That I did. But I just went about it the wrong way. That's all. I wouldn't listen, and that wouldn't be the first time." Robert fell silent. "Thad is the young man your father wrote us about, isn't he? The one you meant to elope with."

"I didn't know Father had contacted you."

"He and Henrietta kept in close touch. Letters every week without fail."

"I remember." There was the lump again, back in the middle of her throat, blocking off every word and every feeling. Noelle groped for the hard-backed chair she knew was nearby and once she'd found it, she collapsed into it. "My father would never have approved of Thad."

"He is not a wealthy man."

"No. And my father thought wealth was important." She thought of Thad working hard to send wages home. "I suppose Henrietta remembers, too?"

"I don't think she's realized that Thad was the man your father disapproved of so strongly. I can still remember the letter he sent us after he'd found out that a poor immigrant's son was beauing his only daughter."

Noelle froze. "Found out? You mean after I told him."

"I only know that Robert was ready to send a posse after him to drive him from the county." Robert sounded sad.

"Drive him from the county?" That made no sense at all. Father didn't know about Thad until that night when she'd been sobbing in her room, jilted. Unless her father had lied to her.

No, not Papa, she thought. But the Thad she'd known had never been a traveler or a wandering spirit, but a steadfast, stay-put brand of man.

He hadn't been chasing dreams, she realized. He'd lost his dreams as surely as she'd lost hers.

"I don't think you should give up wanting a horse ranch." She was surprised how resolute her words were. The lump in her throat had vanished. "You should simply hire someone very good to learn from."

"You wouldn't happen to have someone in mind?"

Was she that obvious? She hadn't realized it until now, but she was starting to get used to having Thad McKaslin underfoot. "He's been doing the work anyhow, and he *is* a gifted horseman."

"As I hear things, he isn't interested in a job or in getting paid for his time here. Something tells me it's because of you."

The cool from the window swirled around her like fog and she shivered, but it wasn't from the cold. She had never seen Thad so clearly.

Chapter Ten

"I'll see you next week, Nellie." Noelle trailed her final student for the day to the front door. "If you stick to practicing your scales for a whole thirty minutes every day, then next week I'll give you something fun to learn to play. Would you like that?"

"Oh, yes!" Nellie Littleton's rush to escape slowed down a bit. "I've been wanting to learn a new hymn."

"Yes, I know." Noelle adored her youngest student. "Now you be sure and practice your scales. I can tell the difference in your playing, so I'll know if you didn't."

"Oh, all-riiiight." The little girl was a doll, even if she did try to get by without practicing the way she should.

Noelle well remembered what it was like to be that age and have piano lessons which were entirely your parents' idea. "I'll see you next week, Nellie."

"Okay. Bye, Miss Kramer!" Her shoes beat a fast rhythm to the front door. Icy wind gusted and then with a quick slam, she was gone. The faint squeak of a wagon wheel told her that Nellie's parents were outside waiting for her.

Noelle listened to the stillness of the quiet house. Sadie was out on errands. Henrietta was in town to fetch the girls home from school. Matilda was keeping an eye on her father. The only sounds in the house were from the crackling fire and the faint clatter as Cook went about her work in the kitchen. Robert had been drowsing in his library the last time she'd checked. Perhaps it was time to check on him again.

The quick tap of Thad's step descending the stairs caught her in midstride. She turned toward the archway, listening to the confident pad of Thad's gait.

She wasn't going to examine too closely why she was glad he'd entered her domain. "Hi, stranger."

"Hi there, pretty lady."

With the smile in his voice and the rustle of clothing, she imagined him standing on the landing, hat in hand, looking storm swept from the conditions outside.

She could not explain why that made her heart pitter-patter. "I didn't hear you come in."

"I reckon it was hard to hear me over the sounds of all those wrong piano notes. Even a cowboy like me could tell someone was playing that wrong."

"Nellie is my most promising student *and* my student least likely to practice. I have hopes her attitude will change in time. Are you on your way home?"

"Not quite yet. I'll wait for your aunt to return from town so I can put up her horse. Then I'll go." The boards creaked slightly as his boots knelled closer. "The mare's foal arrived safe and sound."

"Solitude had her baby?" Pleasure warmed her. "Is it a little filly or a colt?"

"A filly. She's deep sorrel like her mother, as shiny as a copper penny in the sunshine."

"She sounds beautiful."

"She surely is. She's a dainty little thing, all long legs and knobby knees. Would you like to visit her?"

"In the stable?"

"I don't think your aunt would want me to bring a horse, baby or not, into the parlor."

"No, you're right about that." She stood, and she looked like a touch of spring in the light pink dress she wore. "As a general rule I keep out of the stable for a few very practical reasons."

"Ah, I think I understand. I promise to look *before* you step."

"I surely appreciate that." Her eyes twinkled.

When she smiled like that, he felt hope trickle into him.

Crystal lamps clattered in his wake, and he felt sort of out of place, like a colt in a glass shop, but she didn't seem to notice, or, he figured, was too nice to comment.

She'd snagged her coat from the wooden tree by the time he reached her and was already shrugging into it.

"You're still so independent, I see." He caught the woolen garment by the back of the collar, as he would help any lady. "Let me help a little."

"I suppose."

He didn't miss her playful smile. This close, he could smell the lilac soap she used and see the stray strands that had escaped her braid to curl like tiny gossamers around her face. For the first time in years, it wasn't the past he longed for.

She took a step back, tying her coat around her middle. "It sounds like thunder out there."

"Yep. It's turning out to be some winter storm." He reached for the door. "You want to reconsider coming out with me?"

"Not a chance."

He turned the knob and cold gusted in. The crisp *tap-tap* of snow faded into the howl of the wind. "You used to love storms."

"I still do." She slipped past him onto the covered porch and faced the wind. "I might not be able to watch the force of the storm, but I can hear the symphony of it."

Snow bulleted under the porch roof, striking them both. He closed the door against the resisting wind, hardly aware of the boards beneath his feet. All he could see—he feared all he would ever see—was her.

"This is wonderful." She held out her hands, palms up, to feel the strike of the blowing snow. "Bitterly cold, but wonderful."

"I get my fair share of weather working outside. It doesn't hold the same wonder for me. Careful now, you keep inching forward like that and you're gonna hit a patch of ice and then where will you be?"

"On my backside?"

"Exactly. You'd best let me help you." His hand engulfed hers.

You will feel nothing, she vowed. Not the past and certainly not an ember of affection.

It took all her strength to keep her heart as if blanketed by a layer of snow. "It works best if I can lay my hand on your arm."

"Sure." He released his grip on her and she slid her gloved hand along the strong plane of his forearm. Even with the thick layer of jacket and sheepskin, she could feel his strength.

That made her wonder more about his life. About all the pieces he hadn't told her. She took a hesitant step forward and he moved with her, nudging her gently to the left and safely down the slick board steps. She felt the softer snow, which meant they were moving over the walking path between the house and the stables.

She found herself asking a question before she had time to think about it first. "Did you like herding cattle?"

"I didn't dislike it. I got to spend time in the saddle. You know how I don't like to be cooped up indoors all the livelong day."

"Yes." That she did remember. She saw the image of Thad in a white shirt and denims working in amber fields beneath an endless, brilliant blue sky. "I suppose you've seen a lot of the West like in those dime western novels you used to read."

"Yep. I've been all over. I've seen the Grand Canyon. The Badlands. The American desert. The prairies so flat and vast you ride for weeks and you think you'll never come to the end of it."

"There's happiness in your voice. You liked traveling."

"I didn't mind it." Thad cleared his throat, trying to bury the truth more deeply. The last thing he wanted was for Noelle to guess it. He made sure to keep between her and the brunt of the gusting wind. "It was an amiable enough lifestyle. I got to sleep under the stars at night. Saw just about everything there is to see in this wide country. Bear and mountain lions and wolves. Flash floods and twisters and blizzard winds so powerful they can freeze a bull's head to the ground."

"Angel Falls must seem very uninspiring by comparison."

"Not at all." It was the only place he wanted to be. Had ever wanted to be. Gazing down at her lovely face, seeing the snowfall clinging to her velvet hat's brim did funny things to his chest. To his heart. To impossible dreams long buried that had come to life again. "It was tough being gone from my family."

"You missed them." She could see that now. "You and your older brother used to be so close."

"Still are. Another good part about being home is that I'm not always having to write a letter. It's better just to walk up to the main house—I'm staying in the old shanty on our place—walk into the kitchen, pull up a chair and share the day's news over a hot pot of tea. I reckon not much in this lifetime has made me happier than coming back to the homestead."

There was the Thad she'd known—had always known. The man Thad had always been. "Then it's a blessing that you're here."

"I'm glad you think so."

Her shoes sank in the deep snowdrifts, and Thad guided her up the slight slope to the stable's double doors. The sweet scent of hay and the warm earthy scent of horse greeted her. The wind-driven snow moved off her face and echoed in the open rafters overhead. She drank in the sounds of the stable, sounds she missed. The movement of the horses shuffling in the stalls. The low-throated nickers of greeting. The rustle of stray bits of straw beneath her shoes.

The steady footsteps at her side were the sweetest sound of all. She could no longer deny it. Not even Solitude's single, gentle whinny could be more welcome.

"The foal is still wobbly on her feet." Thad drew her

to his side of the aisle and to a stop. "She's in the corner right now, all folded up in the straw next to her ma."

"I can hear Solitude breathing, but that's all. She's so quiet." She tried to picture it, the beautiful red horse standing over her newborn foal. Noelle gripped the top rail of the gate. "Hi, girl. I came to say hello to your baby."

The mare exhaled in an expressive whoosh.

"It's hard to say what Solitude meant by that," Thad interpreted over the rustling sounds in the straw and the solid clink of the mare's hooves. "But my best guess is she's saying it's about time. She's torn between coming to see you and staying with her baby."

The storm chose that moment to surge against the northwest side of the stable. The far-off boom of thunder startled the few other horses in the stables, sending them into loud neighs of protest. Robert's un-manageable stallion took to racing around his stall, sounding like a half-dozen stampeding buffalo all by himself.

Suddenly, she felt the mare's hot breath on her face. She put one hand out and Solitude pressed her nose into it, nibbling affectionately.

Thad's arm brushed hers as he reached to stroke the mare. "She knows you pretty well, I see."

"Solitude was my mother's favorite mare. I gave her to Uncle Robert, since I had no need for a horse. Mama understood Robert's horse dreams."

Thad was silent a moment. "What happened to your horse dreams?"

"Life has a way of taking them away." She traced her fingertips along Solitude's velvety nose.

"True, but life also has a way of giving new dreams."

Thad's hand covered hers and nudged her hand higher. "Are you looking for the star? It's right here."

She felt the swirl of fine hair, where Solitude's perfect white star was. How had he known? she wondered. She tried to imagine the beautiful red horse in her mind. "Dreams. I don't burden myself with make-believe anymore. Just the things that are here and real, and that matter."

"Like this horse. She's the mare your mother once loved."

"Yes." No one had ever seen her so clearly. She'd missed that, too. The straw rustled and four small hooves beat an ungainly rhythm in her direction. "It's the baby."

"Her mane is just like a bristle broom stickin' straight up. Her tail is a red mop. She has her mother's long, long legs." His baritone dipped low as he chuckled warmly. "Whoa, little filly. Those legs keep tangling you up. Slow down."

"I can hear her. Oh, she fell again. Be careful, little girl."

"She's got her front legs crossed, and her hind end is splayed, but she's getting up. She's wobbling, but don't worry. She's going to figure it out."

Noelle listened to the uneven thumps of the foal's ungainly steps. She was aware of Thad moving closer to lean his forearms against the rail. His arm brushed her shoulder. The only thing louder than the cadence of the storm against the roof was her heart. "Has my uncle named her yet?"

"Nope. Not when I was up chatting with him. He's sure looking better day by day. Well, now she's got her front legs straightened out. Here she comes."

"Oh, her whiskers tickle." Noelle's laughter was soft and full of heart. "She's as soft as warm butter. She's lowered her head. I can feel her ear."

"She's got her neck outstretched, giving your skirt ruffle a look. She can see it beneath the hem of your coat."

"She's going to be a sweetheart like her mother."

"Chances are." Although he was no longer looking at the foal, but at the woman Noelle had become, still full of wonder and tenderness.

Now he saw something more. She had a strength that was so subtle he'd almost missed it. He had to look past her beauty and beyond her loveliness to what lay quietly beneath. Now that he saw it, he could not look away.

"Solitude, I didn't mean to ignore you." Warmly, Noelle moved to stroke the mare, and that ruffled skirt hem fluttered with the movement. The foal startled and her long legs splayed in four different directions. Down she went with a skid and a look of puzzlement.

"Is she all right?"

"She looks a little taken aback, but her ma is reassuring her." He watched while the mare checked her foal over and gave her a tender nudge. "It's gotta be tough when everything is brand-new, even your own feet."

"She's back up." Noelle tilted her head slightly, listening carefully to the foal's movements. "Did I startle her?"

"Your skirt ruffle gave her a moment of terror."

"That was exactly Henrietta's reaction when I went to pick up this dress from Miss Sims's shop."

Thad laughed, he couldn't help it. It had been a long time since he'd laughed so readily. "You have quite a protector in your aunt."

"I certainly do. Henrietta is very shielding of me."

"Rightfully so." He reckoned he felt the same way—always had. Always would.

The foal, with her mama watching over her, inched forward, nose down and neck stretched as far as it would go trying to figure out that scary ruffle.

His heart ached as he watched Noelle hold out her hand slowly, palm up, waiting for the filly she couldn't see to come to her.

He'd given up his dreams and put others aside for later, but it looked to him as if she'd lost all of hers. She had no marriage, no children, no horses she'd gentled and trained, not one of the things they'd talked about long ago.

He would give up all of his goals yet if it could give her what would make her truly happy. The foal gave a nip at her hem ruffle, which she could probably feel judging by the way she smiled. He wished she could see the dainty pretty filly as she braced her four long legs awkwardly.

The mare came close to press against Noelle's hand. "You have a beautiful baby, girl. You did great."

Solitude nickered warmly, a proud mama.

Thad reckoned he would give just about anything in his life or anything yet to come for Noelle to smile for him the way she did the horse. The longing for it was so keen, he felt sliced down to the quick of his soul. He was no longer much of a praying man—he used his prayers for her—but this one time he wanted to spend one prayer on himself and ask that she, just once, look at him with trust and love. The way she used to.

"Thank you, Thad." Her heart rang in those words. "Thank you for seeing the foal safely here. And for... *everything.*"

She smiled at him, and it was tentative and unsure, but he was glad for it all the same.

"No trouble at all." He felt much taller, suddenly, at her side.

After spending the last hour listening to the soft bed of straw rustling and the soothing nickers as the mama spoke to her sleepy baby, Noelle sighed with contentment. She hadn't felt this happy in a long time. Maybe it had something to do with seeing Thad in a new light.

Or, she realized, maybe, because she was now blind, she had to rely on a deeper way of seeing—with her heart. Understanding why he'd left was coming to her as softly as a Brahms's air.

"I suppose it's time to leave Solitude and her baby alone together." She regretted saying those words. She wanted to make this moment last forever.

"You're shivering. You must be getting cold." Thad moved closer with a rustle. "I kept you out too long."

"Not nearly long enough." She wasn't sure if she was talking about the time spent with the horses or the time spent with Thad. Maybe both.

"I can bring you out to see the little filly again."

"That's very generous. I just might accept your offer."

"Then I just might come for you tomorrow about this time."

She let her smile of pleasure be her answer, because she didn't trust her voice. No, her emotions were tangled up like a knot in a skein of yarn.

"Come with me." His intonation was light and friendly.

She reached out and before she realized it, her hand

was on his. She could feel the roughness of his skin and the calluses on his palm from years of hard work. His were a man's hands, strong and capable. As he was. It was impossible not to respect that. To respect the man he'd become.

As she let him guide her down the aisle, the symphony of the storm accompanied them. The rise and fall of the low-noted wind played a haunting harmony to the steady, steely beat of the iced snow against the roof. The *chink-chink* of the stallion circling his stall clanged like a melody. The wind moaned in the rafters above. Thad's boot steps added a dependable percussion as he guided her into the storm.

What was she going to do about the man and her suspicions about the past and about her parents? She did not want to think about the past.

The symphony of the storm crescendoed as they stepped out into the yard. Snow hailed like shards of ice stinging her face and pinging against her coat. The wind gusted so hard, it blew her a step backward. Thad was there, his hold strong on her, moving to block the cruelest brunt of the storm.

Yes, she reminded herself, it was respect she felt. Respect that made the spark of caring within her glow a little more brightly. She could feel the change in the air from the lightning strike and the nearly instant strum of thunder. "That was close."

"Too close." His hold tightened on her. "We're out in the open here. We've got to run for it."

"In the snow?"

"Then we've got to lunge for it." He shouted to be heard over another boom of thunder. "Maybe I'd best carry you."

"Try it, and I'll never speak to you again. I'm blind, not incapable."

"I knew you were gonna say that." Standing out in a storm like this was a dangerous notion, so he tightened his hold on her, the only tenderness he was allowed. "Ready?"

Lightning tore apart the sky, cleaving the dense twilight curtain of snow. Blinding white light sizzled to the right, and an unearthly blast of thunder masked the explosion of the strike. He couldn't see what had been hit, but it had been near enough that he could smell it.

"C'mon." He ran, bringing her along with him. He had a good tight hold on her arms. There wasn't a chance he would let her fall. They ran together, and he bowed his head against the onslaught. How long before the next strike? And how close would it be? The wind swirled, holding them back like an inhuman force.

"We're almost to the house," he shouted above the roar of the storm.

To his surprise, she only stumbled once and then, in a blink, they were on the walkway in the lee of the house. She dropped the hems of her coat and skirts, which swirled at her snowy shoe-tops and swiped at the curls plastered against her face. She turned into the wind and let it batter her. "It's magnificent."

You are magnificent. His pulse slowed. His breathing stalled. A terrible pain traced like lightning through the dark sky and tore apart his hard exterior. It was a change that felt more dangerous than lightning, more powerful than the wind, more life sustaining than the rain.

She was the reason his eyesight blurred. She was the

reason his heart stirred to life and why he could not look away. The sight of her filled the empty places in him like the rain pooling on the low places of the earth. He felt whole. He felt healed. He felt at peace with the past. It was like hope and faith creeping back into his soul.

Her smile brightened as the wind kicked up a notch. "I can almost see the angle of the snow."

With the dampness curling the tendrils of her hair and the cold crisping her delicate complexion pink, she looked radiant and rosy. So beautiful it made his teeth ache. It was all he could do to talk past the tight squeeze of his throat. "It's nearly sideways."

"And falling like hail." She closed her eyes as if she were looking inward for the image. "What color of gray are the clouds?"

"Right overhead, they're as dark, and as purple-black as an angry bruise. Can't see much else, as it's nearly a whiteout."

"I hear another boom of thunder. It's definitely moving away. I can't remember the last time we had a storm like this."

I can. He sidestepped closer to her and told himself it was to better shield her from the snow's touch, but that wasn't the only reason. No, not at all. "You're shivering, and the temperature is dropping. I don't want to turn you into an icicle."

"I've been cold before. Besides, I'm having fun."

"That may be, but the last thing I want to do is to get on Henrietta's bad side. That aunt of yours is a fearsome woman."

That made her laugh but it did not make him forget the memory of her and another storm. They'd been at her house in town, standing on the back porch out of sight of any nosy neighbors They were hand in hand, heart in heart, watching the blizzard blowing down from the mountains and across the prairie like a miracle of white.

Noelle whirled toward the driveway. "Someone's coming. It must be Henrietta back with the girls."

He turned in time to see a dim shadow in the snowfall. Miss Bradshaw broke through and into sight pulling the sleigh. There was no blizzard powerful enough on earth to disguise the stern look on the aunt's proud face—probably one of great disapproval. The girls, back from school, stared wide-eyed in the back-seats as Henrietta reined in the mare.

"Inside, girls!" she commanded sharply. "Noelle! I'm shocked at you, risking your health in this way. Why, you're soaked through, by the looks of you, and wearing only a cloak! Not your heavy winter coat. Young man, what are you thinking? No good can come from this. Noelle is very frail. I expect a severe case of pneumonia at the very least."

He realized what she must see, Noelle's hand in his and alone. The hope in his heart withered like a seedling caught in a late frost. He took a gulp of freezing air and reeled in his feelings. For a moment he'd captured a small piece of heaven. For a moment, they were the way they used to be.

He'd almost forgotten that there was the past and the choice he'd made standing between them.

Thad squared his shoulders and met the aunt's gaze straight on. He hadn't thought of Noelle as frail, but he could not argue with the older woman's concern. It was a concern they shared. "Pardon me, ma'am. I was just seeing her inside—"

"Henrietta," Noelle interrupted. "I'm fine. You fret too much. You know I love a good storm."

"You must get your lack of good sense from your mother's side." With what looked like a wink, the older woman climbed out of the sleigh, refusing the offer of his free hand to help her.

If he wasn't mistaken, there was a twinkle in her eyes, a knowing glimmer that made him wonder just how much she'd been able to understand.

Yes, he was serious about Noelle. It ripped his soul in pieces to feel her take her hand from his, to take a step away. Was she remembering what he'd done to her? Seeing a man who'd hurt her?

"I'd best go." His palm felt cold as he stepped away. Lonesomeness set in, beating him like the snow. "Hope I didn't get you in the henhouse."

Her unguarded smile was all the reassurance he needed. "It was worth it. Henrietta's censure isn't enough to go back on your word, right? You'll still take me to see the foal again?"

"I'll see you tomorrow." He tipped his icy hat in the aunt's direction as he took Miss Bradshaw by the bridle bit. "You'd best all get in out of this storm." He paused while another finger of lightning crooked down from the veiled sky. "It's likely to get worse before it gets better."

He turned away so he wouldn't see Henrietta Worthington and her daughters take Noelle into the fancy house and away from him—where she belonged.

Chapter Eleven

Henrietta barreled through the parlor, the teacup rattling in its saucer with her every step. China knick-knacks and crystal pendants on the lamps clinked and chimed at her approach. "Where you young people get your notions, I shall never know."

Noelle squeezed the damp from her braid with the towel, trying to decide what on earth to say. She opted for silence as she heard the teacup clatter onto the side table and caught a whiff of Henrietta's rose fragrance before the matron marched away and came to a sudden halt. The *thwack-thwacking* sound had her imagining her aunt venting her humor on the innocent sofa pillows.

"If you catch a chill and your death, then I shall know who to blame." Henrietta paused. "A man who has made himself useful around here ought to have realized that much! I hope he is not about to make the same mistake as the last stable hand."

"I can assure you that is not a possibility." Noelle gave her hair a final squeeze and folded the towel.

"Oh, do not be so certain," Angelina commented from the hearth where she was warming up from the long ride from the schoolhouse. "You two looked terribly cozy—scandalously cozy—when we drove up."

"Cozy?" Noelle had to laugh at that, although it wasn't humor she felt. No, any thought of serious feelings between her and Thad only brought up that tangled knot of emotions that hurt more than she wanted to admit. She set the folded towel aside for Sadie to pick up later. "Thad was walking me to the house. He had to be close to guide me. You know that, Angelina."

"Yes, but he's a very handsome man and it didn't look as if being near him was a hardship," Angelina said knowledgeably. "I think he's smitten with you."

Smitten? No. Noelle filled up from toe to top with an aching regret. How could she tell her cousin that it was far too late for that? Any loving feelings Thad had to have once felt for her were long destroyed. They had to be.

Thad was a good man with a good heart. Of course he would always care for her. Her eyes smarted with understanding. It was all starting to make sense. All his kind words and the gentle things he'd said earlier which had made her so angry came clear. How he would always care for her.

And she for him, she realized. Her fingertips felt wooden and clumsy as she inched across the small table, searching for the cup and saucer. Regret and the weight of lost dreams burdened her. No, even if she were not blind, it was too late for a second chance.

Henrietta gave another thwack on the unsuspecting

pillows. "I'll have no more talk of this tonight. Robert, are you comfortable? Do I need to help you back upstairs? I shall call Cook to help me—"

"No!" Robert may have been still terribly weak from his injuries, but his tenor boomed. "No, my dear, I've had enough of that room. I'm quite comfortable here."

"Supper shall be served soon, I'll see you upstairs then." Henrietta sounded as firm as her footsteps on the wood floor. "No argument."

"I thought the man was the lord of his own home?" A small smile warmed her uncle's words.

"Yes, and a woman is the queen, so you will obey me. I'll not take no for an answer." While not a word was said, deep-felt love was there all the same in Henrietta's tone.

An abiding love that made Noelle sigh a little. That she could not know the same love, the kind that grew stronger and richer with the years, would always be a great, lost dream. She inched her fingers in the direction of where she thought the teacup was, and fortunately located the rim of the saucer without upturning the cup or burning her fingertips on the steaming hot tea puddled in the saucer.

"Noelle—" Robert changed the subject "—I wish I'd been up to a trip to the stable. I would have liked to see our newest addition."

"Solitude's foal is adorable." She set the teacup gently into its saucer, aware of Thad's nearness. Although he didn't make a sound, she knew. He was close—in the kitchen perhaps? "Have you named her yet?"

"Not yet. You wouldn't happen to have a suggestion?"

Thunder cannoned again. There only seemed one

obvious suggestion. Thad's boots tapped a distant rhythm at the far end of the house. She tried to make her voice sound normal and unaffected. "You should name her Stormy."

"Then Stormy she is!" Robert chuckled. He sounded happy. "I think this horse-raising venture of mine might be taking a turn for the better."

"It could hardly get much worse!" Henrietta commented.

"Ooh, did you see that?" Minnie's words echoed in the dining room's coved ceilings.

Thunder crashed overhead, rattling the windows. Another round of lightning, Noelle realized as she gingerly sipped the hot herbal tea, and the strikes were terribly close. She remembered how Thad had described the storm to her. It was best he stay out of the dangerous weather. "Thad can't ride out in this."

"Sure he can," Henrietta answered. "He has a horse, does he not?"

The tea caught in her throat. She coughed as Angelina answered. "But Mama, it's a lightning storm. He could get struck."

"And he might not. Goodness, Noelle, are you all right?"

Noelle set the cup in the saucer with a splash. "F-fine. I should have kept my thoughts to myself, I see."

"I inquired about the North County McKaslins," Henrietta said by way of an answer. "Your Mr. McKaslin is only a disinherited cousin. Apparently his father was nothing but a disgrace, much like the younger brother is turning out to be."

"So," Angelina teased. "How old is the younger brother?"

"I'll not rise to that bait, missy," Henrietta scolded, although she was struggling not to laugh. "How you test me. Don't think I've forgotten about the incident at school. After dinner, you're to go straight to your room."

"I detest being banished. There's nothing to do upstairs but to read my Bible—"

"Exactly the guidance you need, young lady. Why rumors swirl about you, I'll never know. I'm of half a mind to take you out of that school entirely. How many times must I explain to that teacher that none of my daughters would ever shove over the outhouse?"

"Many a time, Mama." Angelina padded across the parlor as another round of thunder rumbled like cannon fire.

The girls began a discussion, speaking over the top of one another, debating the truth or rumor of Angelina's misdeeds at school, and Noelle took her leave. Keeping careful track of her steps, she made it to the kitchen as quickly as she could.

The moment she pushed open the kitchen door, she heard the maid's quick steps. "Sadie, is there a chance you could set an extra place for Thad?"

"Mr. Worthington has already requested it."

"He did?"

"When you and Mr. McKaslin took off for the stable, miss." Sadie sounded in a hurry as Cook slammed a pot lid down like a crash of cymbals. "Dinner is a bit late tonight. McKaslin is on the back steps, if you got to wondering where he may be."

"Thank you, Sadie." Noelle ran her finger against the far wall, to keep out of Cook's way. The scents of roast beef and simmering gravy hung in the air. Uncle

Robert had already thought to invite Thad? Intriguing. Thunder rattled the windowpanes and the crystal teardrops of the lamps as she opened the back door.

Icy wind slammed into her, but she hardly noticed it. She felt warm and as light as a May day. "Look what rascal has come in out of the storm."

"A rascal?" Thad's chuckle was as warm as hope, as welcome as rediscovered dreams. "I suppose you're right about that." There was a rustle, as if he were hanging up his coat. "Your uncle was kind enough to invite me to dinner with you all."

"Yes, and I think I was the last to know about it."

"That right? I'd thought the invitation had originally come from you."

"It would have, if I had thought of it sooner."

"Is that so?" How about that? Thad felt the hard shell of tension in his chest ease a notch, making it easier to breathe. She breezed past him like warmth and light, and he could not help but follow. Some things like ice and snow and February storms were as inevitable and unstoppable as his affection for her.

He closed the door tight against the pounding weather, glad for the wave of warmth that washed over him. The delicious aroma coming from the stove made his stomach growl. The rare chance of walking at Noelle's side made him feel alive again in his heart and spirit—places he'd thought had been in the dark for too long to survive.

"I can hear Sadie settling the serving bowls on the table," Noelle said over her shoulder as she followed the wall to a closed door. "Prepare yourself for the Worthington inquisition."

"The what?"

Her laughter was a gentle, musical trill as she pushed open the door.

He moved close to help her with it and time seemed to freeze. For an instant, anyway, as he noticed the damp curls of her chestnut hair—she'd unbound her braid and combed out her hair and it fell in a cascade of color and light around her heart-shaped face and past her delicate shoulders. He barely noticed she looked beautiful in the dress of white and gold she'd changed into because the sight of happiness on her face was drawing him more than any beauty.

"Just you wait and see," she said as the door opened fully.

He tried to imagine the entire Worthington family taking his measure with a whole new outlook.

The family was already seated around the elaborately set table. He hardly noticed the room and its blue-and-silver wallpaper, crystal lamps and highly polished woods because of the way the women in the room were studying him, the younger ones with curiosity and the older ones with assessment.

Henrietta, regal at the foot of the table, squinted her eyes at him. Her mouth pursed. "I hear from Robert we owe you yet another thanks. You saw the new foal safely into the world. I hear there was a complication."

"Just had to get her hooves heading the right way, was all." Thad shrugged. "It wasn't anything Robert couldn't have done himself if he'd been up to the task."

Robert nodded in greeting from the head of the table. "You're a humble man, Thad. I can learn a lot from you."

"I've been around horses all my life." Thad took

care not to trip on the carpet as he followed Noelle
around the table. The whole house was fancy for his
tastes, and he felt as discomfited by the surroundings
as by the females watching him with unblinking gazes.
"I'm a cattleman, mostly."

"Is that so?" Henrietta's gaze narrowed. "Are you
done with your wandering all over tarnation? Or is that
the life you intend to return to?"

He gulped, a little taken aback. Noelle had stopped
at a chair beside the oldest Worthington girl, and he
held her chair while she sank into it. "No, ma'am. I've
come home to Montana to stay."

Noelle turned toward him, searching his face as if
she could see him plainly.

Was that hope he saw? Or sadness? So many uncomfortable emotions were muddying his mind, he couldn't
seem to tell up from down.

"Very well then, I suppose that will do." The way
Henrietta said it, it didn't sound good at all. Not at all.
She gestured toward the empty chair beside her. "I'm
determined to get at the truth of your character. You will
sit next to me, young man."

Where she could keep a good close eye on him, no
doubt. Thad swallowed hard at his murky emotions, but
couldn't seem to dislodge them. They were made worse
by Noelle and the way her emerald gaze followed the
sound of his steps around the table, sparkling with mer-
riment. Good thing she was enjoying this because
sweat was starting to bead up on the back of his neck.

As he took his chair at the table, he couldn't shake
the notion that Henrietta was out to find his every flaw.
She was bound to find quite a few.

"When you went on those cattle drives, did you

sleep on the ground with your saddle for a pillow?" the girl directly across from him burst out.

"Y-yep."

"Do you really call the cows little dogies? Did you tell tall stories around the campfire like in the dime novels?"

"Angelina!" Henrietta looked scandalized. "Those are hardly appropriate questions for a young lady to ask." Henrietta's oblong face looked severe, or maybe it was the tight way she'd pulled her hair back, so that her face looked drawn back, as well.

Well, he should have expected that. He had no illusions. All he had to offer was a savings account that used to be bigger and an old shanty that was three times smaller than the dining room.

Thad shifted again, and the chair wasn't getting any more comfortable. He'd be more at ease sitting in a sticker bush facing down a porcupine bare-handed.

It was a saving grace when Robert spoke. "Lord, bless this food we are about to receive."

Thad realized that hands were folded and heads bowed all around him and he did the same.

"—keep us mindful of our many blessings. Thank you for bringing us together again, as friend and family, and teach us dear Lord to better love one another. Amen."

Thad looked up to a course of "amens" and where did his gaze naturally go? To Noelle.

"So, where did you learn all of this horse knowledge?" Henrietta passed him a bowl of dinner rolls and she gave him a stern look over the crusty tops. "Did you attend some kind of training?"

"Training? No, ma'am." It sure looked as if he'd hit

a rocky trail with this woman. He got the notion that the Worthington Inquisition was just getting started. "I learned what I know from growing up on my family's homestead."

"I see. No formal education?"

"Just the local school."

"No academy or college?"

"Begging your pardon, ma'am, but do I look like I've been to college?"

"No, but it was a hope."

He took a dinner roll and passed the bowl to the youngest girl, who looked at him as if he'd turned into a horse right there before her eyes.

Yep, he was feeling mighty uncomfortable. As he accepted the bowl of creamed potatoes from a tight-lipped Henrietta, he caught Noelle's amused expression across the table. She had to know that he was suffering. She didn't seem to mind it at all.

Well, she *had* warned him.

"I got a good look at that mustang you ride." The girl across the table—Angelina?—dumped a spoon of buttered peas on her plate. "Was he once wild? Did you catch him in a roundup? Did you break him?"

"Yes," Robert said from the head of the table. "Tell us about your mustang. A plucky breed, as I understand it."

"Sunny is a mustang?" Noelle asked breathlessly.

His pulse ground to a halt. Regret bit him like barbed wire. He forked a helping of roast beef on his plate, knowing what no one else knew at the table. She'd once dreamed of raising her own horses—mustangs, native to this rugged country. It was a dream they'd shared long ago.

"I'd just finished a drive on the Northern Trail and

was on my own, heading from Baker City in Oregon to my next job. It was a long haul following the Yellowstone River and there wasn't a town in sight, so I chose a spot near water to camp. Something woke me up around midnight. My horse was nervous, so I got up with my Winchester thinking there was a hungry wolf or mountain lion nearby, but it was an injured colt."

"Was he still a foal or was he more grown-up?" the littlest sister asked wide-eyed.

"He was probably six months old, I reckon. When I got up to him, he tried to run, but couldn't get up. He'd been shot."

"Shot?" Noelle gasped.

"On purpose?" Angelina burst out.

"Hard to tell but I don't think so. Likely as not he caught a stray bullet from a hunter, since we were far up in the high country. I searched for his mother, too, after I'd patched him up, but there was no telling how far he'd wandered hurt like that. I found out later there was a wild horse roundup a few days before that." He picked up his fork and knife with a slight clink. "I always figured that's how he got separated from his ma."

"It's lucky you found him." She could see the image in her mind, the dark night, the campfire, the caring man and the fragile colt.

"I always figured I was the lucky one." Thad cleared his throat for all the good it did. There was no hiding the fondness in his voice. "I wasn't sure he'd last the night, but he had spirit and surprised me. I named him Sunny because he was a palomino pinto. His coat is as bright as a summer day."

"He took to you like a best friend." Noelle could see that, too.

"Did you break him like a bronco?" Angelina asked again, her voice resonating with excitement. "He was a wild horse, so did it take longer than a tame horse?"

Noelle took a bite of her dinner roll, but her attention remained on Thad and his answer. She suspected she wasn't the only one since the clink of silver slowed around the table. In her heart, she already knew Thad's answer.

"Sunny was and is my best buddy. He's no more wild than I am, and when it comes down to it, breaking a best friend isn't my way of doing things."

"That's how the last horseman Papa hired did it." Angelina ignored her mother's throat clearing. "He got up on the horse's back and stayed on while the stallion kicked and bucked like a bronco. It was exciting."

"Probably not for the horse," Thad pointed out.

How was it that she knew Thad so well, after all? Noelle searched for her glass of water with careful fingers, listening to more questions fired from around the table, including one from Uncle Robert.

The meal progressed as Thad told of how he taught his colt to trust him. He painted a vivid picture of working with the mustang on the journey to his next job, introducing him to kindness and campfire bread and friendship. How he'd worked with Sunny in the fresh, green, wild grasses.

She could see Thad, gentle and patient and dependable, never giving the colt a reason to doubt his kindness. She could picture man and colt together in the rugged mountain wilderness, surrounded by yellow, red and purple wildflowers and crowned by majestic mountains. The honey-gold colt and the dark-haired man painted an image she wanted to believe in.

The lightning storm had passed by the time the maid cleared the dinner plates, and Thad had helped Robert back upstairs, so he'd taken his escape. The mercury had dropped well below freezing as he said his goodbyes and left Noelle with her family. But the way she'd smiled at him, and the hope in his heart stayed with him through the frigid ride home.

As the wind-driven snow battered him, memories of her kept him cozily warm. He couldn't seem to forget how she'd bitten her lower lip in worry as he'd told of Sunny's first cattle drive two weeks later, and how he'd got swept away in a stampede. Likely as not come to a sad end, but the little guy had made it. Thad kept him on a shorter lead rope from then on.

The sigh she'd made of delight wasn't something he could forget, either, when he'd told of the evening, a year later, when he'd been trying to spark a campfire with a flint and looked up at the sound of thunder. It was a herd of wild horses streaking across the plains and there'd been no mistaking the yearning in Sunny's eyes. So Thad had climbed to his feet and slipped off Sunny's halter. The yearling had taken off with an eager whinny, bolting after the herd and out of sight.

How lovely she'd looked, graced by the lamplight, and captivated by his story as he told of standing in the knee-high grass, feeling nothing but lonesome, when a low welcoming whinny sounded in the dark—Sunny had come back to stay with him.

Had he been alone with Noelle when he'd been telling that story, he would have said it had felt like a sign on that lonely night. He'd been traveling too long, miserable living out of his saddle packs and Sunny's return seemed to give him the hope that heaven was watching over him after all. Maybe there were still dreams to be had, and that he shouldn't give up all hope.

But since he hadn't been alone with her, he'd kept those words to himself. They seemed to whisper within the chambers of his heart, in the lonesomeness within that he'd not been able to shake. He'd missed her. He'd been lonely for her these long years, for his best friend, for the woman he'd wanted to marry, for his one true love.

Distant thunder rumbled through the mantle of cloud and snow, but the cold and dark did not feel as bleak as it once had. Thad nosed Sunny toward home.

Noelle shivered in the cold as she knelt in prayer. The storm howled like an angry wolf outside the bedroom window. She ended her nightly prayers as she always did. *I pray that You will watch over Thad, Father. Please see to his happiness. Amen.*

She rose, teeth chattering and dived under the covers. Cold had sunk into the marrow of her bones and the sheets felt as cold as the air in the room. The flatiron at the foot of the bed gave off blessed heat, and she scrunched down to find the warmth with her toes.

"Amen," Matilda whispered. Her teeth chattered, too, and the thwack of the quilt told that she'd covered herself completely beneath the blankets.

The house had quieted. Henrietta's voice came faintly through the walls two rooms down the hall as she wished Minnie good-night. A door shut and then silence.

Surely Thad had made it through the storm safely. So, why was she worried about him? She rolled onto her side to contemplate that. It made no sense because she knew he'd managed to drive cattle and ford dangerous rivers and crest mountain summits for years successfully. Surely he could manage to find his way home through one blustery whiteout.

She had to be honest with herself. It wasn't his safety she was worrying over. It was her feelings for him. For the man he'd made her believe in tonight with his tales of strength and steadfast gentleness.

That was the Thad McKaslin she'd fallen so hard in love with, she would have defied her beloved parents and a life of security for the chance at her dream—to love him for all the days of her life.

How could that Thad, the one she'd known so well, have forsaken her? He was not a man who could break a promise, let alone a vow of love and forever. That man was the one she'd glimpsed tonight through his honest, plain stories of befriending a wild colt.

He'd probably meant to tell of his horse-gentling philosophy, but she'd heard something different—a man who was trustworthy and steadfast and committed. The man Thad had always been.

A sharp rustle came from Matilda's side of the room. She must have thrown the covers off her head. "I'm too cold and tired to read tonight. Can I read two passages aloud to you tomorrow?"

"Of course. I'm half-asleep as it is, and I hate to trouble you anyway. You know that."

"It's no trouble. I'm just greatly fatigued. I think my mind is overworked from those thrilling stories Mr. McKaslin told at dinner."

"Yes, they were very enjoyable." And for her, personal, although that wasn't something she was about to admit to anyone, even to someone she trusted as much as Tilly. Why, she could hardly admit the truth to herself. "Angelina was enthralled. Do you think she's going to torment your mother with a new desire to run off and herd cattle?"

"Probably. It's Angelina's lot in life to torment poor mama. She ought to be careful or Mama just might make good on her threat to send her to finishing school."

"Think of all the outhouses to overturn there. Angelina will be quite busy."

"True." Matilda chuckled. "He likes you, you know. Really likes you."

"You mean Thad?" Noelle ran her fingertips over the lace edging the pillow slip. "You've told me this before, but I only have f-friendly feelings for Thad."

And there were practical reasons, of course, why she could never risk her heart on him again. Reasons that could not be changed. She groped for the edge of her sheets to pull them up to her chin.

Matilda's mattress ropes squeaked as she leaned to put out the light. "Good night, Noelle."

"Good night, Tilly." She rolled onto her side and closed her eyes, knowing she would dream this night of a wide-shouldered man and his wild horse.

Chapter Twelve

As Thad watched Noelle standing at Solitude's stall alongside her uncle, who was leaning heavily on his stout wooden cane, he tried not to take it as a sign. Of course Robert was feeling strong enough to venture outdoors. It only made sense the first place he'd visit was his horses and had asked Noelle to accompany him.

It didn't mean that she'd changed her mind about *his* offer. That was the story he was trying to sell himself. He wasn't sure it was working. As he patiently waited for the stallion to approach him, he knew one thing— Noelle's face and manner, when she'd greeted him earlier, had been warm and friendly. Not polite and cool, as it had once been.

It didn't hurt to hold out a little hope, did it?

"You've done wonders with these spirited horses of mine," Robert praised as he limped closer, leaving Noelle alone at Solitude's stall. "I knew you were helping out with the stable work and heavier chores around here. What I didn't know was that you've been working with these horses."

Thad kept eye contact with the ill-tempered stallion and kept the apple in his pocket. "I'm only doing what needed to be done."

"But your work with the horses. Triumph is standing still. A first for him, I believe. It's amazing."

"Just a little horse know-how is all." Thad shrugged, keeping his attention on the horse because looking at Noelle would hurt too much. He wasn't sure what risk his heart could afford to take. He'd been up half the night, unable to sleep for working out his plans for the day—his plans for her. "It doesn't much seem like work to me."

"You've made an impressive difference."

"Hate to argue with you about that, sir, but in my view, these horses have a long way to go."

"They'll get there." Robert leaned heavily on his cane, but despite the obvious pain he was in, he was grinning ear to ear. "I'd best get back in before my wife hunts me down and drags me back. She's not keen on this horse-raising venture of mine."

"Do you need help, sir?"

"I'll manage."

There she was, right in his line of sight. Thad gulped hard, and, since Triumph had decided to be a gentleman and stand still without showing his teeth, he palmed him the apple. The stallion took the treat and then lunged back with it, his temper showing as he shook his head like a bull in full charge.

"That stallion does sound more well behaved than he has been." Noelle sparkled with good humor. "He doesn't sound as ornery when he kicks the wall."

"This one has a long row to hoe, but he'd be all right in the end. I'm happy to work with him."

"That's good of you."

"I can't have your uncle getting kicked like that again, not if I can help it." That had her smiling. He loved her smile; he loved everything about her. She tilted her head slightly to one side, as if focusing on the approach of his footsteps, and the soft fall of her hair brushed her face.

"I think we're alone now." She paused to listen. "Yes, we are. There's something I've been wanting to ask you."

"Uh-oh. That sounds plenty serious."

"You have no notion of just how much." She reached out to him, her sensitive fingertips finding first the air, then the edge of his sleeve. "I'm sorry I didn't wait for you to bring me to see Stormy. Robert asked me and he was so excited to be feeling well enough to venture out here. I didn't have the heart to turn him down."

"Sure. I understand that. The question is, do you have the heart to turn me down."

"Turn you down? Why ever would I—" She paused, tilting her head to the side to listen closely. "I hear something. A clink of metal."

"Yep."

"What are you up to, Thad McKaslin?" There was rustling, too.

His chuckle thrummed through her spirit like a harp string. "Guess. It was something you used to love to do. I found this out, and so I asked you for our first—"

"—date," she finished as the *clank-clank* came again. What did he have there? Probably it had something to do with the stables and horses, but for the life of her, the high-noted, pleasant steely sound made her think of one thing. "That can't be ice skates."

They clanked again. "And exactly why is that so impossible? I brought your old pair from home. It seems they were still in the barn where I'd left a few things."

"The skates you'd bought for me." Pleasure filled her up like a warm sip of hot cocoa. "I spent many an hour twirling on one pond or another while you patiently froze on the bank."

"I didn't see it that way. I always figured it was a privilege just to be with you."

"Still a sweet-talker after all this time."

"Hey, it's only the truth, but I'm glad you think so."

Was that a smile in his voice? It was, she was sure of it, warm and sweetly handsome. She sighed a little, remembering how captivated she used to be by the sight of his smile—and now, by the sound and feel of it.

"Come take my arm," he offered, his baritone resonant with warmth and promise. "Let me take you out on the ice."

"To skate?" A sweet longing filled her with a sweet force. Longing to be twirling on the ice once again, she told herself firmly—and *not* longing to spend time with Thad.

Or was it?

With his hand firmly on hers, he coaxed her toward the back door. "You used to be a good skater."

"Yes, but I'm likely to fall on my nose. Or worse. It might be a complete disaster."

"I'll keep that from happening, I promise. I'll be right there with you, seeing for you."

How could she keep from caring for Thad now? Every beat of her heart grew stronger because of his words, his presence and the promise that made her feel free again.

"I'll never let you fall." He used that wondrous voice of his against her, replete with humor and unspoken dreams. Quiet, secret dreams that had her heart opening and her wishes coming to life.

Wishes she could not give life to.

He guided her along the uneven path with a gentle hand—not a domineering one—on her elbow.

"Sit here." His baritone dipped low. With quiet tenderness, he helped her settle on the garden bench.

She hardly noticed the cold trying to seep in through her layers of wool and flannel. The burn of the wind, the twitter of winter birds and the scent of wood smoke on the air faded away. There was only the crunch of snow beneath his boots, the rustle of his clothes as he knelt before her. His scent of hay and horseflesh and leather and his soothing presence was all she could think about. All she could notice.

He lifted her right foot onto his knee, and emotions that had sat like a heavy lump in her chest began to unravel, one aching thread at a time.

She could no longer hold back the question that had been troubling her. "I think I know why you ran off instead of marrying me and why you left me behind."

The ice skate slipped from his fingers. "Let's leave the past where it belongs."

"I'm not speaking about the past. I'm talking about this moment. Right now. What's happened between us since you've come back."

"There's no sense in digging up what's done."

"But—"

"Trust me, Noelle. It's for the best if we don't talk

about this." He shook the snow off the skate and fit it to her shoe. All he wanted to do was to keep her safe and happy and thriving. It was the only way he was allowed to love her.

And love her he did, with all the broken pieces of his heart and all the lost pieces of his soul. He was more than the nineteen-year-old boy he'd once been, and his love was more now, too. Fuller. Deeper. More everlasting.

More selfless. Which was why he took a long drink of the sight of her, savoring each careful detail. The heart-shape of her lovely face, her high cheekbones and sweetly chiseled chin, her jeweled emerald eyes, her cinnamon hair, her creamy complexion, her delicate features, her small slender hands that felt so dear when he held them in his own.

He reached for the second skate. "I need your other foot."

"You've taken over my uncle's responsibilities around the house and yard." She switched feet, allowing him to take her left foot in his hands. "You've gone beyond your duty as our stableman. You're the kind of man who does the right thing, who works hard, who can always be counted on."

"I take my work seriously, is all."

"No, you are the boy I fell in love with, and you've always been the man you are now. I see you, Thad. All of you."

He squeezed his eyes shut. Her words were an answered prayer. If he'd ever had one for himself, it was this. For her to see that he was the kind of man who would never hurt her, who would always do what he could for her greatest happiness. Without condition. Without end.

He clamped the blade into place on her shoe and checked to make sure it was on good and tight. He ignored the chill seeping through the knees of his denims and the gnawing of regret.

She reached forward as easily as if she saw him, and her fingertips brushed the collar of his coat, then the scarf at his throat and finally cupped his jaw. "You left me thinking something had happened to you. You left me waiting, stubbornly believing in you. Even after I learned you'd left the county for good, it took me a long time to give up believing that you had to leave for some reason and you would be coming back to me. That's how strongly I believed in you. In noble, good, unfailing you."

My dear, beloved Noelle. He pressed his jaw against the fuzzy sweetness of her gloved hand. Here was the chance he'd always wished for—to tell the truth, to right the wrong and win her back. He gently moved away and climbed to his feet.

There was nothing more precious to him in all the world, and there never would be. Her loveliness was something he would never tire of, the sight that would refresh his weary heart the most. She was everything good and womanly and rare in this world, and the heart of his deepest dream come true. A dream he would not hurt for any reason.

Her happiness was more important than anything he could ever want for himself. Maybe bringing her here, where mist swirled around the frozen pond like lost dreams, hadn't been the best idea. "You might think that breaking my promise to you that night came pretty easy."

"It had once been my impression."

"I can honestly say it was the hardest decision I ever made."

"I understand that now." She held out her hand, confident that he would take it, that he wouldn't leave her sitting alone in her darkness.

He took her hand to guide her. She rose lightly to her feet, balancing easily on her blades, and he tried not to notice the thud of his heart hitting his soul. He loved her more. He'd been a fool to think he had ever stopped loving her. The love he had for her had not vanished. It had simply bided its time, quiet and dormant as the trees in winter, waiting for spring to come.

The dreams he'd given up on were there, alive after all. He swallowed hard against the pressure building in his chest. "I did what I thought was best at the time. I hate that I left you waiting and hoping. I know what I did came at a cost, but I did what I had to do, what I thought was right."

"I know that." Her emerald eyes, her face, her voice, her manner all shone with that truth. "My father forced you out of town, didn't he?"

The blood in his veins stilled. How did she know? Had she guessed? And if she had, if she knew the truth, there was the temptation to tell her the rest of it. But was it the right thing to do? He could not seem to move, although her skirts whispered as she stood, wobbling on the thin blades. He caught hold of her, keeping her steady when he was the unsteady one.

Forgiveness. It shone in her emerald eyes and radiated in her smile. The way she turned to him, the way she trusted him meant more to him than anything in the world.

"I know how you loved your folks, Noelle. I can't ruin their memory for you."

"You won't. Whatever they did, they did out of love. That's what you did, too."

She understood. An enormous weight lifted from his soul. His throat closed and he could not speak. The burdens of the past, of the wrongs her father had done to him and his family, and the misery he'd suffered melted away.

She looked like a little drop of heaven—or at least his notion of heaven—full of goodness and mercy and kindness. Mist clung to the gossamer curls caressing her sweet face. "My parents were wrong and misguided and they had no right to interfere, but they're gone now. And if there's something to learn from this, then it's that our time here is so very short. I don't want to waste another moment in heartache. Take me skating, Thad."

She held out her mittened hands, and it felt as if she were offering him a second chance. They'd navigated the short way to the head of the little pond where mist curled over the ice like wishes. "Straight ahead a few steps. That's right."

They toddled together the short distance to the pond's edge. The surface was rippled and uneven. He took the first step and braced himself to help her onto the slick surface. "Easy now."

"Oh, I'm out of practice." Her right blade slid forward, and she wobbled as if losing her sense of balance.

He caught her by the elbows and muscled her around. Her gloved hands fisted in the fabric of his coat as he steadied her. "Are you okay?"

"It's going to take me a moment to get used to this." Her hold on him was a trusting one. "Which way am I facing? So I can get a sense of direction."

"The house is in a straight line behind you. The orchard is to the left."

"That means we have the whole length of the pond ahead of us."

"Yes. Are you ready to take a spin?"

"More ready than you know." She moved to the inside, so she wouldn't catch her blade on any stray branch or stem. She looked fearless.

She was amazing. Thad couldn't take his gaze from her as they took that first sweeping step. She was his perfection. She pushed off into the unknown as if she were not afraid of falling.

"Look! Thad, I'm skating."

"Isn't that stating the obvious?" Her happiness was catching and he wouldn't stop the joy dawning within him even if he wanted to.

She laughed, coming to a shaky stop. "Yes, but I can't believe it. It's just like I remembered it."

"How's that?"

"That it must be close to what a sparrow feels flying across the frozen ground." Her touch on his arm was light. "How long do I have before I run out of pond?"

"Don't worry, I'll turn you before you hit land. Ready?"

"Ready."

They pushed off together, and he was drawn by her— by everything about her. Tiny silken wisps of hair had escaped her braid and curled around her face. Joy shone from her like light from a midnight star, and he felt touched by it. Joy shone into him and there was no stopping the power of it or the truth. They glided together in short sharp bursts, and he nudged her into a curving arc that had them circling to the far side of the pond.

"We're heading back toward the house," he told her, so she could keep her sense of direction.

"I can feel that." She lifted her face into the air. "The wind is coming from the north. It's starting to snow."

"Is it?" He hadn't noticed. He could only see her. But now that she'd pointed it out to him, sure enough, there were the tiniest flakes glinting as they fell. They began to cling to her chestnut hair and the wool of her coat like tiny chips of diamonds.

Maybe it was the love he felt for her seemingly turning the snow to jewels, the ordinary into the rare, but being with her again like this, at her side, taking care of her, *did* feel extraordinary.

"I want to twirl." She shakily nosed her blades into the ice, fighting to keep her balance.

He braced his legs, tensed the muscles in his arms and made sure she stayed upright. "Twirl? I don't see why you can't."

"Me, either." She flung her braid over her shoulder and inched away from him. "I don't want to accidentally smack you in the jaw."

"Don't worry. I know how to duck."

"You have good reflexes, too, so I don't know why I'm worrying." She couldn't help laughing, she felt so happy. Bliss bubbled out of her. "I should be able to spin and not fall down. That's my theory."

"It's worth testing out. I'll watch over you."

"I know." She held out her arms and glided in a small loop. Hoping she wasn't heading straight into trouble, she hurled herself into the dark and let the skates slice a perfect circle.

She knew when she hit the track of her first revolution that she'd done it, just as she could feel the air crisping against her face and whispering through her hair. Their movements on the ice were like music; the melody of her quick, light blades and, in counterpoint, the heavier and deeper gait as Thad kept up with her.

She kicked off and for one perfect moment, she was free, gliding into the unknown. She soared over ruts in the ice with the cold wind and tiny snowflakes stinging her face. Never had she thought she would be able to do this again. Joy lifted her up until she wasn't certain if her skates even touched the ice. It felt as if she were gliding on clouds.

"Turn!" Thad called out, and she drew up short.

Putting her arms over her head, she gave a little kick with her toe and twirled. Around and around she went, spinning faster and faster. What fun! The sound whirred in her ears and uplifted her heart.

When she stumbled, Thad was there, catching her like her own personal guardian, holding her in his strong arms.

Safe, just as he'd promised.

The world tilted sideways, and she clutched his shoulders, but it wasn't because she'd lost her sense of balance.

No, she was losing her heart.

"You're glowing," Thad said as they left the pond behind, the skates clinking together with his every step.

Noelle practically floated up the path. She was so happy, she had to be doing more than glowing; she felt as though she was radiating joy the way the stars did light. "I haven't had so much fun since—" Her heart gave a squeeze. "Since the last time I was out with you."

"Me, either. And to think I only fell the once."

"You made a loud crash, too." She couldn't help teasing him, just a little.

"I landed so hard on my backside that I'm surprised I didn't crack the ice."

Laughter hadn't come this easily in a long time. She heard the same lightness in Thad's voice and felt it in his touch as he guided her back to the house. "It's been such a perfect afternoon, that there's only one thing wrong with it."

"What's that?"

"It's coming to an end." She sighed, feeling the pathway level out. She knew without needing to ask that the front porch steps weren't far away. "I—I just really liked skating."

"I know just how you feel."

Did he feel this, too? Her knees turned to butter and she was thankful for his strong arm that guided her safely onto the boardwalk. Snow crunched beneath their shoes. Fragile snowflakes brushed against her face and caught in her lashes. She rubbed at them with her free hand, and her eyes burned.

This was not fair. Being with Thad made her feel whole—and not damaged—again. For a length of time out on that ice, she'd felt normal. Unfettered. Free. She knew that when Thad withdrew his arm from her hand and left her, she would be in darkness again.

No, this was not fair, she thought, but it was the way God meant her life to be. As she caught the edge of the rail, she prepared for the icy steps, pulling a little away from Thad, so as to brace herself for the inevitable.

He turned to her outside the front door, his boots shuffling a bit on the pieces of ice and snow. "I won't be around much after tomorrow. Finn's getting out. I've already spoken to Robert about it."

Oh. The air whooshed out of her lungs. She felt deflated. Her heart squeezed. "A-are you leaving us for good, then?"

"You knew I couldn't stay."

She knew. Sadness ribboned through her spirit, taking the joy from the afternoon with it. She straightened her spine and set her chin. Of course, she had to be practical. Thad had a whole life to live and dreams to find.

She counted her steps from the rail to the doorknob and when she reached out, her hand found the china knob perfectly. "I guess this is really goodbye."

"Not a chance, pretty lady. I'll be by when Robert is up for a few lessons on handling horses. And I'll be by to see you, if that's all right?"

To see her? As a friend, she wondered, or as more? She turned the knob and forced her feet to carry her across the threshold and she counted her steps before she turned to face Thad. She lifted the guards around her heart firmly into place. Hurting, yes she was hurting, but she forced a smile onto her face. "I'd like to see you again, Thad. You'll al-always be a friend."

Utter silence. He didn't speak. He didn't move. Not a shuffle or a rasp or an exhale.

"Noelle" came Robert's voice from his chair at the far end of the parlor. "Invite Thad in for a chat, won't you?"

"No," Thad answered smoothly, quietly, before she could agree. "I've got to get home. Work to do."

"Work?"

"Aiden's land. We're about done building another barn. Next there's the fences to mend, harnesses to repair, and as soon as the snow melts, we'll be turning sod."

"What about your plans for your own ranch?"

"It doesn't change my obligations to my brothers. Don't look troubled. I don't mind hard work. I figure the Lord set a good example. He worked six days out of seven."

"I thought you were no longer a praying kind of man."

"I guess I'm more of one than I thought."

He took a step back, hating that the time had come to leave. The thud that seemed to rattle his chest was his heart falling even more in love with her.

Friends, she'd said. And that she'd like to see him again. Friends was far more than he'd expected. How about that.

He hesitated on the top step. "I'll be coming back around to see you."

"All right. I won't even pretend not to be home when you do."

She smiled and it was a sight that chased the chill from the air and the snow from the sky.

As he tucked down the brim of his hat and headed out into the increasing snowfall, it seemed as if he walked in sunshine.

Chapter Thirteen

Noelle hadn't realized how much she'd been listening for any sign of Thad until he was gone. Oh, he'd found someone to replace him—although no word of it had been mentioned. A worker had shown up to carry in the morning's wood and tend to the stable work.

After the girls had left for school, Matilda had come in to quietly mention that Thad had sent the youngest brother of the Sims family. But there was no mention of the older boy—Emmett Sims—as Matilda poured a second cup of tea and carried it away to the library with a slight clatter. The mention of the Sims family had upset her.

That's all my fault. Sadness eked into her, dimming the warm touch of the morning's sun through the dining room window. Her well-meaning words in town before Robert's accident haunted her now. She'd meant to protect innocent Matilda, that was all. But as she was listening to the crackle of the fire echoing in the empty room around her, she remembered how it had felt to twirl on the ice and know that Thad was at her side. It had been pure joy.

What had happened to her? On the ice she'd caught a glimpse of the real Noelle—the one who'd once known how to live and love. The one who used her heart, her whole heart.

Noelle reached for the teapot with trembling fingers and found the crest of lid and round of the handle. *You might think that breaking my promise to you that night came pretty easy,* Thad had said. *I can honestly say it was the hardest decision I ever made.* His words troubled her like little teeth taking a bite of her soul.

She'd blamed him, judged him and—for a time—despised him. She'd let those things into her heart, into her soul, and although she'd told herself she'd found forgiveness and had handed her pain up to God, it was not the whole truth. The stain of it, like tarnish on silver, remained, and shame filled her.

She slipped her forefinger against the rim of her teacup and poured with her other hand until she felt the lap of the beverage against the tip of her finger. She set down the pot with care. She'd held all that pain in her heart—without meaning to and in spite of her best intentions—and for what? Thad had done what he'd thought best in leaving her. She knew her parents well enough to see clearly what they had done. Her father, bless his soul, would have used any means to protect her, for that's how he would have viewed it.

She'd been the one to change her heart and her life. She'd been the one to stop believing. To stop living. To stop dreaming. Long before the accident took her sight. She'd decided life and love were about sensible decisions and emotions—nothing else.

She scooped a lump of sugar from the bowl and slipped it into her cup with a plop. The house seemed silent around her. It was best to be steeled to the truth in life. It was best to be practical. She almost said so to Matilda but held back the words.

Once, like her cousin, she'd been young and filling her hope chest with embroidered pillow slips and a girl's dreams. Maybe that was a part of the way life went. Maybe she would be a different woman if she'd been able to hold on to some of those dreams, or at least the belief in them.

But she was a woman without dreams.

She took a sip of tea and turned her mind to her music lessons for the rest of the morning. While there was no sound of Thad—no lazy snap of a training whip, no rhythmic trot of a horse he was working, and no familiar gait in the yard outside—her mind turned to him. Always to him.

If her heart squeezed with caring, then it was an emotion she could not afford to acknowledge. Wherever he was this morning, she hoped the Lord would bless him and hold him safe.

After attending Sunday service, Noelle felt more at peace. Of course, the delicious roasted goose and trimmings for Sunday dinner might have helped, too. Full and content, she sipped at her piping hot cup of tea while Sadie padded around the table, clearing away the dessert plates. She might not have seen Thad for the better part of a week, but he was never far from her thoughts.

The family's cheerful din rose up around her. There was some discussion as to the extent of Angelina's bad behavior earlier in Sunday school. Voices rose and fell in discussion, and Noelle had to wonder. If her parents had not intervened, she would be married to Thad. Would she have children? Would she and Thad have been happy? Would she still have her sight and her parents? Would she still be the full-hearted girl she'd once been?

"Noelle, are you feeling well, dear?" Henrietta's concern broke into her thoughts. "You look troubled."

Troubled? How could she begin to explain? "I'm fine, truly."

"You were overheated at the dress shop yesterday. It's a wonder you haven't caught your death. A heater in every room is lunacy. What are people thinking nowadays? You ought to lie down for a bit."

"Goodness, no." She couldn't resist teasing her aunt just a little. "I actually feel quite healthy. Perhaps that is due to that overly warm dress shop."

Angelina burst out laughing. "Yes, Mama. We must get a heater in every room. Maybe even a furnace."

"It would be very practical," Minnie chimed in. "We wouldn't have to wear our woolen underwear all the time. It's scratchy."

"Girls." Henrietta did her best to sound shocked at the mention of undergarments, but there was the warmth of amusement in her voice. "Settle down and stop this teasing. We're at the table."

"Where we could use a heater," Minnie pointed out. "I'm always stuck in the drafty corner."

The maid padded from the direction of the kitchen. "Looks as if we have company on the way."

"Company? On Sunday afternoon?" Henrietta's chair scraped against the floor, as if she were standing up to take a peek out the window. "Goodness, it's a horse and sleigh. I don't know that horse. Whoever could it be?"

There were rustles of movement as if everyone were taking a look. Robert's low chuckle was sheer amusement. "It looks like a caller coming for one of the girls."

"A suitor!" Angelina sounded intrigued. "But Mama won't let us have a beau until we're eighteen."

"Perhaps it's for Matilda," Minnie offered.

"Oh, there would be no one coming for me." Matilda's tone was light.

Noelle wasn't fooled. She didn't know if she was the only one who could hear the quiet despair—or, maybe it was just empathy. Matilda might be without prospects, but she wasn't the only one. She regretted her words to Tilly.

Dear, Lord, she prayed with all her heart. *Please let it be someone for Matilda.*

"I know who that is!" Minnie's voice hit a few high notes of delight. "It's Mr. McKaslin."

Thad? Her teacup hit its saucer with a clatter.

All around her chairs were scraping back, shoes beat away from the table, and Robert chuckled warmly. "I wondered how long it would take that fellow to get up his gumption."

"The gumption for what?" Noelle asked him.

"You'd best get your coat. Looks like he's coming up to the door."

Sure enough, the door was rasping open and Henrietta's voice rose above Angelina's and Minnie's footsteps. "Mr. McKaslin! What a pleasure to see you on this fine afternoon. What can I do for you?"

"Is Noelle at home?"

So he'd come for her, just as he'd promised. Noelle tried to ignore the buzzing expectation in the air and everyone's advice. From Matilda's quietly spoken,

"Oh, just what I'd been praying for!" to Robert's advice, "Go on, now, go have a nice time," to Angelina's shocking comment, "I'm predicting a May wedding. June at the latest."

She truly hoped Thad had not heard *that*. She was on her feet without realizing it. Matilda had her elbow and guided her to the front door. Henrietta thrust the coat into her hands. And Thad was there, his unmistakable presence had her turning toward him, and she felt his smile with all of her heart.

He thought this was funny, did he? She stepped through the open doorway and let him help her into her coat, aware of her family members' careful and excited scrutiny.

"Goodbye, now!" Henrietta practically sang. "You be back in a couple of hours, Mr. McKaslin."

"Yes, ma'am."

Thad sounded as if he were smothering laughter, and the moment her coat was fastened and he took her hand in his, she could feel the connection between her heart and his. That rare, emotional bond they'd always had was here again, anew, and she felt the strong bright happiness that matched her own.

He'd come for her as a friend, just as he'd said. She let him guide her down the steps and along the path.

She was going to enjoy these moments she had with him because she had learned the hard way in life that nothing lasted. Everything changed. Before she knew it, Thad would be busy with his ranch and his dreams, and she would never see him again.

She waited until the door shut firmly behind them before she apologized. "I don't know what has overcome my aunt, but she has jumped to conclusions."

"So I heard. Everything."

"Angelina's comment, too?"

"Yep."

He was probably not put into a panic at the mention of a wedding—in the way of men in general—probably because it was a bold impossibility. As surely as the ground was at her feet, there was no way Thad was harboring any wedding thoughts for her.

She knew better than to think it. When he let go of her hand, she stood in darkness, listening hard to hear what he was doing. There was the softest rustling sound—of a lap blanket, perhaps?—and then the prettiest jingle of bells sang out in a short burst. The horse must have shaken his head with impatience.

"Whoa there, boy. Stand still for the pretty lady." Thad's patient voice must have reassured the horse for there was no more shaking of the bells.

Just the ring of appreciation in her heart. "You're taking me for a sleigh ride?"

"Yep, and I'm grateful you've agreed to come along with me. I need the help." His hand found hers again.

"Help? What do you mean?"

"I bought this saddle horse for Finn, and I want to break him to the harness. So I need to take him out for a drive, and I was afraid I'd get lost."

"You need me to help you find your way around the countryside?"

"Don't think I could do it without you."

"Then it's good you came by, although the reason for asking me is going to disappoint Henrietta terribly."

"Funny. I didn't think she liked me much." He took her by the elbow, helping her, always helping her. Tenderness filled him right up. "I've got the riding blankets out of the way, so go ahead and climb on in."

"Do you know what my aunt values in a man more than affluence and social position?"

"Ah, I've got the good sense not to buy a horse that will kick me."

"No." She chuckled; she couldn't hold it back as she settled onto the cushioned seat. "Character."

"Character, huh?" He leaned to tuck the soft fur robes around her. "Then I'm all out of luck."

Oh, she loved his humility. She loved how caring he was with her, and how his sense of humor could make a cold February afternoon seem like a treat. When he had settled in next to her beneath the warm robes and had gathered the reins, she decided not to tell him that ever since her accident she didn't like driving fast.

She took a deep breath and let the icy air tingle in her lungs. The tingling seemed to drive out the last of her uncertainty. She would not allow herself to be anxious, not with Thad driving. He could handle any horse and any situation. She trusted him.

"Why isn't Finn training his own horse?" she asked, because she was curious. "Does that mean that he's not doing well?"

"Oh, he's doing just fine. Finn doesn't have the patience for serious horse work. He's better at other things. We have him putting on the sides of the new barn Aiden and I put up before the last set of storms came in."

"In this weather?"

"We figure it's penance for all that he's putting us through. Work him hard, and maybe he'll get on the straight and narrow."

"What was he in prison for?"

"Stealing a horse. He was lucky he wasn't hung. There's still a lot of vigilante justice in these parts." Thad's chest closed up. It was hard to talk about, especially to her. The differences between them suddenly felt as wide as the sky and about as impossible to fly across.

"You hurt for him."

Her sympathy touched him. It did more than that, her sweet face was marked with understanding, and it reassured him. "There's no way to measure how hard we all took this. He's smart and talented and he has a good heart."

"Sort of like his older brother?"

Now, that was just what he needed to hear. Snow brushed his cheek like grace, changing his heart, changing his life. Thad took a shaky breath. "Finn's got our pa's weakness for liquor."

"And it's hard for him to resist?" When he didn't answer, she nodded once, as if she understood why without words. "You want him to be stronger than that."

"Yes. That's right."

"I've felt that way about a family member." Her forehead pinched. "My parents. I am sorry for what they did to you. My father was a man who could be very persuasive. What did he say to you?"

"That you wouldn't be happy living a simple life with me."

"And you believed him?"

Her voice, her face, her eyes vibrated with pain. A pain he felt like a dagger sink into his heart. What else could he do but to tell the truth. "I didn't want to. I wouldn't let myself."

"You left me because my father threatened to demand payment on your mortgage, didn't he?"

Thad bit his lip. Hadn't the truth hurt her enough?

"You don't have to answer. I know it's true." She tucked the robe around her more tightly, as if unable to say more. She was hurting, clearly she was hurting.

"It's tough when the people you love aren't the way you want them to be." The cold scorched his face like fiery ice, and yet it was warmer than the pain that settled in him. He was no longer too numb to feel it. Because of her.

"And so you know, my father was wrong," she said. "All I wanted then, all I needed then, was you."

Her words were like coming home. Like Christmas morning and happy new year and every birthday rolled into one. The beautiful world was all around them, so he began to describe it to her. "The mountains, their faces are hidden in the clouds. The sky is a darker shade of white guarding over the white prairie. The snow is quiet today. Nothing sparkling or glistening. Just a still silent white."

A small smile curved her rosebud lips.

They rode on in silence, gliding over the rise and draw of the rugged plains. They listened to snow whisper and tap, and shared a quiet that felt companionable. Peaceful.

Meant to be.

The sleigh was slowing, and before she could ask why, she heard the waterfall. Angel Falls. She loved the cascading music of the charging water. Even before she lost her sight, it was one of her most favorite sounds. Maybe because she'd built so many dreams around it. It was painfully ironic that she had inherited this property from her father, one of the last investments he had acquired before his death.

"That sounded sad." Thad drew the horse to a stop.

She tilted her head, listening carefully but there was only the snort of the horse, the water falling and the whirl of snow against the dash of the sleigh. "What sounds sad?"

"You. You sighed."

"Did I?" She wasn't aware of it. Then again, it was hard to feel anything. The tangled ball of emotion had returned and expanded like regret in her soul. "Is the water gray like the clouds? Or green from the mountain snowmelt?"

"Green as moss."

She closed her eyes, searching for a visual memory of the falls in winter, but the one that came to her was vivid with color and cheerful wildflowers polka-dotting rich green fields.

"The snowfall is as gray as the clouds," Thad told her. "The snow is white, but it's pure white and gray shadows and a thousand shades between."

She couldn't see it. She couldn't let herself. She struggled to dim the memory in her mind's eye of rainbows the sun made on crystal blue water. And there, on the rise where the meadow met the hills, she used to envision a log house with wide windows glinting in the sunshine and a porch to sit and watch the falls in the evening's light.

A dream. That's what she remembered, and the loss of it thrummed along the broken strings of her heart. The regret swelling in her soul seemed to block out even those colors and that light.

The wind whirring in her ears stilled, as the horse drew the sleigh to a stop.

Thad leaned closer. "We have a lot of memories

here. Remember how we would come here the summer I proposed?"

"I r-remember." Those memories stuck in her throat like sorrow. "You proposed to me on the rise of land, where we would always picnic."

"I would come here on my lunch and you would slip away from your mother's garden parties."

"Yes, I would bring a basket of some of the goodies from the kitchen."

"Cake and cookies. Lemonade and sandwiches. I don't know why I especially remember the ham sandwiches."

"Our cook made excellent ham sandwiches."

Suddenly they were laughing together, and the sorrow and the regret lifted away. "It was enough just to be with you," she remembered. "To talk and laugh and walk side by side."

"I remember holding your hand." He took her hand in his, fitting their fingers together with such deliberate care.

Still a perfect fit. As if they were made to be together. Thank heavens. He kept a tight hold on her hand and did not let go.

"You wouldn't happen to be attending Lanna and Joe's wedding?" he asked.

"Yes, as it's the first big social event of the year. We've been preparing for it since the New Year. All the girls need new dresses and bonnets, gloves and shoes. We've kept Miss Sims's dress shop in profits for the last month."

"I thought that might be the case. You're probably going with the Worthingtons?"

"Yes, as I have a difficult time driving to town these

days on my own." She liked that he chuckled, just a little, at her joke. "You'll be there?"

"Count on it. You wouldn't mind saving me a spot on your dance card?"

"I would, but Henrietta does not approve of dancing."

"Then will you save me a minute or two to chat with you?"

"Only a minute. My social card is very full." She smiled, quipping again. She simply felt so…happy. It was Thad. He made her happy. This—being with him, talking with him and laughing with him—was a perfect moment in time.

"I'd rather have a minute with you," he said, "than to have a million minutes without you. I saw your face that night at supper when I told your family about Sunny."

"It was an incredible story."

"I never forgot your dreams, Noelle. They were mine, too." His tone dipped and he paused. In that instant of silence, she could not know how his face looked and what emotion lurked there.

She longed to see him. To know all the little things about his dear face that had changed—and those that had stayed the same.

He broke the stillness between them. "I always wanted to hunt down whoever owned this property and buy it for you. Of course, I was a kid back then. I had no notion of how expensive this land really is."

The wind burned her eyes. Surely it was the wind and not sadness. "I wish I had known that."

"You wanted to build a life here, too, remember?"

Did she. The colors filled her mind as love for him did her heart. She couldn't take the pain of it. She curled her fingers around the hem of the robe and felt the icy caress of wind against her face. She could never be a rancher's wife now.

The confusion of her emotions ached within her. "That is a lost dream for me, Thad. A child's dream."

"That's not necessarily so."

She didn't know how to tell him that he was wrong. The swell of wind and snow moved between them like melody and harmony. How did she speak of the remnants of her hopes and the ashes of her future to the one man who knew the value of what she'd lost? Of what she would never have again?

"Some of my hopes have been lost, sure," Thad said with an easy note. "But I've gained some along the way, too. I suppose it's like anything else in life. It doesn't work out the way you want, but sometimes in the end you wind up somewhere better than you expected."

"That sounds awfully optimistic for you."

His chuckle sounded good-natured. "I admit it. You've changed me."

"Oh, I don't think—"

He squeezed her hand to interrupt her. "You've given me dreams again and I thank you for it."

Noelle turned away, letting the concert of snowfall and waterfall fill her senses and create a silence between them. A silence she desperately needed.

"I suppose I'd best turn the horse back. I want to get you home well before suppertime. I don't want to earn Henrietta's wrath. I reckon I'm already walking a fine line as it is."

She managed a weak smile. "I'll have you know that my aunt holds you personally responsible for Angelina deciding to become a mustang wrangler."

"I didn't know proper young ladies from fine

families were allowed to be wranglers." He sounded amused.

"They aren't. But when you're sixteen, you have to dream. The world is so full of possibility."

"It still is." There was an unmistakable smile in his voice.

The reins hit the dash, the horse carried them forward, and she listened to the song of the sleigh's runners on the snow. The murmur of the waterfall faded to silence behind them. Thad's hand remained tightly on hers. He did not let go.

Chapter Fourteen

The land office was quiet midweek. Noelle shifted uncomfortably in the hard, ladder-back chair and signed her name on the page where the agent had pointed out for her. The scratch of the pen seemed loud.

There. Done. She handed the ink pen and the legal document to Mr. Dorian on the other side of the desk.

"Are you sure about this, Miss Kramer?"

She hadn't been so certain about anything. This simply felt right. "Yes. You'll contact Mr. McKaslin today?"

"I'll send a message out to him immediately."

"And you won't let him know this land belongs to me?"

"I'll respect our agreement, Miss Kramer, don't you worry. Your father was a good man. He helped me keep my home when times got tough for me, and I owe him. I'll do my best for you."

"Thank you, Mr. Dorian."

Love was complicated, just as people were. She would never understand why her father had pressured

Thad so, but maybe she now knew more about what forgiveness truly was. She knew that her father had done the best he could for reasons he thought were very sound. How could she fault his love and her mother's, when they were lost to her now?

Signing this paperwork to sell her father's land, was something she did with love, too. She was finally understanding what it meant to be only human, frail at best, and like all humans complete with shortcomings. Wasn't her blindness, after all, only a shortcoming? It was not a punishment from God, and not something which had damaged her.

If blindness was her price for surviving the accident that should have killed her, then she was grateful to God for sparing her. She was grateful to Him for bringing Thad back into her life.

She rose to her feet and stood a little straighter. "Mr. Dorian, thank you for your time. You'll be in contact?"

"As soon as I have Thad McKaslin's offer for you." The chair across the desk scraped, as, presumably, the land agent stood. He took her hand in a gentle, business-like shake. "Would you like me to see you to the door?"

"No, thank you. I counted my steps when I came in." She withdrew her hand, oriented herself and counted her way to the door. With every step she took, the joy inside her soared a little more, but the sadness did, too, and both together moved through her spirit like melody and harmony.

The moment her shoe touched the slick boardwalk, she took a deep breath of winter air and listened to the chime of ice melting from the rooftops. She tried to imagine Thad's happiness when he received the note from the land office. Finally a good piece of ranch property for sale, he might think, and at the price he could afford. Yes, he would definitely be very happy.

Joy burned within her, balanced by sharpening sorrow. She wanted him to have his dreams and the life he'd always wanted, even though she could not have hers.

"Noelle?" Matilda's gentle alto broke through her thoughts. "We had best start making our way over to the church."

"Yes. Do you have our gifts?"

"They're in the sleigh. Mama will see to it. She's fetching the girls from school first. Here, take my arm. The boardwalks are so slick with all the snow melting off the roofs."

Dear Matilda. She had such a good heart. Sweetness ached through her remembering herself as an innocent, starry-eyed girl who believed in a fairy-tale kind of love.

Dainty footsteps came their way. "Noelle? Matilda? Why aren't you at the church?"

She recognized the dressmaker's soft country cadence. "We are on our way. Would you like to walk with us?"

"What a kind invitation." Miss Cora Sims sounded pleased. "As you know, I'm attending the wedding alone, and I have no one to sit with, as both of my nephews refuse to be anywhere near a wedding. You know how young men can be."

Matilda's grip tightened again. Noelle could not resist asking, "Is Emmett well?"

"Keeping busy enough with his teaming. Oh, there he is. Emmett, yoo-hoo!"

Matilda's grip turned into a stranglehold and she leaned close to whisper. "Mr. Sims is driving his team and wagon over."

There was no excitement. No interest. Not a single note of hope. Just a simple, plainspoken statement. That was all. It was as if the air had drained from the wind.

Noelle winced. Matilda, bless her dearly, had taken her poor advice to heart.

There was no time to speak of it, for suddenly there were the muffled plop of horse hooves in the top layers of the melting snow, the jangle of harness and the low-noted groan of a wagon's axle.

"I've been waiting for you, Aunt Cora." Emmett Sims had a pleasant, quiet voice, and his words held affection for his aunt, not censure.

"I was held up by a last-minute customer. I apologize. Noelle, would you and Matilda like to ride over with me?"

The good Lord had a way of making things right. Noelle did not hesitate, even when Matilda took a step back and started to say, "No thank you—" She spoke right over her cousin. "Yes, Cora, your offer is completely providential. We accept."

"I'm so glad," the seamstress said warmly.

It was a mystery how she had managed to stay a spinster all these years. Noelle felt that was something they had in common, and vowed to ask Cora over for tea and get to know her better.

Boots hit the boardwalk nearby—it must be Emmett climbing down from the wagon. "Let me help you ladies up. You first, miss?"

Was that her imagination, or had his voice dipped a notch, as if he were shy or, perhaps, a little taken with Tilly?

"Oh, yes, thank you." Primly, coolly, Matilda answered.

Noelle imagined the moment when Emmett reached out with his gloved hand—he was a teamster, he was probably wearing leather driving gloves—and the moment when Matilda smiled up at him. Was this the first time he had noticed her? Did he think her pretty? There was a tap of shoes on the wagon boards, and the springs rasped slightly as Matilda settled on the seat.

Before she knew it, Emmett had kindly but capably helped her up onto the narrow seat, and Cora followed. There was a quiet steadiness to the young man. Later, when they were alone, she would ask Matilda what he looked like, what color his eyes and his hair were.

The reins slapped the dash and the horses clattered to a quick start. Noelle held on tight to the edge of the seat and prayed. If Emmett Sims held a secret caring for Tilly, wouldn't that be perfect? She could not have a happy ending, but she wanted one for her cousin. In fact, she was going to do her best to make sure it happened. She would trust the Lord to guide her.

It was a fast ride to the church with the icy winds blowing against her face and tearing her eyes. The watery touch of the sun did nothing to warm her as she accepted Emmett's hand down to the slick pathway that led to the church door. Merry bells pealed in the steeple above, drowning out the everyday sounds of the horse and foot traffic. She stood disorientated until Cora touched her hand, guiding her out of the crush of those hurrying to the church at the last minute.

"Tell me, Noelle, is your cousin sweet on my nephew?"

"Why are you asking?"

"It's simply wishful thinking. I have never seen him take such care with a young lady." Cora sounded pleased.

Noelle took that as a good sign. Suddenly Matilda was beside her, a little breathless and unusually quiet. She didn't utter a single word, much less make one sound, as Emmett Sims's boots stomped on the wagon steps—presumably to knock off the slush sticking to them—and called out from above. "Good day, ladies. Miss."

How perfect that they both seemed to be sweet on one another.

Noelle knew he was safely out of sight when Matilda caught her by the hand again and they took careful steps in the slick slush.

"Thad McKaslin is standing in the back of the church," Matilda whispered the moment they'd inched through the vestibule. "He appears to be intently looking for someone."

Joy shivered through her spirit, unbidden and powerful. Her heart squeezed with longing and love for him, and she did her best to quiet those feelings, to stow away those emotions. "Perhaps one of his brothers?"

"No, dear cousin, I think he's waiting for *you.*"

The happiness gathering inside her took over with a quiet wonder. She didn't need Matilda to tell her the moment when Thad spotted her in the crowd. Although the organ music and the rumblings of the guests filling the long rows of pews hid the sound of his gait, she could feel him like music in her soul.

"I would like to sit with you," he said simply, kindly, the friend that he was.

The friend which he had to be. They both knew it. She managed what she hoped would pass for a smile. "You would be most welcome, Thad."

Where Matilda and Cora had gone off to, Noelle did

not know. She only knew Thad's innocent touch as he led her down the aisle and protected her from the crush of the crowd. He stood so close to her, she could smell the soap on his shirt and the winter wind on his coat. Why she could distinguish the quiet, steady draw and exhale of his breathing in the swell of noise in the sanctuary, she could not explain. Her every sense seemed tuned only to him, to this man who meant much more than a friend to her. And always would.

"I saw you arrive in Emmett Sims's wagon."

What a strange tone in his voice. Noelle took another shuffling step and her hoops bumped against him. "He was taking his aunt to the church and they were kind enough to bring us along."

"Kind enough? He seemed rather happy to be doing so, if you want my humble opinion. I didn't like it."

There it was again, that sharp tone that was unlike Thad. Whatever for? Then realization struck her like the bench post against her toe. Thad was jealous? Why? "It's my suspicion that he's sweet on Matilda. Don't tell me that you are—"

"No-oo. No." Thad's answer came so quick, lightning would be slower. "Oh, your cousin. Sure. They probably went to school together, just like we did."

Noelle inched along the bench, careful not to step on anyone's shoes. "Did you truly think Mr. Sims would possibly be interested in me?"

"Well, I, uh—" He didn't answer.

What was wrong with him, anyhow? Before she could joke with him a little more, a gloved hand caught her by the wrist.

"Noelle!" Henrietta's voice was full of smiles. "I've

been saving a place for you. I did not know Mr. McKaslin would be joining us. Robert, scootch down a bit."

"We're awful crowded as it is."

"Scootch!" Henrietta was adamant. "We have plenty of room, Mr. McKaslin. Don't you even dream of going anywhere else. It's a privilege to have you sit with us. Noelle, dear, sit right here."

Noelle let her overly helpful aunt guide her onto the pew, although she hardly needed the help. She was just too amused to think of an argument. What was the matter with everyone today? First Thad, and now Henrietta. It had to be the wedding. It jumbled sensible people's reasoning abilities. Thad worrying that a younger man would be interested in *her,* a blind woman. And now Henrietta.

She was thankful she was not so ill-affected. The music changed; the sanctuary's buzzing and whispering and rustling silenced, and she imagined the minister and the groom had taken their places.

The "ahs" that rose told her that the bride must have swept into sight. Lanna must look lovely, she thought, and happy. Noelle laid her hand on Thad's arm and whispered in his ear. "Tell me how beautiful she looks."

"She can't hold a candle to you."

With those words, he'd won a little bit more of her heart. Noelle said nothing more. It was wisest not to.

"Why is a lovely lady like you sitting alone in the corner?"

Thad and his sense of humor—*he* had been the one to leave her. Noelle drew herself up straighter on the chair, brushed a stray curl out of her eyes and shook her head once, very slowly. She hoped she was giving him her best schoolmarm look. "The man I was with left me here all alone so he could get some punch."

"His loss is my gain." The chair creaked softly beside her as he settled into it. "Sorry I took such a long spell. Your uncle caught me in line for punch and started jawing my ear off. Sounds like he's happy with the younger Sims boy."

"I believe so. And so far, the young man has not made any show of interest in one of my cousins."

"I bet your aunt is ecstatic that her daughters are safe. I'm toeing a narrow line as it is." He caught her hand.

The small glass cup was icy against her palm and the sweet scent of lemons and limes tickled her nose. "Can't you tell that she likes you?"

"She has been unusually glad to see me with you. You think she'd be concerned about your reputation."

"My reputation?"

"Hanging out with a cowboy who doesn't have a wealthy family or social connections."

While his tone was light, there was something in his voice. Something serious. Her pulse skipped a beat. Could he be serious about her? She took a sip of the tart punch. No, she was reading too much into things. Perhaps it was her heart, wishing that he at least loved her, too, a little.

Because she loved him. Very much. She could no longer deny it. She cherished this man. She honored him. She wanted nothing more than to love him for the rest of her days.

"I think my reputation would be greatly improved being seen with you tonight." She kept her words as light, but they were honest, too. "Do you see your family anywhere?"

"I haven't seen hide nor hair of them. I know Aiden was planning on bringing Ma, but I didn't see them in the church. Of course, it was crowded. Half the town must have been there."

"And here, by the sound of it. That must mean your mother's health is still improving?"

"She's holding her own. She ought to do better once the warm weather decides to show up. That could be June, knowing this part of the country."

"And your younger brother?"

"We made him stay home tonight. We didn't want him getting into any trouble here."

"By trouble you mean…?"

"Getting his hands on some alcohol. Maybe thinking about joyriding with someone's horse tethered up outside. We were hoping jail would have straightened him up. Shown him that life is a serious matter."

"It didn't?"

"No. He's bitter. He's full of hatred. It's not a good situation."

"And he's your little brother." Sympathy marked her face, making her all the more comely. The dress she wore was the color of lilac blossoms and made her look like a princess. "You must want so much for him to live well and be happy."

"That's what I want." Thad swallowed against the hard emotion. The helplessness of it nibbled at him. "I can't make a grown man's decisions for him. Aiden and I are doing our best, but we're both here tonight."

"And he's home alone?"

"If we're lucky, he is." His throat stung. "The thing is, I could have gone down that path myself."

"You?" She looked at him as if she saw him perfectly, the man he was, down to the soul. "No, not you."

His Noelle, so beautiful and unguarded, she made his spirit soar. She looked at him as if he were ten feet tall. Admitting the truth, well, it was tough, but she may as well know everything. "After I had to make the decision to ride away from Angel Falls, I knew what I'd done to you. It about broke me. You were my dream, Noelle, and all I saw was a future without you. A life without you. You were about all that I'd ever thought of living for."

Her eyes brightened with tears and she turned away so he could not see the emotion on her face.

He would always be able to see into her heart. "I was hurting bad. Very bad. After a long hard day in the saddle when the cattle were down for the night we'd all gather around the campfire. Whiskey would get passed around and it h-helped. I didn't feel anything for a long time, and that was all right by me."

"Oh, Thad." She kept her face turned away. She set her cup aside and then folded her empty hands.

"Once I realized what I was doing, I haven't had a swallow since. I'm not the sort of man who will follow my father's path in life. But I can see how easy it might be for someone else to. I know Finn doesn't think he has much to live for. He's just existing. Spending his days one at a time."

"I've been guilty of that, too."

"You?" That surprised him. The woman who'd made the most of her life in spite of her blindness. The woman who could have any man in the room proposing to her, judging by the looks she was getting from several of them. The woman who still chose to be with him.

When she straightened, her eyes were bright with unshed tears. "I'm so sorry for your brother. It's easy to fall into the habit of walking through life. It's safer. Because you don't have to risk as much. You don't have to really feel."

Yep, he was standing on that spot himself. He'd been afraid to move a step forward. He couldn't see how this would work for them. He didn't know if Noelle still had the same dreams. He didn't know if she would want him for a husband.

Still, he had to try to find out. He was already so far in love with her that he couldn't see straight. His every breath was because of her. He took her folded hands in his. "Come. Walk with me."

"You don't want to listen to Chopin?" she teased, although she stood as quickly as he did.

"To who?"

"Haven't you noticed the piano music coming from the ballroom?"

"It's tough for me to notice anything when you're nearby. Any man of good sense would be as muddled in the presence of such a beautiful woman." Thad's gait fell in rhythm with hers. "Did I say something wrong?"

"No, not at all, if your intent was to perjure yourself."

"I was only telling the truth, Noelle. You'll always be the loveliest woman in any room to me."

"Oh, Thad." Her poor heart couldn't endure any more of this. The moment they stepped onto the front porch, the icy air swept over her, cutting through her, and she prayed for the cold to numb her clear to her soul. It didn't. She was left with her impossible love for him.

"You must stop saying such kind things to me. You'll spoil me."

"That's my hope, darlin'." Still sounding light-hearted, he accompanied her to the rail, where the great silence of the night stretched out before them. The streets were quiet, the town settling down for supper-time, and the noise of the party was behind them.

She tried to imagine the sky. Was it velvety dark with white sparkles of stars? Or one depthless stretch of black? Wondering about the sky was far easier than thinking of the man at her side. She shivered; she'd forgotten her cloak.

"Here. I can't have you freezing to death." There was a rustle of fabric and then the weight of his coat on her shoulders. "Your aunt wouldn't like it if I let you catch a chill. She might not let me in the house the next time I came calling."

Calling. Why had he chosen that word? Her entire soul squeezed with longing for what could not be. Surely he was making a small quip, that was all. There was no way Thad McKaslin was coming to court her. It didn't matter how deeply she wished for it to be so.

She tucked away her sadness and lifted her chin a notch. "After what you've done for our family, Henrietta would welcome you with open arms no matter what."

"Then I guess I don't have a single worry. I'm planning on taking you for another sleigh ride this Sunday afternoon."

"Oh, and you're simply assuming that I will agree to go with you?" she teased, hoping it would chase away her doubts.

His warm, wonderful rumble of laughter did that for

her. He moved one step closer. Then another. "I'm hoping that I'm the one man you can't say no to."

"Maybe. Maybe not. You will simply have to wait and see."

"I don't have to wait. I think I already have my answer." His hands cupped her chin, such a tender gesture.

Surely, it was one of friendship. It had to be one of friendship, right? She couldn't help pressing her cheek against his callused palm. "You are a tad sure of yourself. Perhaps I intend to say no."

"What? And miss your chance to drive a real mustang?"

"You'll be bringing Sunny?"

"Yep, and there's no reason why I can't let you take the reins for a spell."

"No reason?" Oh, it felt like an answered prayer to laugh with him again. "Other than the reason that I can't see where I'm going, you mean?"

"Well, I'm sure I'll keep an eye on your driving."

"Yes, that would be prudent, although I'm sure Sunny is smart enough not to let me drive him into a tree or a fence post."

"If this warmer weather lasts, we might have to go horseback riding instead of driving."

It was not the past she saw, but a future. Riding beside him, laughing in the summer sunshine, so happy and in love. It was a future she could not have. "Now you're using my lost dreams against me."

"Not against you. Never that." His voice dipped tenderly, gently.

With the sift of snow blowing in from beneath the eaves and the wish filling her soul, she thought for one breathless, sweet moment that he was going to kiss her. Really, truly, lovingly kiss her. Her soul sighed with longing. Her spirit ached with the wish.

Then a hush of a footstep told her they weren't alone. "Thad?" A woman's gentle voice spoke. "There you are. They're serving dinner. Oh, is that Noelle?"

Thad's mother. Embarrassment burned her face to the roots of her hair, and Thad's touch fell away from her face, but he did not step away. No, he remained solidly at her side. His hand crept around hers.

Noelle felt her face heat. "H-hello, Mrs. McKaslin."

"Noelle, dear, call me Ida. Aiden is holding a small table for us. Will you join us?"

"I would love to." What could it hurt? Come tomorrow, he would receive the land agent's news, and, God willing, he would be starting to work on his dreams.

Dreams she could not share with him. No, that would be the privilege of some other lucky woman, one who could see, one who could do what she, Noelle, could not.

For tonight, she would treasure simply being with him.

Hand in hand, and heart to heart, she let Thad lead her out of the cold night and into the hotel's warmth.

Chapter Fifteen

It was late evening by the time dessert was served and finished in the hotel's finest room, and later still, Thad thought with a yawn, as he made his way to the coatroom. Plenty of Angel Falls's finest gentlemen were gathered outside the back door, in the shelter of the porch. He thanked the young gal at the counter and slung the small pile of coats over the crook of his arm.

"Thad McKaslin!" Abe Dorian emerged through the smoky doorway. "I hadn't thought you would be here tonight. Don't know as to why."

"I went to school with Joe and Lanna."

"Of course you did. Got too much on my mind, I guess." Affable, Dorian gave a shrug. "If you were at the wedding, then you weren't home this afternoon to get my note."

"Your note?" Could it be? Thad didn't dare get his hopes up. "A good piece of ranch land didn't come up for sale, did it?"

"Good? My son, it is prime property. The owner is asking a reasonable price, too. She's inherited it some time ago and decided to sell only this morning." Dorian's dark eyes twinkled. "I thought of you right away."

And of a sure sale, if what he said of the land was true, Thad thought. "Which piece is it? Is it close to town?"

"It's the northeast quarter section right at the falls."

His pulse skipped five beats. He almost dropped the coats. Had he heard that right? "Did you say at the falls, not below it?"

"That's what I said, son. Prime land and it's at the price you want."

Noelle. He could see her through the crowded room. His gaze went to her as inexorably as snow to winter and the stars to the night. Emotion closed up his throat so tight, he couldn't speak for a spell.

"I gave you first crack at it." Dorian hitched up his fine black suspenders. "Do you need time to think it over?"

"No. That's one piece of land I've always wanted to own. Never thought I could." His heart full, he didn't lift his gaze from her, from his Noelle.

If he could have one dream, why not another?

"Then stop by the office first thing tomorrow and we'll make it legal. You have yourself a good evening, son." Dorian, sounding pleased with himself, returned to the back porch.

Thad stood stock-still, unable to move, unable to blink. She was at their small table, interested in something Ma was saying to her. There were so many things he wanted to remember about her on this fateful night. The way lamplight shone like liquid red satin against the highlights in her hair. The curve of her face was delicate perfection, and the slope of her dainty nose just right.

She made him believe that real love was enough. That in the end good happened if a man worked hard enough.

I'm gonna marry her. He felt the decision with all of his soul's might. He didn't remember walking down the hallway or crossing the room. He only knew that he was suddenly at her side, where his heart had led him.

"We were just talking about you." She turned toward him, a smile shaping her lovely mouth and happiness alight on her sweet face. "I was telling Ida and Aiden about how you've managed to almost tame the two impossible horses my uncle bought."

If he blushed to the tips of his ears, he wasn't going to admit it. "It wasn't much. Glad to help."

"It proves you have a great gift with horses, Thad." Her soft, slim hand found his arm and rested there so naturally. For one brief tender moment, she betrayed her feelings for him. "I know this time your dreams are going to work out. You wait and see."

"I was just speaking to Mr. Dorian." Wrestling to keep his emotions under control, he handed his ma her coat, and then Aiden his. "He said there's a piece of land along Angel River for sale."

Aiden cheered up at that. "Which parcel?"

"It's near the falls." Thad came back around to Noelle's chair and settled his hand on her shoulder. There it was, the connection between them, so binding and infinite that he could feel his spirit turn around her like stars around the North Pole.

"What luck." Aiden's voice came muffled, as if from very far away. "That's prime land. I can't remember the last time anything upriver from the falls has been for sale."

"No one deserves it more than Thad," Noelle said quietly, sincerely.

She captured his heart all over again. Yep, he was in a bad situation, loving her as he did. His soul hurt with the strength of it.

"I'm grateful for this chance." His tone was raw and real, betraying his feelings. That embarrassed him because he wasn't talking about the land.

Noelle leaned toward him, as if she were unaware of his turmoil and his adoration. "It looks as if you will be able to have your horse ranch, just as you've always dreamed."

He prayed it wasn't only the land she meant, for she was part of his dreams. He carefully shook out the folds of her wool coat. "Think your uncle will let me see you home?"

"Maybe." There was that mischievous smile again, the one he loved so well. "But there you go, assuming I'll want to go with you."

"Darlin', I know what you want." Yes, he could see that clearly, too. He helped her slide back her chair and then into her coat, tenderness filling him up so there was hardly any room left to breathe. Hope could do that to a man.

The whisper of the falls came quietly at first through the soft music of the night, a quiet whir above the low-noted air whizzing past her ears, hardly noticeable at all. Then rising in volume until it was the dominating sound. It was a solemn chorus of water and snow and hope against the steady *chink-chink* of Sunny's shoes upon the ice.

It had been a perfect evening. The excellent meal

was improved with excellent company; there seemed to be no one more dear than Thad's gentle mother. And to have spent the entire evening in Thad's presence, at his side, sharing simple conversation, had uplifted her. She still felt as light as the airy, spun-sugar snowflakes dancing lazily against her cheeks and eyelashes.

She knew where they were without a single word from him. It wasn't the sound of the waterfall alone, but Thad's wistful sigh. "Are you planning on going into the land office tomorrow morning?"

"You know I'll be there well before they open. Just trying not to let myself get too excited." The amused notes in his voice told her he was grinning ear to ear. "I'll try to be dignified for your sake."

"For my sake? I'm not Henrietta. As much as I love her, I do not think reputation and decorum are everything." She smoothed the buffalo robes covering her skirts, to give her hand something to do. Many secrets lay inside her heart. It would not do to give him a single hint of them.

"Then I can let out a whoop?"

Now she was grinning ear to ear. "I have no objections."

"I'd better not. Best not to scare any fellow traveler up ahead. They may take out their rifle, thinkin' I'm a wolf. And considering how I look, who could blame them?"

She felt the laughter bubbling up. Oh, no one could bring summer to her life the way he could. She could tell he was slowing the sleigh, for Sunny's gait slowed. Taking a long hopeful look at the land? At his land? She hoped he was not only grinning ear to ear but glowing with happiness from the bottom of his soul. "What's the first thing you're going to do with the land?"

"The first thing?" He fell silent a moment, and the crash of the falls began to ebb a tad. "I ought to fence it, but seeing as Aiden, Finn and I have been repairing fence for the past month, I'm not too keen on starting out digging one hundred and sixty acres of fence posts."

"If not the fence first, then what will you do? The stable?"

"No. I'll start on a house."

A home. Her chest wrenched. How could she be ecstatically happy and deeply sorrowful all in the same moment? "T-tell me about it."

"It'll be two stories. Not big, I can't afford something grand, but a nice-size parlor to spend winters cozy by the fireplace without feeling cramped and still have plenty of room for all the bookshelves I intend to build."

Exactly what she herself would have wanted. "W-with big windows and a porch for quiet summer evenings?"

"Yessiree. With a roomy kitchen for my wife."

"W-wife?" Agony filled her. She clamped her lips together, set her chin and braced herself for the sorrow.

As much as she longed to be the woman who could marry him, his happy future mattered more. Her sadness faded away like one last long note, leaving only peace in her soul. "You are ready to settle down. You must have someone in mind."

"I've got my eye on a real nice lady." His baritone warmed gently. Perhaps he was worrying he was hurting her feelings.

Her love for him shone so strongly within her that she felt as if she were glowing, too. Happy for him, deeply and truly happy, she leaned back in the seat, sure, so completely sure, that God would bless Thad in this new part of his life. "Do I know her?"

"I think you do. Maybe you might offer your opinion on the plans for this house. I want her to have a roomy place to do all the kitchen work easily and not so close that she catches her skirts on fire on the stove."

"Very easy to do," Noelle agreed.

"And a sunny spot for the kitchen table, a place where you just want to sit over a cup of tea and spend time jawin'."

"I can imagine it. A lot of cabinets and a roomy pantry—you could spend some of your winter months making them for her. A round table between the corner windows and a place for boots and coats to dry." The future she could see might have once been her dream, but it felt right sharing it with him. "There will be children one day who will need a place to come in from playing in the snow and warm up."

"Children." His baritone dipped intimately. When he spoke next, his voice vibrated with emotion. "Now, I hadn't quite got that far. Except for four upstairs bedrooms."

"Four sounds like a nice number."

"It surely does." His heart was full to bursting as he nosed Sunny off the main road. "I've been thinking about building a little cottage behind the main house for my ma. Aiden's taken care of her all this time, and I feel as if it's my duty now. What do you think of that?"

"As long as she would want to move. She has her own house."

"Yep, and with both of my brothers there, too. It's my hope Aiden will come to marry again one day, and then she'll be feeling in the way again." He gripped the reins more tightly. He could feel his dearest hopes ready to come true, and it was so much to lose. "I would like her close. I've missed her, and she can feel good helping to take care of things at my place. She likes taking care of the people she loves."

"Then it sounds like a good solution. She would be closer to any future grandchildren."

There she went, mentioning children again. Thad couldn't say what that did to his heart, but he was fairly sure it would never beat normally again.

"As long as she got along well with your wife," Noelle pointed out sweetly, "it sounds perfect to me. Does this mean there will be another wedding soon?"

"I'm praying that's the truth."

"Praying? Does this mean you're a praying man again?"

"Maybe. You never know." The Worthington manor came into sight, windows ablaze with golden lamplight. It looked like the family was already home. "About this wedding of mine. Think you'd like to attend?"

"Absolutely beyond a doubt. It's what I've been praying for."

How about that. Thad reined Sunny to a stop outside the porch. He climbed out from beneath the snug buffalo robe and circled around the sleigh to help Noelle out. Powerful love for her broke him wide-open, and it was greater than anything he'd ever known. Incapable of speech, he simply took her hand in his, and led her with care up the porch steps. Joy lifted him so far up, he couldn't feel the boards beneath his boots, for there was only her. Just her. In his thoughts, in his heart, in his soul.

She broke the silence between them when they reached the door. "You will let me know how tomorrow goes with the land agent?"

"I will. The moment the land is mine, you will be the first one I tell." He acted on impulse and again cradled her face in both his hands with all the tenderness in his soul. He wanted more than anything to tell her he would take care of her, that he would do his best for her, and how great his love was for her.

As if she realized that he intended to kiss her, she tipped toward him an infinitesimal amount. Her eyes widened with such honesty, and they were the color of his dreams. Her smile was every last piece of his heart.

"Good night, Mr. McKaslin." The serene notes of her voice blew through his spirit like the rarest of joys.

He opened the door for her. "Good night, Miss Kramer. I'll talk to you tomorrow."

"Good." Her smile was the last thing he saw as he tipped his hat to her and left her in the care of her aunt, who was in the act of charging toward the door.

Maybe it wasn't so polite to run off, he thought, as he took the steps two at a time, but he wasn't a parlor-sitting kind of man. And he wanted to end the evening when it was perfect. Just perfect.

The snow fell soft and airy as an answered prayer. His boots sank up to his ankles in the new blanket of snowfall and he rubbed Sunny's nose before he slogged back to the sleigh. Funny how it did feel as though God had been watching out for him in the end. That He hadn't forgotten a simple hardworking man after all.

Thad settled on the seat, pulled the robes tight and gathered the reins in his gloved hands. Snow tapped on his hat brim and slapped his cheek as he turned Sunny in a lazy half circle, nosing him away from the bright lights of the Worthington home and into the cloying darkness.

Maybe things just take time to work out for His good; that's all. Maybe that's what he'd lost sight of when he was so far from home and everyone he loved, his heart dashed. Faith had been a painful thing for a long spell, and now it was hurting in a whole new way.

The wind kicked up, cold and shrill, so he knuckled down his hat against the stinging snowflakes. That pain seemed to spread through his chest like wildfire. For whatever reason, he was being given a second chance with Noelle. What he didn't know was that gratitude could hurt, too.

Noelle's words tonight came back to him. *It's easy to fall into the habit of walking through life. It's safer. Because you don't have to risk as much. You don't have to really feel.* Maybe that had been his problem more than he'd realized. He'd gotten awfully used to walking through his life instead of feeling it. That made it tough to know anything much of value, including God's presence.

You didn't give up on me and I thank You for it.

Thad gave Sunny more rein, but the mustang already knew where he was going, heading toward the falls, toward home.

In the bedroom she shared with Matilda, Noelle carefully poured the pitcher of warm water and measured the rise of the water level in the porcelain basin. The pitcher clinked gently onto the stand, and she felt the curls of heat from the water's surface against her face.

Happiness still strummed through her, and it was a good feeling, and a welcome change. She splashed water on her face and reached for the bottle of soft soap she liked so well. The lilac scent always reminded her of late spring, when the earth was warm and the sun's warmth a welcome friend.

She lathered and scrubbed and rinsed, going over the evening's events in her mind. Whatever God's purpose in all of this—her blindness, Thad's coming back to Angel Falls, his plans for a ranch and a home and a family starting to come to fruition—she could not know. She could only trust that He was bringing them both to the greatest good for their separate lives.

She patted her face dry in the soft towel and rehung it on the bar. Footsteps marched down the hall like a division of soldiers coming closer.

"Angelina!" Henrietta's voice echoed above the strike of her shoes. "I am shocked. Simply beside myself with agitation at what I've only just heard from your father."

And what shocking behavior would it be this time? Noelle wondered as she sprinkled tooth powder onto her toothbrush. Knowing Angelina, it was bound to be most entertaining.

Robert's cane tapped after Henrietta. "Now, now, dear, it's not as bad as all that—"

"Not that bad?" Henrietta's outrage echoed in the corridor. "Caught smoking behind the outhouses! I cannot think of why Clarissa Bell would accuse you of such a thing!"

Poor Henrietta, Noelle thought in turn, for it was not easy being a general in charge of such troops. It took a lot of internal fortitude to stay in denial about Angelina's rebellion, which was not acceptable for a Worthington.

Matilda's steps padded a little heavier than usual

down the hallways. "Uh, I don't know why Mama is going on about Miss Bell. You know that Angelina was smoking behind the outhouses. The more Mama refuses to see it, the more outrageous she behaves."

Noelle heard a muted clunk, realizing that Tilly was carrying the warmed flatirons for their beds. She rinsed and dropped her toothbrush into her cup by the basin. "Henrietta loves her daughters so much, she cannot find a single flaw in any of you."

How she wished she still had her own mother to do the same.

"Mama made comments all through dinner how she thought my wedding should be, much grander, of course, than Lanna's." The bedclothes rustled and snapped. "Who does she think I'm going to marry? No one has ever come calling. I'm not exactly pretty like my sisters are."

"You are lovely in your own way."

"That's another way of saying that I'm plain." She sighed deeply.

"No, dear heart, not at all." Poor Matilda. Noelle remembered when she had been that naive and young—it had been like walking with her heart wide-open. Fairy-tale love could lift a girl right out of her shoes. She might have walked on thin air for the better part of her courtship with Thad—and probably had for half of this evening, too.

"I'm just starting to fear I'll have to live with my mother forever." Tilly sighed again.

Noelle listened to the rustle and chink as the flatirons clinked into place. "I know what it is like to have a heart full of love to share and no one to give it to."

"Perhaps we shall be old maids together. I'll read to

you at night, and study from the Bible as we do now.
I'll take care of you."

"I would not wish such a fate for you, to take care
of me. You deserve a good man to love you truly." She
went to her bedside table. "I owe you an apology, Tilly."

"Whatever for?"

"I gave you some bad advice about Emmett Sims."
She pulled open the drawer and felt for her buttonhook. "I should have told you that I hope he feels the
same way about you, and if he does, to hold on to that
love and protect it from all things."

"But I thought—"

"I told you that love is frail and not to place all your
hopes on it, but there is nothing greater than love. The
Bible tells us so. I think I'm finally understanding. God's
love for us is not trifling or fleeting or simple. It is the
greatest strength, the greatest loyalty, and it is complex.
Love is the only thing strong enough to put your hope on."

"Is that what you did once? With Thad?"

She had thought it was love—and Thad—at fault,
but that was not true. As she unhooked one button and
then the next, she thought of all that had happened, all
that she had lost.

Oh, Papa, how could you have done such a thing?
Her father's intervention and his stubborn will had
changed her life. He had destroyed her one real chance
at loving Thad. Now it would be forever too late. Thad
was going on with his life. She had to go on with hers.
Maybe Matilda would have a better experience.

"Don't give up hope, Tilly." She started loosening
her other shoe. "Perhaps we ought to have our next
dress purchases delivered. What do you think?"

"Oh, Mama would not approve of that."

"Spring is almost here. You might need a few new dresses and bonnets. I can arrange it when I'm in town next."

"Oh, I would be too embarrassed. As much as I wish for it, I don't think Emmett Sims is interested in me." Matilda, the dear she was, didn't sound sad, only wistful. Her bed ropes squeaked as if she had sat down on the edge of her mattress. "A few more years, and I'll be on the shelf. I'm never going to get married."

I know the feeling. Noelle ached for her younger cousin. "I would hold out hope, if I were you. Something tells me that Mr. Emmett Sims might have noticed you."

Tilly remained quiet, but there was hope in the air.

The floorboard outside the door gave a tiny squeak. Was it Angelina? Noelle wondered, as bare feet padded quietly into the room.

"Angelina!" Tilly scolded in a low voice. "You are not supposed to be out of bed. Didn't Mama just hand down a punishment?"

"Yes, but she's helping Papa, so she won't know that I'm out of bed unless you tell her." Angelina's whisper floated closer.

Noelle felt the foot of her bed dip and turned toward her troublesome cousin. "Do you really think it's wise to smoke cigarettes? It's a poor choice for you for many reasons."

"I know, but I was bored. I told Mama I didn't want to wear that frilly lacy dress. I looked like I was about to go to a convent. Or get *married*." It took no imagination at all to see Angelina rolling her eyes. "She's really planning them, you know."

"Planning what?" Matilda asked.

"Our weddings. Meredith and Lydia aren't home from finishing school yet, and she's almost planned a seven-course meal for each of them. And a string quartet, but not for dancing. She started to ask what I wanted, and that's when I needed a bit of fresh air."

"You mean smoky air." Noelle couldn't help jesting.

"Ha-ha." Angelina was probably rolling her eyes again. "Noelle, you'll be the next to marry, anyhow."

"*Me?* Why would you say such a thing?" She tugged off one shoe and then the other. "I'm the last woman any man would marry. Men are looking for a helpmate, not someone they have to steer around the parlor."

She set the buttonhook inside the drawer, careful to keep a smile on her face. "Matilda's will be next."

"Oh, I don't know." Tilly's voice sparkled with humor. "We all thought Mr. McKaslin was rather devoted to you throughout the evening."

"Devoted?" Angelina sounded equally as amused. "Now tell the truth, Tilly. That handsome cowboy of Noelle's isn't merely devoted. He is utterly in love with her. He is a courting man. Valentine's Day is tomorrow. I would bet—"

"Don't bet, Ange," Tilly argued.

"I would *bet*," Angelina emphasized, her rebellious streak showing, "that he proposes before tomorrow is done."

Noelle's jaw dropped and she sputtered for air. Thad, propose to her? For one brief instant, joy flooded her soul. Then drained away, leaving her in shadows.

No, he would need a wife who could help him with his dreams and not keep him from them. She remembered his plans for a wife, a wife who could cook, a wife who could tend children and, she figured, who could work alongside him with the horses.

It hurt, she couldn't say it didn't.

Somehow, she kept the smile on her face. "What an outrageous thing to say. Angelina. *This* is how you get into so much trouble."

"What? I'm telling the truth. The way he looked at you wasn't like anything I have ever seen before. Tell her, Tilly."

Matilda sighed. "I didn't want to mention it. I know it will make you sad. But it's true. All through the wedding ceremony and the dinner at the hotel, his gaze never faltered. He adores you, Noelle, and in the right way. The real way. The loving way that lasts forever and nothing can break."

Noelle opened her mouth to argue.

Angelina was already talking. "He doesn't seem to mind that you can't see. Something like that doesn't stop true love."

"What am I going to do with you two?" She could only shake her head, doing her best to hold down the sorrow that was hers alone. She was no longer an idealistic girl seeing romance and fanciful possibilities instead of practical, real life.

Somewhere deep inside her she wished she could.

"I hear voices, Matilda and Noelle!" Henrietta called from down the hall. "It's well past your bedtimes. In my day, a young lady was asleep before nine or it wasn't proper!"

"We'll say our prayers now, Mama," Matilda promised earnestly over the nearly imperceptible pad and rustle of Angelina tiptoeing from the room.

Noelle pulled her nightgown from her bureau

drawer, listening to the squeak of floorboards as Matilda knelt down to pray. There was a damp chill in the cold that crept through the walls and she shivered as she unbuttoned her bodice. She wondered if a change in the weather was coming.

Good. The sooner this snow melted, the quicker Thad could start building his dreams. For that was her most cherished dream, she realized as she stepped out of her dress and untied her petticoats. Her only dreams were now for him.

She was starting to see that life, like music, was a careful balance of melody and harmony, of sweeter notes and deeper ones. As she slipped her nightgown over her head and knelt beside her bed, she thanked the good Lord for both.

Chapter Sixteen

This had to be the best day of his life, family problems aside. His troubles at home seemed manageable from his current outlook, Thad thought as he dismounted in front of the Worthington stables. The sun was shining, he was the proud owner of a real fine spread and was carrying an engagement ring in his shirt pocket. Knowing that she would say yes just made it easier to feel on top of the world.

"Howdy there, McKaslin!" Eli Sims came through the open stable doorway to take Sunny's reins. "Good seein' ya. Looks like you beat the storm here."

Thad hadn't noticed the dark clouds overhead. He was in too good a mood to let them trouble him now. "Guess so. How's things going for you here?"

"I can't thank you enough for finding me this job."

"I'm glad it suits you." Thad grabbed a package from his saddlebag before Eli could take Sunny in out of the cold. "How's that stallion treating you?"

"He's an ornery one. You come to work him some?"

Thad glanced up at the house, where wide windows

glinted with lamplight. "Maybe in a bit. Has Noelle's last student of the day left yet?"

"Yep. Left a while back," the young man called over his shoulder before he disappeared with Sunny into the shadowed aisle.

Nerves kicked his stomach. Slushy snow squished and skidded beneath his boots. He clutched the package, going over all the decisions he'd come to. He'd already run it past his ma. Normally he took Aiden into his confidence, but he suspected his older brother was still sour on love and marriage. Best to figure out how this was all going to work on his own.

Ma seemed to think moving into a little cottage next door to him was a fine idea. In fact, there had been no way she could have disguised her happiness at his plans. He knew she was unfulfilled with only gruff Aiden and independent Finn to mother. Hadn't she been spoiling him too much since he'd come home?

Surely Noelle wouldn't mind some of that spoiling. The nerves in his gut took another hard kick. At least, that's what he was hoping. Hadn't she liked the notion when they'd talked on the ride home last night?

Stop worrying, man. His pulse beat like a runaway train down a steep track with such force, he began to wheeze as he headed up the walkway. The brick stones were wet from snowmelt, as were the steps of the porch.

Noelle. He saw her through the window. She was sitting in an armchair near the hearth with sewing on her lap. Her chestnut hair was loose, framing her lovely face and tumbling over her shoulders. She was beauty itself in a rose-pink dress, looking like spring had come early to this hard land.

His spring.

First off, he had to stop wheezing so hard. He stood on the top step and drew in a calm breath. Now all he had to do was raise his fist and knock on the door and lay his heart, his pride, his dignity and his future on the line. Not a fearsome prospect at all, right?

Just knock. He did it, one knock was all he could manage. He waited, hoping—praying—someone had heard it. He took a step back and tried to buck up his courage for the next difficult event. One thing was for sure, he'd be feeling a whole passel better once she'd said yes and he could relax.

The door swung open and instead of the maid looking up at him, it was his Noelle. "Thad, is that you?"

"How did you know?"

"I recognized your gait and your knock." She opened the door wider, waltzing backward a few steps, her rose-pink skirts swirling around her ankles. "Come in. My aunt took the girls to town, and Robert is out with Matilda for her first driving lesson."

He managed to force his feet forward and into the warmth of the house, surprised his watery knees could hold him up so well. "You're here all alone?"

"Not exactly alone. Sadie's upstairs cleaning and Cook's in the kitchen. Would you like some tea? I'll call Sadie—"

"No." Had she gotten lovelier overnight? He had never seen her so beautiful, but then he was biased. "No need to go to any fuss. I came to talk to you—"

"About the land sale." Her smile dazzled him. "Come, sit and warm yourself by the fire and tell me everything."

"It was good luck mostly." He closed the door and followed her to the hearth. She moved with grace, as she always did, walking almost as if she saw where she was going. She caught the edge of the chair's arm with her fingertips and settled into it, waiting for his story expectantly.

He sank down into the chair opposite her. His damp boots squeaked once on the wood floor. Heat radiated over him like his dazzling love for her. His chest cinched so with powerful affection for her, he didn't see how he was going to be able to get the words out.

Maybe it was best to talk about the land sale, as she'd asked. "It's a stroke of luck that this section came up for sale. I've signed papers too fancy for me to read, and I still don't believe it."

"It's not luck." She said it with confidence. "That land was intended for you."

Faith wasn't what he'd come to talk about, but it was the truth. It had to be the truth. The hard journey of the past five years had led him here, to this shining, shimmering hope. God had been watching over him after all. Knowing that gave him courage.

"I have something for you." He placed the wrapped package into her hand. "It's for Valentine's Day."

"*What?* No, this can't be—"

"It's for you." She sure looked surprised. "Go on. Open it."

"But, Thad I—"

"No arguments." He was out of words, so he knelt before her. "Aren't you curious about your present?"

"All right." Her fingertips inched across the spine of the volume. "Is it a *book?*"

Thad lifted it for her, because it was heavy. "You're

thinking, this is an odd gift since you can't see to read, am I right?"

"I can have Matilda read it to me." She unfolded the paper to reveal the black leather cover.

"No need for that." He opened the thick vellum pages with care and slid the book onto her knees. "This is one book you can read. It's raised print. Go on, you can feel the title."

"It's the Book of Psalms." She turned toward him and it wasn't only tears that stood in her eyes. He saw her heart and her soul, all she was, all wrapped up in surprise and joy. "I love the psalms."

"You always did." It did him good to see her so happy. He loved her without end. He would do anything for her. The need to cherish and protect her left him iron-strong. Now all he had to do was ask the question, and she would be his. His intended, his fiancée for all the world to see, and soon enough, his wife.

His *wife*. That would have brought him to his knees, if he wasn't there already. "I remember how much you used to love to read, especially your Bible."

"This is extremely thoughtful. And expensive."

He brushed the tendrils away from her sweet face. "Go on, give it a try."

Her sensitive fingertips skimmed over the top of the page and found the raised numeral. Her face brightened until all her heart shone sweetly. "It's the twenty-third psalm. I can feel the letters. Why, I can read them. 'The Lord is my shepherd; I shall not want.'"

"How does it feel to be reading again?"

"It's an answered prayer." Happiness filled her completely. "'He maketh me to lie down in green pastures; He leadeth me beside the still waters. He restoreth my soul.'"

"Glad you like it."

"Like it?" This is—" She looked at him with tears in her eyes. "I don't know what it is. It's—just. Thank you."

Those tears broke him open completely.

God, if you're listening, a little guidance would be a help. Thad swallowed, not expecting to be heard for he knew the Lord was busy, but he asked anyway. He covered her hands with his, psalm book and all.

Noelle leaned closer to him, her unspoken question on her face. The soft gray daylight kissed her sweetly, or maybe it was his own love for her making her seem so dear, so perfect in all the ways that mattered.

"Noelle, some things have changed an awful lot in the five years since I've been gone. Surely both of us have." He had to take a pause because his heart was beating as though he was running on a steep uphill slope.

"Thad, you sound so serious."

"That's because I've never been more serious or more sure." Nothing had mattered so much before this moment. He gathered up his strength and kept going. "I want the job of making you happy for our lifetimes to come. I want to be with you in those green pastures. Marry me."

"What? What did you say?"

"Marry me, Noelle." His tone was complete love and pure wonder. "Be my wife."

"Wife?" She repeated the word blankly. Her mind was like a midnight fog. Nothing seemed to penetrate it. "You want to m-marry me?"

"You needn't sound quite so horrified," he quipped. "This shouldn't come as a surprise. Isn't that what we talked about last night?"

"What talk?" Panic crept up her spine like hungry ants at a picnic. Noelle vaguely felt the book slide off her knee and heard the distant thunk as it hit the floor at her feet, but it was hard to notice anything beyond her fears. "Do you mean our talk on the sleigh ride home?"

"That would be the one." His hands were comforting, his voice soothing. "I don't want you to be so distraught, sweetheart."

"I—I—" She couldn't make any words come. The panic was crawling into her throat now, and a horrible sorrow taking root in her chest. A dark, agonizing sorrow.

"I love you." His baritone broke through the sorrow. "Surely you know that I do."

His love for her made it worse. She could hear Shelton's words echoing in the chambers of her mind. *You're damaged goods, now. What use are you?* Henrietta's loving reassurances after she'd woken up from the buggy accident. *I'll take care of you now. I'll never consider you a burden.* Well-intended words, but even Henrietta, her own father's sister, had used the word *burden.*

"I was hoping," Thad was saying, "that you'd come to love me, too."

Love him? Love was too pale a word for the deep abiding devotion she held for him. "Y-you are supposed to marry someone else. Someone b-better."

"Who could be better than you?" He said those words as if he could not see the problem.

Her dear, sweet, good-hearted Thad. Did he truly not understand? What did she say? She longed to throw caution and her very real concerns to the wind. She wanted to wrap her arms around him, accept his proposal and spend the rest of her life as his wife.

His wife. Her soul soared at that very notion. Having the privilege to love and cherish and honor him day by day, year by year for the rest of her life felt like her heaven on earth. Sweet longing filled her with such force, it threatened to lift her right out of the chair.

And what about what Thad wanted? Her joy faded. Her longing vanished. She had to keep her feet on the floor and tight hold of her common sense. A marriage between them would never work. Not if he wanted to realize his dream of running a ranch. She could not help him with that, not the way she once could.

That's what he hadn't realized, she thought. He was acting on his past feelings for her. He still viewed her as he did five long years ago when the world seemed full of possibilities and their love unshakable.

She knew better now. She was wiser. If her heart cracked into a million pieces, she had to ignore the pain of it. She had to do the right thing. The best thing for Thad.

And, yes, for her.

He broke the silence. "It shouldn't take you this long to say yes to marrying me. Not if you want me."

She withdrew her hands from his—and her heart, too.

"You do love me, darlin'. Don't you?"

"Love isn't the question, Thad." She sat very still, gathering up every bit of might she had and yet it wasn't enough.

"Then what is the question, darlin'?" So tender his words. So loving.

Sorrow dripped through her. "I c-can't marry you."

"You sound so sure about that. Why not?"

Because I won't trade my dreams for yours, she ached to say. Because I don't want to be a burden to the one man I love beyond all else on this earth.

Her soul squeezed with pain, making every inch of her ache. She covered her face with her hands, unable to say the truth. Unable to bare herself so fully.

Not even Thad would understand. He would say all the right things, about how her blindness didn't matter to him, and that was not the truth. It couldn't be the truth.

She swallowed hard against the burn in her throat. He hadn't seen her real limitations yet. She had worked extremely hard to adapt to the constraints of her blindness, but he didn't know that. He only saw what she could do and not what she couldn't. She had to do the right thing for them both.

"Noelle? Are you crying?"

"N-no." She would make that the truth. She set her chin and blinked hard against the heat behind her eyes. "I don't know what else to say to you, Thad. I c-can't marry you."

"You haven't told me why, darlin'."

His tenderness tore her apart. Fear left her helpless. Truly in the dark, she reached out in prayer. *Help me, Lord. Don't let my words hurt him.*

There was no answer, not one in her heart, not one in the darkness. Outside the house another gust of wind slammed against the house, rattling the windowpanes, jarring her soul.

"Tell me, sweetheart, just tell me the truth."

"Which truth?" She squeezed her eyes shut. Torn, so torn. Saying no to him was like ripping out her soul.

"We're simply not suited, Thad. Not anymore. You said it yourself. You've changed. I've changed. It's too l-late."

"No. No it's not. I won't believe it."

"Please, I—I can't marry you."

"But this is our second chance."

Her eyes were luminous and her face filled with such sweet longing that for one blissful moment he thought she was going to say yes. To tell him that she loved him truly and forever, as he loved her.

He knew he'd thought wrong when she seemed to withdraw from him. The longing slid from her face, her lovely expressive face that would always be so dear to him.

"No." Her rejection came quietly. Tenderly. She bent forward and her hair fell in a curtain to hide her face and her emotions.

They were not secret to him.

The psalm book lay on its back on the floor between them. He lifted it carefully, dusted it off so it was as good as new and laid it on the small table beside her chair. Although she'd said no to him, the great abiding love he had for her did not fade.

It would never fade.

"Guess I'd best get going, then." While he didn't say it as a question, he meant it as one. He watched her carefully. She nodded once, that was all, as if trying to shield her heart from his.

He climbed to his feet, holding his soul still against the pain he knew was coming. Like a lethal blow, there was no pain at first, just the shock filtering through him like cracked ice in his veins. He took a step backward, waiting, hoping, praying she would reach out to him. That she would stop him before he made it to the door.

She didn't. He opened the door and forced his feet across the threshold. It took all his self-restraint to keep from looking back at her one last time. To keep from reaching out to her when he knew she was hurting, too.

How had this all gone so wrong? He closed the door with a click and let the wind batter him. Snow lashed at him like a boxer's glove, and still he could not move off the porch. He'd left his heart behind in that room, and he couldn't leave without her.

What was he gonna do? Stand here forever? He had to get moving before the shock wore off. Before the pain set in and the sorrow with it. It was bound to be bad—he'd experienced this before. He'd ridden away from her once, and he knew the emptiness of living his life without her love. How was he going to manage it a second time?

He started down the stairs, and her words stuck with him. *We're simply not suited, Thad. Not anymore.* Not suited? And what did that mean, anyhow? His boots crunched in the slush and snow on the walkway. Big, fat flakes fell from a gray sky as he crossed the yard to the stable. *You said it yourself. You've changed. I've changed.*

I haven't changed that much. He stopped stock-still between the house and the stable, realizing that wasn't true. Not true at all. How about that? The hardness from years of unhappiness and a tough life on the trail had fallen away somewhere, sloughed off him like a too-large, worn-out coat.

He was no longer bitter and unbelieving. He was no longer thinking God had stopped noticing the troubles of an average man. He no longer believed life was about hard work and that relationships ought to be, too. He'd found himself again—the man he used to be—because of Noelle. Because of her love and God's grace.

Why had she said no? Why had she turned him down? He'd thought she'd loved him. He'd thought she wanted him to love her.

"Hey, Thad!" Eli called above the rush of the storm. "I saw you comin'. I've got Sunny for you."

"Thanks, Sims." Thad seized the reins from the younger man, nodding. "You'd best get inside before this gets much worse."

"Will do. Looks like we're in for a hard blow." Eli waved his hand and took off.

Sunny wheeled around, eager to get home and out of the weather. Thad grabbed the saddle horn, ready to mount up, and realized the house was in his view again. There she was, standing in the window, veiled by the bleak snow. His heart turned over. His soul filled with longing.

It's too late, she'd said.

Too late.

Swift pain like a dagger's tip to his heart stole his breath and weakened his knees. He took a stumbling step, leaning on the horse's shoulder for support, and somehow he scrambled into the saddle.

The wind gusted, driving cold that hit like bullets. The snow had turned to rain, soaking him down to the bone. She'd said no to him. He had to respect that, although it tore out his heart.

"C'mon, Sunny. Take us home."

The mustang obliged, heading swiftly down the road. Lucky thing, since the sorrow was setting in. It wasn't easy riding away from his dreams a second time.

* * *

Noelle listened to the rain sing against the parlor window. The wind lifted and fell like a cello's haunting tones. The limbs of the hawthorn tree outside the window rubbed against the eaves with a tuba's low notes. The fire in the hearth crackled in counterpoint to the gusts of wind and beat of rain. It was a haunting symphony, one that spoke of sorrow and regret.

Regret for the lost years between them. Regret that she never had a voice in Thad's decision to leave. Regret at the years she'd wasted. Regret that there would be only wasted years ahead without real love.

She swiped the last of her tears from her eyes. She knew for certain that she would love only Thad forever. *I'm hoping for a wife one day. Someone who sees life the way I do. You work hard, try to do what's right and at the end of the day rest up for another hard day on the ranch.* Her blindness separated them more successfully than her parents' had. There was no solution to that.

She heard her cousin's hurried gait well before the door opened on a chorus of wind.

"That rain is cold." Matilda shut the door behind her, dripping water on the floor. There was a rustle as if she were shedding her sodden wraps and her shoes squished wetly on the floor coming closer. "I need to sit by the fire and warm up. Papa said maybe we're in for a spot of good luck. This could be a warming spell that brings us an early spring."

"I hope so." Noelle prayed her voice sounded normal and feared that it didn't. "Then you can take me for rides in the buggy. How did your driving lesson go?"

"Fine. We rode up to the waterfall and back. It's roaring with all the snowmelt and rain."

"The waterfall has never frozen in the winter, not in my memory." Her love for Thad was like that, she realized, never ending, always replenished. Alive in her heart when it was the last thing she needed or wanted. "Would you like me to bring you some tea?"

"Please. I can't remember the last time I've been this cold."

Tea. Yes, that sounded like something soothing to do. She rose from her chair, ignoring the ache that burned her eyes and tightened her throat. She didn't want to talk to anyone, not even to Matilda, about Thad's proposal. They would pity her, and that was the last thing she wanted. The last thing she needed.

She skirted the end table and headed across the parlor. Grief lodged so tightly within her she could hardly function. Her pulse thudded in her ears so loudly that the strike of her shoe on the floor muted. There was Thad at the edges of her memory and glued to her soul.

Who could be better than you? he'd said with complete sincerity. *I love you,* he'd said with utter honesty. *This is our second chance.* His tender plea filled her mind again and again. This is our second chance.

If only it could be. She had to stop thinking about this. About the tender love in his voice, even when she turned him down. And the defeated cadence to his gait as he walked away from her. What she could not think about was the future without Thad in it. Without a prospering ranch, and happiness, buckets of happiness. She could almost see it, vivid, so vivid, those fields of green dotted with grazing horses. The two-story house where drying laundry snapped on a clothesline and children played in the yard—

She froze in midstep, confused. Where was she? She'd forgotten to count her steps. She didn't know if she was about to walk into the window or if she was on a collision course with her aunt's whatnot shelf.

"Where did you get that book?" Tilly broke the silence.

"I-it was a gift." Outside the symphony of the rain crescendoed to a roar, confusing the sounds in the room, confusing her.

"From whom?"

She turned toward Matilda's voice, using it like a compass. "Just someone."

"Thad came by, didn't he? Angelina was right. Too bad he didn't propose, too. Wouldn't that have been something?"

A rush filled her ears. The sound of her heart breaking all over again. She spun on her heel, careful to keep track of her orientation. She guessed how many steps would take her through the archway and into the dining room.

"Noelle?" Tilly called out. "He really didn't propose, did he?"

Her step faltered right along with her heartbeat. She reached out a hand to catch the corner of the dining table and caught air.

"Noelle? Are you all right?"

Two more steps and she tried again. There it was, the beveled, polished edge. She gripped it with relief. Her knees were wobbling so she lowered herself into the nearest chair, glad that her cousin hadn't noticed how lost she'd been.

How lost she would be from this day on.

Chapter Seventeen

In the warmth of the town's dress shop, Noelle ran her fingertips across the skein of fine crochet thread. Her mind should have been on deciding if the yarn had the right weight and feel for the lace tablecloth she wanted to make for Matilda's hope chest. But when she heard the name "McKaslin," she couldn't seem to concentrate on anything other than what the shop owner was telling Aunt Henrietta.

"—should have been helping his brothers with the spring planting," Cora Sims was saying over the *thump, thump* of fabric being pulled off the bolt to be measured. "That boy is trouble waiting to happen. He's on a bad path for sure."

"It's all in the upbringing." Henrietta's voice echoed across the length of the shop. "I haven't had one bit of trouble with my children. I've taken a firm hand right from the start and made it clear there were standards to be upheld."

Noelle bit her bottom lip, remembering the uproar at last night's dinner table when Angelina had announced she wasn't going to finishing school like her sisters and wanted to take to the cattle trails instead. Since she heard Matilda choking as she struggled not to laugh, she wasn't the only one amused by wonderful Henrietta.

"This is the color I want," Tilly said when she was able. "Light blue."

"A light blue tablecloth sounds lovely to me. We need ten skeins."

"I'll count them out," Matilda said eagerly. "Mama's busy with Miss Sims."

"Is she ordering more spring dresses for your sisters?"

"Yes. She's taken charge as usual and I don't think Angelina is going to be very happy. Mama's chosen two different pink fabrics for her."

"Pink for Angelina? That's wishful thinking on your mother's part." Noelle tried to imagine the shop full of new spring fabrics so soft and bright and pretty, but her imagination was not the same these days. Nothing was, not one thing, since she'd let Thad walk out of her life over a week ago.

Thad. The thought of him still hurt in the broken places of her soul, where she'd banished her love for him, although it still lived.

The noise of the rain on the roof, the shop conversations and the background din from the streets outside faded away. Regret filled her until she was brimming over. Thoughts of him carried her away to the steadfast comfort of his hand on hers as she swirled over the ice of the pond at Thad's side. Once again, she heard the deep rumble of his cozy chuckle in the stable with the new foal nipping at her skirt ruffles. Once again she felt the bright dreams of lush fields and grazing horses standing at Thad's side.

It's not possible. Stop thinking of him. She squeezed her eyes closed, but that did not begin to stop the colors of her heart. Her heart did not see reason. Nor did it understand that there could come a day when Thad realized he had made a mistake. That the dreams they'd once shared were not something she could give to him as his wife.

Is that the real reason? a logical, sensible voice asked at the back of her mind. It was a question she could not let herself answer.

"Did you want to get that, Noelle, dear?" Henrietta bustled her way to take the basket of goods. "I'll be glad to get this totaled up, if you and Matilda want to go browse at the cobbler's."

"Yes, thank you."

Although she kept a good memory of the shop, she was glad when Matilda guided her around a new fabric display and on toward the door. The bell jangled overhead as they scooted outside into the cool spring air. The damp stung her face as she bundled up against the rain.

"Oh!" Matilda squeaked with surprise. "There he is."

Thad? Noelle turned toward the sounds of the street, wondering where he was, if he was well, if he looked happy, if he had all that he'd wanted. Love blazed up from the locked-away chambers of her heart, and she longed for him the way gray skies longed for blue.

"He tipped his hat to me!" Matilda's whisper was tremulous. "Oh, he smiled at me from the street, where he sat on his wagon seat, and as his horses drew him past, he reached up with his hand and tipped his hat brim. He was smiling just a little, nothing flashy or bold, just *polite*. Oh!"

Her pulse turned hollow. Emmett Sims, not Thad. Disappointment weighed her down like a blacksmith's anvil. And it made no sense whatsoever because it wasn't as if she were holding out a single hope that— No, not one single hope that there was any way Thad would love her enough—

No, it's not what you want for him, Noelle. She kept her spine straight, gathered up her resolve and smiled at her cousin's joy. "Perhaps Mr. Sims fancies you more than you've thought."

"Perhaps. We shall have to wait and see is all."

"I'm not fooled you know, by your reserve. Inside you are floating like a cloud."

"How did you know?"

"I've felt that way myself." She tucked away that memory, too, not of being young and in love, but of all the ways she loved Thad more now. And always would. "I've lost count. Where are we on the boardwalk? Is that the bakery?"

"Yes. I can smell the cinnamon buns."

"I think we need to celebrate, don't you? Henrietta needs to go to the post office before she catches up with us. We have plenty of time. We'll have iced cinnamon rolls and tea, which ought to put us in a much better mood for shoe shopping."

"I think you're right." Matilda took a better grip on her arm. "Come with me."

As Noelle turned on her heel to let her cousin guide her to the door, she thought she felt a feather brush against her soul like a touch from heaven. But there were no other footsteps squishing anywhere close by on the rain-soaked boardwalk. Just the sucking of mud at horse hooves and wagon wheels and the concerto of the rain falling.

Strange. Shrugging, she followed her cousin into the shelter of the bakery.

"Thad?"

He ignored his older brother's voice as he watched Noelle step inside the bakery across the street. Affection tied him up in knots, for he could still see her through the gray sheets of rain and the street traffic and the bakery's window. She was feeling her way for a curving chair back and, after three tries, found it and, with care, settled onto the seat.

"You and Finn are both useless," Aiden quipped from the row filled with buckets of nails. "Both of you aren't doing a thing to help me. I should have left you two at home."

"Don't go tossing me into the same stall as Finn." Thad couldn't seem to rip his gaze away from the bakery shop window. "I'm not the lazy one."

"Hey!" Finn's voice rose up from the back corner of the store. "Watch who you're calling lazy!"

Aiden came close to peer through the window, too. "You've been watching her since you spotted her enter the dress shop. Tell me again how you think her saying no was for the best."

A dagger through his gut wouldn't hurt as much as Noelle's rejection. No, nothing in this life could hurt him like that. But it was a private pain. "Between Finn, helping you with the ranch and working on mine, I haven't had a whole lot of time to ponder it."

"Perhaps you'd best start right now, since you've got

time to stand idle at the window." Aiden strode off, hiding a small smile.

Think about it? He'd been doing nothing else but going over the last two months in his mind. He was sure he had won her back. He was sure she'd felt the same way. She loved him. He knew that. She hadn't bothered to deny it. Yet something worried at him that he could not shake and could not look at because it hurt too much.

He hadn't given up on her. He would never give up. Seeing her again hurt enough to bring him to his knees, and yet, could he look away? No. He could not turn his back and walk away from even the sight of her.

She looked subdued, without the joy he'd seen in her when they'd been together. Across the street, the bakery owner was serving a pot of tea. Two plates of enormous cinnamon rolls were on the table. Noelle was exchanging pleasantries, smiling sweetly to the older woman who ran the place. Her fingers nimbly searching for the flatware and the sugar bowl, unaware that as she spooned sugar into her cup half of it landed on the tablecloth.

He remembered, too, how Matilda had guided her along the boardwalk with care, and earlier, in the shop, helped her around the displays in the dress shop. Her words came back to him, haunting him, always haunting him. *You've changed. I've changed. It's too l-late.*

Now he heard a different meaning. When he'd feared that she had meant they were no longer suited, that she no longer wanted a life as a simple rancher's wife, perhaps that wasn't what she'd meant at all. No, maybe she'd been speaking of something else entirely.

Oh, Noelle. His heart crumpled with love for her. Tender affection swept through his soul like a flash flood, leaving him sure. Absolutely sure. His vision blurred for a moment as he watched her take a sip from her teacup and then lower it into its saucer by touch.

Understanding rained through him like a March squall. The last years of his life, so tough and lonely, suddenly made sense to him. He knew now where the good Lord had been leading him all along—home to his precious Noelle.

"Thad!" Aiden called from the front counter. "Are you coming or not?"

"Coming." He tucked his heart back into his chest, went to collect Finn and followed his older brother out the door.

"I am insulted. That's what I am." Aunt Henrietta bored through the parlor like a runaway train on a mountain grade. Crystal lamp shades clinked and chattered as if in fear. "The nerve of the territorial governor! Suggesting that I perhaps tend to my realm of home and children instead of complaining about modern progress!"

"Clearly the governor is in error." Noelle's fingers stilled. She counted the stitches of her new project—a patchwork quilt—with her fingertips. "You've spent a lot of time composing letters trying to make a difference for us all."

"I hardly expected them to listen to a woman, but I did not expect being insulted." There was a *thwack, thwack* as Henrietta beat one of the decorative pillows on her best sofa before dropping onto it. "For the first time in my life I think it's a pity that woman do not have the vote. If I did, I would vote such a man out of office."

"Well, you should," Noelle said as kindly as she could. She recognized the touch of drama in her aunt's tirade. "He clearly does not appreciate a woman with good sense."

Across the hearth, Noelle heard Matilda struggling to hold back a chuckle.

"Precisely. It gives me pause. I may have to admit those suffrage women in town have a good argument." There was a clicking of steel needles—Henrietta, gathering up her knitting.

Matilda apparently could not hold back her amusement any longer. "But Mama, you don't approve of women wanting to vote."

"I don't. But in light of this uncomplimentary letter, I do not know what the world is coming to. Perhaps I should give an ear to their cause. Clarissa Bell is in my prayer group. I shall speak to her today. Yes, that is exactly what I shall do."

Noelle carefully slipped her needle into the quilt block she was sewing. It was hard to be certain above the music of the spring storm, but she thought she heard a horse in the driveway. Perhaps it was Cora Sims arriving early for an afternoon of sewing. With any luck, maybe her nephew, Emmett, had driven her.

She slid her work into the basket at her feet. "Is Robert still in the stables?"

Henrietta humphed. "Out working with that mare the way Mr. McKaslin taught him. He refuses to give up on that animal. If he gets hurt again—"

Noelle rose from her chair, thinking of Thad. Her spirit lifted as it always did. Always would. "If Thad says so, then Robert should keep the mare and work with her. It will be all right."

"Mr. McKaslin has not been coming up to the house lately." Henrietta's voice turned thoughtful over the ambitious *click-click* of her knitting needles. "And here I had believed him to be most enraptured with you, the poor man. Utterly besotted. Did you see it, too, Matilda?"

"Yes. He's very sweet on you."

Sweet on her? Her heart broke all over again. She headed straight for the door before anyone could guess at her feelings. Or her failures. "Me, marry? I'm on the shelf and have been for long enough to gather dust. Far too long to try to tidy me up and marry me off now."

"You're young and as lovely as could be." Henrietta rose to her defense. "Mr. McKaslin is a man of character, and so he is deserving of you. He ought to propose to you and consider himself blessed with you for his wife."

Dear Henrietta, so loyal and true. She could not understand. Noelle lifted her cloak from the tree, fighting the sorrow. Grief suffocated her. She slipped the wool fabric around her shoulders. "I'm too set in my ways to adjust to marriage. I rather like being a prickly spinster."

"That you could never be!" Henrietta sounded deeply amused. "Trust me when I tell you Thad could not take his eyes off you."

Suddenly Matilda was at her side. Noelle startled. She had been too upset to hear her cousin's approach. Everything was wrong, everything was amiss, since Thad had asked her to marry him.

Since she'd had to say no to him.

It was for the best. She tied her hood snug beneath her chin and opened the door with determination. She'd done the only thing she could do, and it was the right thing.

But her life without him was dark. It was like being blind all over again.

Outside on the doorstep, the wind gusted with a spray of wet. Raindrops fell like striking lead, ricocheting off the earth, making it hard to hear the horse's progress up the road. Bleakness washed over her like the heart of the storm. She gripped the porch rail, letting the rain strike her. Would Thad be working in this gale anyway? Would he be working on that house of his? Or in the fields turning sod with his brothers?

Wherever he was, she hoped he was happy. She would gladly give all of her happiness through her lifetime to him.

Matilda joined her at the rail. "If you married Thad, I could help you. It's not far at all to his new place at the falls, and I can drive now."

"Oh, Tilly. You're like a sister to me. I don't want that life for you, always having to help."

Noelle hung her head, letting the rain batter her. Why wasn't Matilda's offer reassuring her? Why did it only make her feel more panicked?

Because your blindness isn't the only reason you can't marry Thad. She swiped the wet from her face with trembling fingers. She no longer felt safe, no longer sheltered. The storm turned angry, beating against her so hard, it was a surprise it didn't blow away her fears like last autumn's leaves.

"It looks as if it won't last long. It's starting to break up to the west." Matilda moved away from the rail. "Oh, there's someone at the stables."

"Mr. Sims, I hope, coming to bring Cora to visit." The ache in her soul beat at her like the storm.

"I don't think it's the Sims. There's no buggy. Just one horse and his rider."

Thad. With him came the sweetness of hope. She fought against it, but there was her great love for him and the slide of her heart forever falling. She steeled her spine and reminded herself she could not let herself love this man any more than she already did. She would not.

And then he said her name.

Chapter Eighteen

"Noelle."

When she held out her hand to him, wet from the rain, feelings came to life within his poor heart unlike anything he'd felt before. True devotion as soft and warm as a prayer lit him up until he felt as hopeful as a spring dawn. He wanted her. Just her.

Only her.

"Th-thad. What are you doing here?"

"It's your worst fears come true, darlin'." He wasn't hurting anymore. He was no longer alone. He was sure beyond all doubt. Rain slanted beneath the porch roof, striking him, and he moved to shadow her from it. Out of the corner of his eye he saw the cousin slip into the house and close the door to leave them alone. "I've come to change your mind."

"About m-marrying you?" Her heart showed on her face, all of her pure longing and sweet love for him so revealed to him. His heart wrenched with hope. Then she turned away, and sorrow crumpled her face. "Thad, you have to leave. I can't go through this again. I hurts t-too m-much."

"I can see that." He laid her hand over his heart. "I can feel how much it hurts you."

"Then why are you here? You have to go."

"No." He stood resolute. "Your pain is my pain. That's the way it is. I'm not going to walk away from you this time."

Her chin shot up, and there, revealed on her lovely face was the truth. He could see it, he could see the hurt and want and other precious emotions on her face. But she could not see his.

So he lifted her hand to his chin, her fingertips to his cheek. "I want you to feel what's on my face, since you won't look in my heart."

"Thad, just leave this be. Please." Tears stood in her eyes, as if refusing to fall. "I told you. You can't turn back time. Not even God can do that. It's too late."

"That's where you're wrong, darlin'." He pressed a brief kiss to her fingertips. Tenderness took him over, and it made him stronger. Better. "It's never too late for God's greatest blessing. So, you can't turn down my proposal over it. It's because I left you once, and you're afraid I'll do it again. Isn't it?"

"Why didn't you come to me instead?" Rain trickled down her forehead. "You didn't love me enough, that's why. You cared for me, I know that, but I loved you more."

"Not a chance, darlin'. Everything has changed these past five years except one thing. My enduring love for you. That's something that will not end."

Another drop of rain trailed down her forehead. The tears standing in her eyes still did not fall.

His heart was breaking for both of them, but this had

to be said. So he said it. "I didn't realize why I left without a word, even with your father's threats, until years later. But you've gotta understand. I was young and down deep, I was afraid your father was right."

"Right that you didn't love me enough?"

"No, darlin'." Tenderness, unmistakable tenderness, made those words intimate and sincere. "I was afraid that one day down the road, the shining way you looked at me would dim. Life is tough, and hardship might rub off that shine. You might get tired of long days of working this hard land just to try to prosper."

"You think I cared about those things?"

"No. Fear isn't rational. You just don't know what's up ahead in your life, or which way the weather will blow. Down deep, I was afraid things might not work out. That we'd be scraping by just like my parents had, running short and losing hope. And that would be the day you would look at me as a failure."

"You think I would have stopped loving you?"

"Maybe. I didn't know. What if I was the reason you wound up losing all of your dreams? What if that day came and the comfort of your parents' fancy home and privileged lifestyle would lure you away from me." He stopped, his voice raw with emotion. "I can see how the thought of losing you that way hurt more than leaving you for good before you had more of my heart. I don't know if you can understand that, darlin'."

"A little." Tears fell in a slow hot roll down her cheek. "A lot."

"But I promise you this. I've matured. I've been out in the world. I've earned my experience the hard way, and I know my worth." Truth rang in his voice, was granite-solid on his face. "I'll stand by you no matter what. I'll never stop trying for you, never let you down and never stop loving you. If only you will give me this chance. This one precious chance to marry you. Please, don't say no."

"I h-have to." She choked on a sob. "You look at the past when you see me. You're trying to fix what hurt you so much. I understand that. But look at me now, Thad. I can't be a rancher's wife. I can't be what you need."

"You *are* what I need. Why can't you see that?"

His honest words tempted her. How they tempted her. Another sob wrenched up from her soul. His face was warm against her fingers. She could feel the faint rasp of his day's growth of beard along his jaw and the set of his jawbone. He meant what he said. At least, he *thought* he did.

If only she could make him understand. She struggled for air and still she could not speak the truth—she had to say the whole and terrible truth. "Can't you see I'm afraid now? Love just isn't enough. Can't you see that?"

"Real love is always enough, darlin'."

"I'm not the woman I was. I can't do most of the work around a ranch house by myself. I'm not wh-ole. I don't want the day to come when you look at me and see a burden. You'll realize all that I've cost you. You'll stop loving me."

A muscle jumped along his cheek. He breathed in air with one long inhale. She trembled in the cold and the uncertainty.

At last he broke the silence. "Fine. Let's say you're right. You say yes to me. We get married. Down the road, I'm working with a new horse and I get kicked hard, just like your uncle did. Let's say I don't wake up right away, but when I do, I can't move my legs. Are you going to stop loving me?"

Tears burned as they spilled down her face. A sob ripped up from her chest. There was only one truth. One bright shining truth. "No. Never. I would only love you more."

"Well now, that's how I feel about you, darlin'." His hands cupped her face tenderly, sweetly. "You are my dream. Marry me. Please. Don't make me live in the dark without you."

She felt the heart of the girl she used to be, the young woman who believed in love and fairy-tale wishes. Her future stood before her, the man who was rubbing away her tears with the pads of his thumbs and pressing chaste kisses where her tears had been.

She felt whole, she felt healed, she felt renewed. She covered Thad's hands with her own, her precious Thad. She could feel the smile changing her face and his love changing her life. "You want me to marry you pretty badly, it seems. Perhaps I *could* be persuaded."

"Maybe you'd best tell me what it'll take to persuade you fully."

"A kiss."

"Darlin', now that's something I'd be happy to do."

When his lips touched hers, it was perfection. Her soul sighed. Her hopes lifted. Every dream within her was renewed.

The front door burst open with a clatter. "Young man! I do not permit such behavior unless you are engaged! Now unless you're—" Henrietta stopped. "Oh, you are! Noelle, I can tell by that smile on your face. My prayers are answered. You two come in. We've got celebrating to do."

The rain chose that moment to stop. Noelle didn't need to ask Thad if the storm had broken. Warm, soft sunlight spilled over her like grace.

Epilogue

August

Noelle felt a tug at the hem of her skirt as she passed by the corral fence and laughed. She'd been laughing a lot lately; she couldn't help it. She was blissfully happy. "Stormy, are you trying to eat my ruffle again?"

"Yep," Thad answered at her side, always by her side. "That pretty green dress you're wearing obviously looks as tasty as grass to her."

Noelle laughed again, letting her fingertips ruffle the growing filly's mane. Solitude nickered gently, patiently watching over her baby. Both had been a wedding gift from Robert.

"Let go, sweet thing." Thad's low baritone rumbled with happiness and humor, too. "That's right. We'll come see you later, after our ride."

"Yes, we don't want to be late. Henrietta likes supper at six o'clock sharp."

"We'd best get a move on if we want to ride the trail

along the river." His hand cupping her elbow was gentle, guiding her down the aisle to where Sunny and Sky, a mustang Thad had bought for her, stood saddled and patiently waiting.

Sunshine kissed her warmly, and the fragrant breezes ruffled the sweet grasses at her feet. It was a beautiful day.

A beautiful life.

Sky nickered and sidled over to nudge Noelle's free hand. Warm breath puffed across her face. Fine whiskers tickled her palm. The mare gently leaned against her, pure affection. Her own horse. Noelle feared she might burst from joy.

Thad's arms slipped around her waist, drawing her against his chest. His voice rumbled cozily. "You're looking mighty happy, Mrs. McKaslin. Care to tell me why?"

"Well, let's see." She let her fingertips trail up the placket of his muslin shirt. "I have a mustang that I love. A ranch I love. A house I love."

"What about me?" There was only pure tenderness in his tone. Only devotion in his words. "What about the husband who adores you?"

She laid her hand on his chest over the beat of his heart. Deep, abiding love welled up from her soul. "My husband?"

"What? You're forgetting about me already?" He was chuckling. His kiss grazed her forehead. "What about your husband?"

"There are no words to say how endlessly I love him." She lifted her face to his. "No number big enough to measure all the ways I love him."

"What a coincidence." His kiss brushed the very tip

of her nose. "For that's exactly the way I love you, Noelle. Without condition. Without end."

She knew. Her heart ached with happiness. The past was healed and now there was only the beauty of their lives together. After a shockingly short engagement, according to Henrietta, they had married in May. Three perfect months of marriage had passed, with each day better than the last.

And now there was a new dream to come true. Thad's hand slipped to her tummy, which was still flat, but that would change soon enough.

His lips slanted over hers in a tender, loving kiss. Sweetness filled her heart. Joy left her dizzy. Hope lived in her soul. Yes, theirs was a love that would last forever.

"Henrietta's gonna be mad at me now." He stole one more kiss. "We're definitely going to be late for supper."

"Perhaps she'll forgive us once we announce our good news." It was her turn to steal one last kiss. "She'll be too ecstatic to be really mad at us."

"I know how that feels. I'm ecstatic, too."

She laid her hand on his, and it was the future she saw. Those four upstairs bedrooms full, the house pleasantly loud with children's footsteps and laughter and play. Ida would be watching over them all, sweet and loving. The evenings would be best of all. She would spend them on the front porch beside her husband, hand in hand, heart to heart.

Yes, it was easy to see her dreams these days. Thad was right. Love *was* enough. And when dreams came true, it was called happiness.

"Are you ready?" he asked.

She grabbed hold of the saddle horn and suddenly she was airborne, lifted by Thad's strong arms. She slipped into the saddle and she smoothed her skirts, while Sky stood patiently. The wind ruffled her hair, and she pulled at the strings of her hat, which was hanging down her back. The Stetson slid up into place and its wide brim shaded her face from the sun's heat.

"Are you settled okay?" Thad asked, handing her the reins.

She nodded, and while he mounted up with a creak of the saddle, her heart brimmed with gratitude for this wonderful life full of blessings. She knew that God had brought her and Thad together again. The good Lord had blessed her with the privilege of being Thad's wife.

She would be forever thankful to Him.

"Ready, darlin'?"

"Ready." She gathered the sun-warmed reins.

They started out together. Side by side they rode into the rays of the sun and through green pastures.

* * * * *

Don't miss Jillian Hart's
next inspirational romance,
HER WEDDING WISH,
available June 2008 from Love Inspired.

Dear Reader,

Thank you so much for choosing *Homespun Bride*. I hope you enjoyed reading Noelle's story as much as I did writing it. Thad and Noelle were young sweethearts separated by her well-meaning parents and have been greatly changed by the consequences of this. Thad has become embittered and hard. Noelle has stopped believing in love and dreams for herself. Then God sees fit to give them a second chance at happiness. I hope you find inspiration in the way the Lord works in Noelle's and Thad's lives and that their journey speaks to your heart, as well.

Wishing you grace and peace,

Jillian Hart

QUESTIONS FOR DISCUSSION:

1. At the beginning of the story, Noelle has adapted to her blindness. What does it say about Noelle's character?

2. When Thad realized he has rescued his first and only love from the runaway horse-drawn sleigh, what is his reaction? What does this tell you about his character?

3. Thad had come to believe that love is nothing at all, not substantial and not lasting. How does this change through the story?

4. As Noelle comes to know Thad again, what aspects of his character does she come to admire—even though she does not want to?

5. How do Thad's actions reveal the kind of man he is down deep? How do his choices impact the story and the romance?

6. Noelle believes that the best of her life is behind her. How has this affected her? How does this change through the story?

7 How important are the themes of trust and forgiveness in this story? Of judgment and withholding judgment?

8. How does God's leading bring Thad and Noelle together?

9. Both Thad and Noelle have been afraid that love is not enough for a lasting happiness. How are they wrong? Have you ever felt this way?

10. How does God guide Noelle back to her hopes and her dreams?

Love Inspired
HISTORICAL
INSPIRATIONAL HISTORICAL ROMANCE

She had made a solemn promise to see her younger sister to safety in California. But the journey across the frontier was a test of courage for Faith Beal. All she had to sustain her was the guiding hand of a stranger who truly seemed heaven-sent. But would the secrets that seemed to haunt Connell McClain threaten their growing feelings for one another?

Look for

Frontier Courtship

by
VALERIE HANSEN

Available March wherever you buy books.

Steeple
Hill®

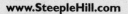

Love Inspired.
HISTORICAL

TITLES AVAILABLE NEXT MONTH

Don't miss these two stories in March

HIDEAWAY HOME by Hannah Alexander
A Hideaway Novel
Wounded in WWII, Red Meyer felt like half a man, and
he was determined to keep his distance from sweetheart
Bertie Moennig. But when trouble erupts on the home front,
they'll have to join forces to solve a dangerous mystery.

FRONTIER COURTSHIP by Valerie Hansen
A wagon train to California became a test of courage and
endurance for Faith Beal. Frontiersman Connell McClain's
care and concern made the trials worth the pain, but would
the secrets that haunt him threaten their budding love?

LIHCNM0208